SHATTERED VOWS
A CRIMSON POINT NOVEL

KAYLEA CROSS

SHATTERED VOWS

Copyright © 2019
by Kaylea Cross

* * * * *

Cover Art and Print Formatting:
Sweet 'N Spicy Designs
Developmental edits: Deborah Nemeth
Line Edits: Joan Nichols
Digital Formatting: LK Campbell

* * * * *

This book is a work of fiction. The names, characters, places, and incidents are products of the writer's imagination or have been used fictitiously and are not to be construed as real. Any resemblance to persons, living or dead, actual events, locales or organizations is entirely coincidental.

All rights reserved. With the exception of quotes used in reviews, this book may not be reproduced or used in whole or in part by any means existing without written permission from the author.

ISBN: 978-1792979316

Dedication

For Deb Nemeth, who helps me bring my visions to life and gives me the confidence to keep chasing my dreams. Thank you for everything you do for my stories.

Author's Note

Here we are at Jase and Molly's book! I've been looking forward to this one since I dreamed up the series and characters. These two have traveled a hard road, and it's my absolute pleasure to give them a shot at finding happiness together. (Plus, Jase is my favorite hero of the series, so there's that, too.)

Happy reading!

Kaylea Cross

Prologue

Molly Boyd clamped her teeth together to keep them from chattering and hunched into a tighter ball in an effort to keep warm, but it didn't help. She was cold all the way to her bones, her sodden clothes sticking to her skin. A summer rainstorm pounded down outside the shelter of the culvert she huddled in—hiding from her ex-husband.

Shock kept advancing and retreating, trapping her in an emotional fog. She'd never imagined she would end up like this. Not even after everything she and Carter had been through.

The left side of her face throbbed. Her cheek was bruised, her eye swelling slightly, and her lip burned where Carter had backhanded her. Her bare feet stung from the scratches she'd sustained in her flight to this lonely culvert at the side of the road.

All of it was eclipsed by the pain in her heart.

She closed her eyes, fought to hold off the memory of him breaking into the house and coming at her with that terrifying, predatory expression on his face. The memory of escaping the house, slamming that branch over his back and running for her life through the darkened woods.

Tears threatened. She shook them off, refusing to give in. If she started crying now, she might never stop, and she had to stay alert because she was still in danger with Carter looking for her.

What am I going to do?

She shivered harder, tucked her knees up tight to her chest and leaned her forehead on them as she fought to keep from spiraling into the black pit of despair yawning at the edge of her consciousness. Jase was coming. She'd called him and he was coming. He would find her, help her, and he'd alerted the cops. He would make sure she was safe—even if it was from his former best friend.

At the faint sound of an approaching vehicle, her insides tightened in fear. She lifted her head, her gaze darting toward the road, dreading the moment the familiar black pickup came into view again. Carter had driven up and down this road earlier, shouting her name through his open window for endless minutes. He would never stop looking for her.

Headlights cut through the gloom. She turned her face away and squeezed her eyes shut, willing Carter away. The divorce papers had set him off, even though he must have known they were coming.

She sat perfectly still, heart hammering against her ribs as she waited, hardly daring to breathe lest the slightest motion give her hiding spot away.

"Moll?"

She flinched at the male voice all but drowned out by the thundering rain, her heart rocketing into her throat. Shit, she was trapped here. Carter was former Special Forces and the waterlogged ditch was too steep. She'd never be able to climb out and escape him if he found her this time.

"Moll. It's Jase."

Jase. The fear receded instantly, the cold inside her

thawing under a tide of relief as she turned her head toward him. She trusted him. Trusted that he would protect her and keep her safe, no matter what.

He was wading toward her through the flooded ditch, a tall, strong silhouette, his jeans soaked to the knees. She couldn't move, couldn't call out. Her muscles were too weak and shaky to obey her.

Gathering her courage as he came nearer, she forced her gaze up to meet Jase's. The instant their eyes connected, she almost lost the battle to keep the tears at bay.

Frowning in concern, he quickly climbed into the culvert and knelt down beside her. Before she could find her voice, he reached out and gently grasped her chin in his warm fingers. His jaw was tight, his aqua eyes burning with outrage. "Did he do this? Did he hit you?" he demanded, voice vibrating with horror and anger.

Molly's fading composure crumbled. All the emotions she'd been holding back crashed over her like a dark wave, taking her under. She leaned toward him just as the dam broke.

Jase made a low sound and reached for her, wrapping his strong, warm arms around her as she laid her head on his shoulder. He ran a comforting hand up and down her back gently. "Are you hurt anywhere else?"

Just her heart, now shattered into a thousand jagged pieces.

She shook her head, her entire body trembling while she choked back the sobs trying to claw their way free of her throat, the humiliation all but strangling her. This was a nightmare. Only she wasn't dreaming.

"All right, let's get you out of here." Jase slid one arm beneath her knees and lifted her, keeping her close to him as he carried her out of the culvert and through the water-filled ditch.

Molly ducked her head against the pelting rain and curled into him. She didn't know what to say. Was ashamed to tell him what had happened.

"I'm gonna boost you up, then come right behind you." He lifted her toward the steeply sloping side and helped her scramble over the edge before climbing up the side. Before she could even get to her feet, he scooped her up again, ignoring her mumbled protest as he strode for his truck, parked close by at the edge of the road.

Molly curled against him, still trying to come to terms with everything that had happened. As well as something…something that was still happening inside her right now.

Jase opened the front passenger door and carefully placed her on the leather seat. The interior was warm. Almost hot compared to outside.

"Hang tight." He disappeared for a moment, opened the rear door to grab something and came back with a jacket. He tucked it around her, did up her seatbelt because her hands were still shaking and shut the door. Once he had climbed into the driver's seat, he cranked the heat to high and reached over to aim the vents at her.

Molly sighed in relief as the warm air flowed over her. The numbness was retreating, leaving a sapping exhaustion in its wake.

Still leaning toward her, Jase reached up to stroke her wet hair away from her face, his eyes worried. "Moll, do you need to go to the hospital?"

"N-no. I'm okay." *You're not. And you'll never be okay again.*

"What happened?" he asked, turning the truck in a tight circle and starting back up the road.

She huddled beneath his jacket and told him about Carter breaking into the house and attacking her in as few words as possible, her voice hitching due to the little gasps still jarring her lungs.

Jase was silent as she finished, his stubbled jaw clenched tight. He shook his golden-brown head, and a deep, terrible shame engulfed her, almost worse than the pain of Carter hitting her.

But there was more to her story. So much more. She didn't want to hide the rest from him and had intended to tell everyone anyway. Just not like this.

"And it gets worse," she added, her voice barely above a whisper.

He looked over at her sharply.

She didn't speak for a long moment, staring out the windshield into the gloom. "I'm pregnant," she finally said, her voice breaking.

Jase's sharply indrawn breath made her cringe inside. He snapped his head back straight to watch the road.

"I know." She gave a bitter laugh. "Unreal, isn't it?" The irony of it might have been funny if it wasn't so freaking sad. She'd always dreamed of having kids one day. But not like this. And now it was even worse that it was with Carter, because it meant that she and the child would always be tied to him.

"I thought you said you guys..."

Hadn't been intimate in months? They hadn't. Except for one time. One lapse in judgment that had turned out to be more costly than she could ever have imagined.

A few beats of thunderous silence passed. Then Jase glanced over at her again, and his expression was so hard it might have been carved out of granite. "Did he force you?" His voice was savage.

"*No*," she answered immediately, though given the shit show of the past few months, she understood why he might wonder that. "No."

Sighing, she explained. "It was a stupid, one-time nothing. We hadn't slept together in months. But he was so damn sad and vulnerable this one night and I didn't know how to help him. I've been on the pill, but for whatever reason it failed."

She shouldn't have slept with him. Her deep-seated

need to heal and comfort had overtaken her usual common sense, and now she was paying the price.

"What am I going to do?" she whispered, feeling utterly lost and alone.

Jase stopped at an intersection and turned left rather than going straight, to his place. "I'm taking you to Beckett and Sierra's."

Horrified, she jerked her head around to stare at him. "No, don't."

"Yes, Moll. You need to be somewhere safe while Beckett and I deal with Noah. Sierra will take care of you."

Nothing she could say or do would change the inevitable, and she desperately needed to be with someone she trusted. Sierra was her best friend.

"Okay," she finally agreed, dreading Sierra and Beckett's reaction. At least she was warming up now, her teeth no longer chattering.

The few minutes' drive to Beckett and Sierra's house passed quickly. Jase turned down Salt Spray Lane and at the top of the hill stood the grand Victorian, its lighted windows glowing warm against the gray backdrop. Beckett and Sierra met them at the door.

Sierra immediately engulfed Molly in a big hug and ushered her inside and took her upstairs to give her dry clothes to change into. "My brother's on the way," Sierra said to her. Noah, the town sheriff.

Time passed in a blur for Molly as she changed and told Sierra everything. Including that she was pregnant. Finally dry and wearing a sweater and jeans that were too big for her, she followed Sierra back downstairs to where Jase and Beckett waited.

She glanced at Jase, standing by the kitchen doorway. His powerful arms were folded across his wide chest, his expression unreadable, but to her it was full of disapproval and a silent judgment that made her squirm inside.

"Thanks for coming to get me," she told him softly. From the beginning, he'd always been there for her and Carter. He was still here for her now.

That clear aqua gaze never wavering from hers, he shook his head once. "I'd do anything for you. You know that."

She did.

Molly looked down at the floor, his words hitting her in the center of her battered heart. She'd had a chance with him years ago on the night they'd met at the bar just off base. He was good looking and funny, and she'd been interested in him for those first few minutes. But then Carter had walked in and the rest of the world had ceased to exist. How different might her life have turned out if she'd chosen Jase instead?

She shook the useless thought away. Playing the "what if" game at this point was stupid. Just as she'd been stupid to sleep with Carter almost three months ago. But she wanted this baby, was already fiercely protective of it.

Sierra's sheriff brother Noah arrived to talk to her. Molly begged him not to arrest Carter and take him to jail, but to send him to a psych facility instead. He was mentally ill and needed help, and he wouldn't find it in prison.

Except they'd already tried every type of therapy and meds after his brain injury and still his mental state had deteriorated to this extent.

Noah explained that it wasn't his call. It was up to the judge who handled the case, once Carter was located and taken into custody.

Beckett and Jase left to look for Carter and she immediately felt on edge, wishing Jase had stayed. He calmed her, made her feel safe.

Anxiety continued to churn in her belly as she answered Noah's questions, struggling to mentally process everything that had happened. It was still surreal. As an ER nurse she'd seen domestic abuse victims countless times over the course of her career. But it had always happened to someone else. She'd never dreamed she would wind up a victim of it herself one day.

Noah left. The storm continued to rage outside. Beckett and Jase hadn't returned, and they hadn't called. Had they found Carter?

Sierra's phone rang. "It's my brother," she said before answering it. A moment later her gaze shot to Molly. "Yes. Hang on." She held the phone out. "He wants to talk to you."

A cold knot of dread formed in the pit of Molly's stomach. Sitting up, she took the phone, her heart thudding. "Hello?"

"Molly. I..." He heaved a sigh and her insides clenched tighter. "There's been an accident."

Her lungs seized.

Carter. She knew it was.

"What happened?" she rasped out.

"His truck went through a barricade and over the cliff a few miles south of town."

She swallowed. "Is he..." She let the question dangle there, unable to voice it aloud.

"I'm sorry. He's gone."

She closed her eyes, put a protective hand to her belly as tears burned the backs of her eyelids, loss and guilt all but smothering her.

Carter was dead. Leaving her to grieve for the man he'd been, as well as the tortured soul he'd become. And most painful of all...

He'd just left behind a child he hadn't even known about.

Chapter One

Five weeks later

"You look like shit."

Jase took the box of tile from Beckett with a grunt. "Gee, thanks, Cap. Feel like it, too." It was Friday afternoon and whatever his system had been fighting the past week had lost the battle. He was freezing and hurt all over.

"Go home, Sergeant." It was definitely an order. Jase had been the Assistant Operations and Intel Sergeant of their A-team for years. They might not be in the Army anymore, but Beckett hadn't lost his commanding officer's authoritative edge one bit.

Jase set the box of tile on the covered shower floor. "I will once I get this tile up." He wanted to at least finish the master bedroom shower so he could come back and do the grouting tomorrow. The master suite was the last thing to finish, and with the funeral next week he wouldn't have much time to put in here.

Beckett sighed and shook his head. "Leave it. I'll do it. Just go home to bed."

"I'll finish this, then go. You and Mac have been here

late every night for the past two weeks helping me with the renos." This was his project, and his responsibility to get finished. The guys had been more than generous with their time and effort to help him out.

He knelt to back-butter the first tile with thinset. Beckett stood there watching him with his arms folded across his chest as Jase began to lay tile, beginning with the second row. "When are you gonna tell her about this?"

Jase pressed the first tile to the wall above the strip of wood he'd screwed in to provide a level line marker. "Soon." He didn't want to show Molly until the whole thing was move-in ready and looking just the way he envisioned.

He'd been keeping an eye out for a house for her. As far as projects went, this one had been pretty easy compared to some they'd tackled together.

The place had been in great shape to begin with, so most of the work had been cosmetic. The painters had finished up a couple days ago, and Jase and the guys had handled refinishing the hardwood floors. New stone countertops had gone in last week, and the appliances had arrived yesterday. Landscaping would only take a couple days, but Jase wasn't tackling that until he got over whatever bug this was.

A resigned sigh. "Move over." Beckett stepped into the shower enclosure with him.

Jase knew that tone, and this time didn't bother arguing. He scooted over to make room. "All those years serving side by side, and this is the first time we've been in the shower together."

Beckett huffed out a grudging laugh. "I'm just glad we're both dressed right now. Shut up and hand me a trowel."

By the time all the tiling was done his hands and feet felt like ice and his face was burning. "Thanks, man," he said to Beckett.

"No worries." Then Beckett nailed him with a warning look. "But if you infected me with whatever you've got, I'm gonna be pissed. Now go home and go to bed before you fall over. I need you at a hundred percent come Monday."

Because they were both pallbearers charged with carrying Carter to his final resting place. And they had to be there for Molly. She may have signed the divorce papers prior to Carter's death, but she'd loved him and the funeral was going to be hard for her.

Before the all too familiar heaviness could invade his chest, he stood and dusted off his hands. "I'm going." He shrugged into his treasured WWII era leather bomber jacket that had belonged to his grandfather, wincing as his aching shoulders and back protested, then dragged himself into the cab of his truck and headed for home on the other side of town.

He checked his phone as he got out in his driveway. There was a text from Lauren, the woman he'd met at the gym a couple months ago. She'd been asking him to go out with her for weeks—just as friends, because he'd made it clear he wasn't looking for anything else. Though he could already tell she was hoping for more eventually. They'd finally set something up for tonight, and now he'd canceled a few hours ago.

Excuse the late reply, I was in a meeting. Sorry you're sick! Text me when you're feeling better so we can reschedule.

Will do, he typed back, though he was actually relieved about having to cancel.

While he didn't want Lauren to get the wrong impression, if it hadn't been for Molly, he would have been totally into her. Which was stupid, because Molly was never going to be his. She saw him as a good friend and that was all.

Didn't mean it was easy to stop hoping that might

change now. And it didn't mean he would stop trying to take care of her—including renovating a house to make it perfect for her.

The sound of a rake scraping over asphalt reached him. His neighbor, Mrs. Wong, was busy trying to rake the cedar needles that had begun to fall on her driveway. She was past eighty and had difficulty walking, let alone doing yard work.

"Hi, Mrs. Wong," he called out.

She stopped and looked up at him between the trees, a bright smile breaking over her lined face. She was an adorable, pleasant and tiny lady who lived alone in her little bungalow. Today she had on one of her homemade knit hats and a matching scarf. "Oh, hello, dear."

Her driveway was almost as long as his, and she had cedars on both sides. With the amount of crap on the driveway, it would take her hours to clean it, and by morning there would likely be the same amount again. "That time of year, huh?"

"Yes." She looked up at the trees with a resigned expression. "I love them most of the year, but I hate cleaning up after them from September through March."

"I can see why." Even if he was sick, there was no way he could let her clean it on her own. She had arthritis—she'd told him so the day he moved in—and would barely be able to move in the morning. "Let me get my blower."

"Oh, no, dear. I can—"

He wasn't listening, already halfway to his garage. He pulled the blower out, overrode all Mrs. Wong's protests and made her go back inside. He blew the driveway clean, then used a push broom to gather everything into a pile and put it in large yard waste bags. By the time he was finished, his body hated his good Samaritan guts and he couldn't wait to crawl into bed.

He was up in his room when another text came in.

From Molly this time.

You free to come for dinner later?

It was amazing how much even a text from her could twist his insides up. *Rain check.*

She started typing a reply immediately and the answer popped up a moment later. *If you're standing me up so you can work on that old car of yours, you can suck it.*

That pulled a grudging half-smile from him. *You mean my baby*, he corrected. The beloved '32 Ford he'd inherited from his grandpa was safely tucked away in his garage, awaiting a lot more of his time and attention before she would be road worthy. *No. Sick as hell, going to bed.*

Without waiting for a reply he turned his phone to silent, dragged his ass into the shower and stood under the scalding hot spray, letting it pound over his achy shoulders and back. A little warmer now, he checked his medicine cabinet but there was nothing in it to help him, so he pulled on sweats and climbed into bed.

Next thing he knew, something woke him. Sounds coming from down in the kitchen. He'd locked the door, so whoever it was knew the key code.

Rolling over, he grabbed his phone to check it. Sure enough, there was a message from Molly from a minute after he'd responded to her initial text.

I'm coming over. Be there in a while.

He flopped back against the pillow with a groan. The nap hadn't helped; he still felt like hell. Rather than get up to find her, he texted her. *I'm awake.*

Seconds later he heard her soft footfalls on the wooden staircase. She paused at his door, and his pulse quickened. She tapped softly.

"Come in." He didn't have the energy to do more than prop himself up against the headboard.

The door opened. Dark, spiral curls appeared, then

the most beautiful face in the world, her light brown complexion of her biracial heritage making her gold-green eyes even more vivid. "Hey." She walked in wearing a snug pair of jeans and a purple top that hugged her round breasts, carrying a tray in her hands. "How you feeling?" she asked as she approached the bed.

"Not good." He waved her off, not wanting to risk making her sick. He didn't want that, especially now that she was pregnant. "Better keep your distance."

"Uh oh, is it the man flu? That's one of worst viruses of all."

He gave her a mock glare. "I'm legit sick here."

She gave him a grin and kept coming. "I'm a nurse. I can handle it." She set the tray down on the opposite night table, then climbed up onto the bed beside him to lay a practiced hand on his forehead.

Jase bit back a groan at the soft, cool touch. It soothed his burning skin, but also something deep inside him. Because it was Molly.

"Whoa, you're burning up. Hundred-and-one at least." She removed her hand. "Did you take anything?"

"No, couldn't find anything."

"Here." She leaned over, dug into her purse and came up with two pills. "Tylenol, extra strength." She handed him a glass of water, waited while he swallowed the pills and set the glass back on the tray. She put her hand on his cheek again, and it was all he could do not to sigh and lean into it.

Being this sick sucked ass. Having Molly nurse him was a definite perk. Aside from his grandma, he'd never had anyone take care of him this way. He liked it, probably more than he should have.

"What other symptoms do you have?" she asked, cradling his other cheek now. "Sore throat?"

"No. I hurt all over, though."

"Nausea?"

"No." At least, he didn't think so. His head was pounding and he was tired as if he'd gone three days without sleep.

"Think you could eat a little? I made you soup. Chicken noodle, with ditalini pasta. Your favorite."

Sick as he was, he couldn't help but smile at that. She'd made him soup from scratch. Knowing her, she'd probably run straight to the store to buy all the ingredients for it as soon as she got his text. "I can't believe you remembered that."

She shrugged. "I like food, so when you told me once that your grandma used to make it for you when you were sick, I guess it stuck." She pulled her hand away. "Are you up for some?"

It smelled awesome, and he hadn't eaten much since that morning. "Yeah."

She reached over and picked up the container with a spoon sticking out of it. "Careful, it's still really hot. I know it's not her recipe, but hopefully it'll do the trick."

"This is great, thanks." He took the container from her, inhaled the savory scent of the broth. There were small, neat chunks of chicken and vegetables in it, along with the little round pasta bits. The last time he'd had this was when he'd been home on leave in Nebraska, shortly before his grandma had passed away. He'd been sick with a cold and she'd made a big pot for him, along with a loaf of her homemade white bread.

"Sure. I put a few other containers of it in your fridge for later, in case you get hungry." With that, she popped off the bed and headed to his bathroom.

Jase sipped at the soup, comforted body and soul by the warmth of it sliding down his throat, and by Molly's presence. The water ran in the bathroom sink. She came back a moment later and sat back down on the bed.

"Settling okay?" she asked.

He nodded and kept eating. It was damn tasty, and

he hadn't realized how hungry he was.

She waited until he finished, then set the empty container back on the tray and began to wipe his face with the cool, damp washcloth she'd brought.

This time he did groan, closing his eyes. "That feels so good." Too bad he had to be sick to get this kind of intimate attention, but he'd take it.

"Good." She pressed the cloth to his cheeks, his burning forehead. "You'll feel better once the meds kick in and take your fever down."

He hoped so. He needed to be better by Monday. "Haven't been this sick in years."

"No?" She set the cloth aside and gestured for him to slide down into the bed.

Jase eased down, every muscle in his body aching in protest, and laid his head on his pillow. "We were in the Spin Ghar Mountains in Afghanistan. I'd been sick for days and could barely carry my pack. At one point Beckett was gonna call in a medevac for me, but I wasn't going to ditch them on a mission. Finally they dragged me into a cave for the day so I could sleep. Carter took care of me." It hurt to think of the catastrophic downward spiral his best friend had taken in the months after his brain injury, but it was nice to be able to talk about happier memories of him with Molly.

At the mention of her ex's name, she paused in the act of pulling the covers up under his chin, her eyes darting up to his. A small smile lifted the side of her mouth. "Did he, now? And how were his nursing skills?"

"The shits."

She laughed and tucked the blankets around him. "Yeah, playing Florence Nightingale wasn't exactly his strong suit. When I got sick he'd bring me a bucket, but he definitely wasn't going to stay and hold my hair back for me."

Jase smiled. "He did his best. I was so cold I thought

I was gonna die, so he shoved me into my sleeping bag next to the fire and curled up behind me in his for the night. Told me he'd leave me to die if I puked on him." He smiled at the memory.

Molly's laugh was a balm to his soul as she sat beside him. "So he spooned you to keep you warm?"

Jase nodded. "He was the big spoon and I was the little spoon." Even though Jase was by no means little. Compared to Carter, though, pretty much everyone was.

Her eyes sparkled as she grinned. He loved seeing that little bit of happiness in her again. She'd been through so much, and this last month had been especially hard on her. She'd left her support network back in North Carolina and moved here for Carter, only to wind up afraid for her safety after his mental health took a bad turn, forcing her to get a restraining order against him and finally file for divorce.

She shook her head, her expression turning wistful. "How can you not love a big, tough bear of a man with a squishy inside, huh?"

Yeah. "Pretty sure Beckett snapped some pictures of it." All the guys had given them a hard time about the two of them curled up together, but Jase had been too sick to care and Carter had just growled at them all to shut the fuck up. "We should ask him if he's still got them."

"I'd pay money to see those." She glanced around his room, at the pictures and framed military mementos he'd hung on the walls and put on the bookshelves. Some from his military service, and his grandpa's WWII service medals.

It struck him that she'd never been in here before, in his most intimate space. Aside from his old Ford, she'd never seen his most treasured things. He liked having her here, though he wished it was under completely different circumstances.

A smile spread across her face as her gaze settled on

one at the far end of the room. "That's a great shot of you and Carter with your granddad."

Jase followed her gaze. He'd put the framed photo in the center of the top shelf where it was most visible.

Jase was in the middle, his eighty-three-year-old grandfather on his left, and Carter's massive form towering above them both on the right. "My granny took it when I brought him back home with me for Christmas just before you guys met." His father's parents had taken him in and raised him from age fifteen, after Jase had lost his parents to a boating accident on a lake that summer.

"That must have been a shock for your grandparents."

He started to smile, stopped when his stomach gave an ominous gurgle. He shifted beneath the blankets, swallowed against the sudden wave of nausea. *Don't you dare*, he warned his body. "They loved him. He was the life of the party, as always. They even dragged us out dancing with them at the legion one night."

She looked at him in astonishment. "As in, swing dancing?"

"No. My granny tried to show Carter a thing or two, though." He shook his head, fought another wave of nausea that made his insides tighten. "God, it was funny to see him out there. He was like a bull in a china shop and he couldn't give a shit because he was having too much fun."

Molly burst out laughing. "I've changed my mind. I want pictures of *that*."

"It was something to see. All the ladies in there were over seventy, and all of them wanted to dance with him. They kept him busy for hours." That had been a great night. Everybody had loved Carter. Hard not to love a guy with that kind of wicked sense of humor and unflagging loyalty. That's why it was so damn painful to think of what he'd become and how it had all ended.

The nausea intensified, roiling in his belly. *Shit.*

He started to sit up, sweat breaking out on his face and back. He did *not* want to puke in front of Molly. She was everything he'd ever wanted in a woman. He didn't want her to see him throw up his dinner.

"You okay?" she asked in concern.

He shook his head, gulped. Tried to throw the covers off him so he could bolt for the bathroom.

He didn't even make it out of the bed.

His stomach turned inside out, forcing the soup back up his spasming throat. Thankfully the container appeared in front of his face. He grabbed it, doubled over on the side of the bed as his stomach emptied itself. Burning his throat and making his clenched eyes water.

Oh, Christ, now he remembered why he hated throwing up so much.

Eyes streaming, still heaving, he gulped in air as the spasms finally passed. When he opened his eyes Molly was there in front of him, wiping his face. She took the container before he could stop her, and—God, no—looked down at the mess.

She studied it for a second then looked up at him, her eyes were bright with mischief. "You don't like my cooking?" she joked.

A laugh burst out of him in spite of himself, then he groaned and pushed the container away. "Make it go away."

"All right." Chuckling, she carried it from the room and returned with another glass of water. "Drink a few small sips of this. Slowly."

He did, feeling miserable as hell. God, he couldn't believe he'd done that in front of the woman he'd craved since the day they'd met.

When he'd taken a couple of sips, she put the water down and stood. "Lie back down. Time to sleep."

Too sick to argue, he did as she said. He was asleep

in minutes, only to wake a couple more times through the night to get sick. Each time Molly was there with a bowl and a clean, cool cloth to make him feel better. Finally he passed out, and the next time he came around, the sky was just starting to lighten through his bedroom windows.

Something rustled beside his bed. He jerked upright, squinting to make out the shape on the floor as his eyes adjusted. Molly was there rolling up a sleeping bag.

She'd stayed? On his *floor*? She was pregnant, for Chrissake.

"How are you feeling?" she whispered.

"Little better." His voice was rough. "I can't believe you stayed. You should have at least taken the guestroom." He'd imagined having her in his bed so many times. Naked. So very naked as she reached for him and he was finally able to touch and stroke her silky smooth skin, taste the tender place between her thighs, find out what sounds she made when she came.

"You were so out of it, I didn't want to leave. I had to drag you back to bed twice."

She had? He didn't remember that. But to make a pregnant woman, let alone the one he was in love with, stay on the hard floor? Nuh uh. And what if she got sick now? "Jesus, Moll."

"I'm fine, I promise. Just glad you're feeling better." She rounded the end of the bed to grab her purse. "I've got a meeting at the funeral home, but I'll check on you later. If you need anything, text me. There's leftover soup—undigested—in the fridge, and I put some applesauce in there too. No dairy, and if your stomach's still iffy, then pick out the chicken when you eat the soup."

"Moll."

She stopped at the door to look back at him, raising her eyebrows.

She was so damn beautiful standing there. He couldn't believe she'd stayed to take care of him when she had so much going on. "Thank you."

She gave him a smile. "Of course. Now get better."

Jase lay there listening to her footsteps retreat down the stairs, then the front door shut. A few moments later, her car engine started.

In the silence, his gaze strayed over to the framed photo of him, his grandfather and Carter on the bookshelf. Jase had given Carter his word he would look after Molly if anything happened to him, and he would, always. No matter how much it hurt.

Chapter Two

CTE. Chronic Traumatic Encephalopathy.

That's what had killed her ex-husband. Although in some ways Carter had been dead to her a long time before he'd driven his truck over the side of that cliff.

Molly stood rigidly at the gravesite as the early September sun shone down on her and watched the uniformed pallbearers carry the flag-draped casket toward them from the hearse. The sight of it as they'd brought it into the church earlier had been a heavier shock than she had anticipated, the finality of it hitting her hard.

Now she fixed her gaze on the blue field of the flag, placed in the traditional manner over Carter's left shoulder. As Carter's former commanding officer, Beckett was positioned next to it. Opposite him was Jase. They looked so strong and handsome in their dress uniforms. Invincible, even though she knew better.

Behind them walked three other Green Berets who had served with Carter at some point, as well as Aidan MacIntyre in his navy blue Royal Marines dress uniform. Aidan had become tight with the others when his unit had carried out joint operations with Carter's A-team overseas.

Together the men carried the casket to the grave,

somber and stalwart. At an order from Beckett, they carefully placed it onto the lowering device. Molly wasn't sure what she felt at that moment. Numb, mostly.

The past few weeks had been an exhausting blur. The funeral had been delayed for over a month after his death because she'd been involved in a lengthy battle with Carter's parents about final arrangements for him.

Out of respect for his last wishes and the man he used to be, Molly had insisted Carter be buried here in Crimson Point. He would have wanted that, to be near her, Beckett and Jase. He would have hated being buried back in Kansas, a place he hadn't visited once in the entire time she'd known him.

In the end, she'd gotten her way. But it meant that Carter's body had been held in a Portland morgue until the other day, when his remains had finally been released to the local funeral home.

As an experienced ER nurse Molly was no stranger to death or horrific injuries, yet she had declined the invitation to view Carter's body. She hadn't wanted her last sight or memory of him to be of charred, blistered skin from the horrific burns he'd suffered in the fire after the crash.

She had agreed to the autopsy, however, in the hopes that the pathologists would be able to find the cause of his drastic mental decline since his brain injury suffered on his final tour in Afghanistan well over a year ago.

All around her the small crowd of people attending the graveside service faded into the background. Her friends Sierra and Poppy were here, as well as her mom and grandmother, who had flown in from North Carolina.

The Army chaplain officiating the service began his remarks. Molly listened with only part of her attention, her hands knitted together tightly in her lap, pressed against her burgeoning abdomen. She was more than four months pregnant now. The unintended result of wanting to comfort Carter during the last stages of their dissolving marriage.

Now she could admit the truth. She'd slept with him that final time to say goodbye, and also partly because she'd been so damn lonely...

Movement around the casket broke her from her thoughts. The Army honor guard took its position behind the grave.

She started a little when they fired the first rifle volley. Jase, Beckett and Aiden stood at attention, holding a salute along with their fellow servicemen in uniform. Two more volleys followed. Three precisely timed and spaced shots, the customary signal that the dead and wounded had been removed from the battlefield and cared for after a battle.

Then the first haunting notes of Taps rang out. Chills raced down her spine in spite of the midday heat, and her eyes stung. Muffled sobbing came from nearby. Carter's mother, seated next to the man she had divorced more than thirty years ago. Though they had every right to be here, Molly still didn't understand why they'd come.

They hadn't been there for Carter, too wrapped up in their own lives to maintain a relationship with him. Not even when he'd been wounded. And most certainly not through his hellish ordeal since.

They hadn't once traveled to see him in the hospital. He'd stopped taking his mother's increasingly infrequent calls months ago. Upon arrival at the church for the funeral service they had given Molly cold looks and an even colder shoulder. She did her best to ignore them, glad they would be gone in the morning. This was about Carter, not them, and she intended to make sure he was buried with dignity in the place he would have wanted.

"In his life he honored this flag. In death the flag shall honor him," the chaplain said.

The honor guard stepped forward and began folding

the flag. Once it was transformed into a neat triangle, one of them approached her and knelt before her. "On behalf of the President of the United States, the United States Army and a grateful nation, please accept this flag as a symbol of our appreciation for your loved one's honorable and faithful service."

Molly took it and held it on her lap, her spine rigid. Since she was technically Carter's ex-wife, the flag should have gone to his mother. But Molly would be damned if that woman would have this last piece of him. Carter would have wanted *her* to have it, not the woman who had given birth to him and then deserted him in his time of greatest need.

The military chaplain said something else and launched into yet another prayer. She didn't hear a word of it, too lost in her thoughts.

Then, one by one, Carter's brothers-in-arms came forward to pay their respects.

Beckett went first, dropping to one knee beside the bare casket. He placed a hand on the lid, bent his head and murmured something she didn't catch. Then he placed a Green Beret pin on the top and raised his hand, curling it into a fist.

Molly flinched as he slammed the end of it down on the pin, punching it into the polished wood. Beckett stood, saluted smartly, and turned away.

Then Jase took his turn.

It seemed to her that he moved in slow motion as he mimicked his former A-Team commander, crouching next to the casket and placing his palm flat on the top.

He held such a special place in her heart, and she ached for him. This ordeal had been every bit as hard for him as it had for her. He had known Carter longer, had been his best friend since they'd gone through SF selection together years ago. Carter's downward spiral had cost him not only her, but Jase and Beckett as well. Men he'd once fought beside and bled with, men he'd relied on for survival during the terror of combat.

Other mourners stood to place flowers on the casket. Carter's mother. Molly's mother.

Molly went last. She handed the flag to her mother, set her hands on the edge of her folding chair and pushed upright. Her knees threatened to wobble for a moment. A strong hand shot out to grasp her upper arm, supporting her. Glancing up, she met Jase's aqua stare. Steady. Watchful. Comforting.

Giving him a nod to let him know she was okay, she stepped forward to face the casket, a white rose in her hand. Her mind was in chaos, too many mixed emotions spinning there to sift through, but guilt and regret battled for supremacy.

Remember the good times.

She'd promised herself the night Carter died that she would focus on the good instead of the bad.

She owed him that, and so rather than thinking of how he had been in the months prior to his death, she thought of Carter's blinding smile in the midst of his thick, dark beard. His contagious belly laugh that could make complete strangers join in. His fun-loving personality, the way he was always the life of the party. Always hamming it up, making sure he was the center of attention.

Life had been many things with him, but boring wasn't one of them. Then that IED blast in Helmand Province had changed everything forever.

She didn't know how long she stared down at the decorated coffin lid. Warmth registered along her left side and a strong arm curled around her shoulders. Jase. She knew it without looking up, from his distinctive, spicy scent. She drew in a deep breath, feeling calmer.

It's time. Let him go. Let him be at peace.

Leaning forward, she placed her palms on the lid and

bent to touch her lips to the sun-warmed surface, right beneath the row of pins that Carter's fellow warriors had pounded into the wood.

"Goodbye, sweetheart," she whispered, speaking to the man he used to be, and the man she hoped he was again now. Wherever his spirit was, she prayed that he was finally at peace.

Placing the rose in the center, she straightened and allowed Jase to escort her back to her seat. Beckett was there too, waiting to help her.

Her throat tightened at the way they took care of her. They had both been there for her at every turn before the night Carter died, and especially since. Helping take care of the final arrangements, walking her through all the steps, the financial and estate paperwork because she'd been overwhelmed and not thinking clearly. What would she have done without them these past few months?

They were both hurting too, especially Jase, who blamed himself for Carter's death no matter how everyone tried to dissuade him of the notion. Molly still didn't know the details, but he and Carter had come to blows the night Jase found her in the culvert. After the fight, Carter had jumped in his truck and taken off. Minutes later, he'd crashed through the guardrail on the coastal highway and plunged over the edge of the cliff.

Even now it was impossible to know whether it had been an accident or suicide. The toxicology report showed Carter's blood alcohol levels were below the legal limit, and they'd found only prescription meds in his system.

The rest of the service passed quickly. One final prayer from the chaplain, and it was finally over.

Molly stood and walked toward the limousine parked on the cemetery road with Jase and Beckett flanking her. She didn't want to stay and watch the cemetery workers lower Carter into the ground. Couldn't stand to hear the terrible thud of finality when the casket hit bottom, or watch them cover it up with dirt.

She stopped partway to the limo, aware of Jase and Beckett following close behind. Watching over her. Ready to do whatever they could to help.

But they couldn't help her now. No one could. She was on her own. She and her baby.

"I want to walk for a few minutes," she told them. During the coming reception at Beckett and Sierra's she would have to play the hostess and visit with everyone, maybe even her in-laws. She needed to gear up for it. "Just need a little time to myself."

Beckett traded a look with Jase before focusing on her. "All right."

Her high heels clicked lightly on the pavement as she walked away, past rows of graves and trees leafed out in their late summer glory. The farther she got from the ceremony, the easier it was to draw in a deep breath. In another few weeks, the glowing green leaves would begin to turn scarlet and gold, then start to fall.

She put a hand to her abdomen and closed her eyes, inhaling deeply. This child might not have been planned, but Molly considered the baby to be a blessing. A piece of Carter would live on, and there was comfort in that even though the thought of having and raising a child on her own seemed lonely and daunting.

As of right now she had only her income to sustain her. Carter's life insurance policy named her as the beneficiary, but the settlement was up in the air until the company could determine whether his death had been an accident or suicide. If they decided it was suicide, the policy was null and void and Molly would get nothing. She had to plan as if she wasn't going to get anything from the insurance company.

A slight breeze blew across her skin, stirring the leaves overhead. She stopped and looked over her shoulder. Everyone was gathered around the grave now, including Beckett and Jase. The cemetery workers were lowering the casket.

Molly looked away and headed back for the limo, keeping her gaze averted from the gravesite.

She glanced up a minute later when she noticed a man in a suit approaching her casually on the path. She stopped, not recognizing him. Mid-to-late thirties maybe, dark-haired, fair skin, dressed in a tailored suit and wearing sunglasses.

He gave her a polite smile and stopped in front of her, his hands clasped in front of him. "I'm sorry for your loss."

"Thank you." He didn't introduce himself. "How did you know Carter?" Maybe he was one of the clients connected to Beckett's renovation company. Carter had been project manager for several months before Beckett had been forced to let him go due to his increasingly erratic behavior.

"We had business dealings together," the man said, and something about his tone struck her as cryptic.

She was about to ask what kind of business dealings, but the mourners were all leaving the gravesite now. Time to go.

She aimed a polite smile at the stranger. "Excuse me."

"Of course." He stepped aside and let her pass, but she could feel his gaze lingering on her as she approached the limo.

At the vehicle she accepted dozens of hugs and other condolences from the guests until she was half-desperate to escape into the back of it and shut the door.

As though sensing her distress, Jase materialized out of the crowd and ushered her into the open back door. Her mom and grandmother were already seated in the back, ever the elegant Southern ladies in their black dresses and tasteful black hats with veils that covered their eyes. "See you at Beckett and Sierra's," Jase said to her, his broad shoulders blocking out the sunlight and the crowd of people behind him as he shut the door.

Thankfully the reception passed quickly. Throughout it, she was keenly aware of where Jase stood nearby, still in his dress uniform. He stayed within sight, keeping an eye on her. She drew strength and comfort from that.

The guests began to leave earlier than she had expected, and she was glad. More than anything she just wanted this to be over so she could put it all behind her and actually move forward instead of feeling like she was just treading water. She'd loved her husband, but he hadn't been Carter for a long time. She'd done most of her grieving before he'd died. Now it was time to move on.

On their way to the door her mom and grandmother invited her to stay at their hotel just outside of town rather than go back to her rental house alone. Molly declined.

Her mother gave her a sympathetic look, then hugged her tight. "You need to come home," she said, the familiar scent of her perfume making tears prick Molly's eyes. She was excited about becoming a grandma come February, and it wasn't the first time she'd tried to convince Molly to move back to North Carolina since the situation with Carter had blown up.

But that was all the help her mother had offered.

Where were you? Molly wanted to demand. *Where were you when I was going through hell and I needed you?*

Her mother had never come to visit her here. Not once, even though she'd known what was going on with Carter, because she had never supported Molly's decision to marry him, and she was angry that Molly had moved away. Molly wasn't sure if she could get past that.

She choked the painful questions back and returned the hug. Asking them now would only cause more pain, and she'd had enough of that already for several lifetimes. Besides, the high road always had the best views.

"Not right now," she answered evenly.

"For a visit at least, then," her grandmother said, standing next to her daughter. Her complexion was several shades darker than her daughter's, and a few darker still than Molly's.

"Maybe. But not right now," Molly said, holding firm.

She needed to find her bearings. Figure out what the rest of her life was going to look like. Running home to North Carolina to hide at her mother's house now was a cop out. She needed to stand on her own two feet and face the future alone for a while. Before this child came into the world, she needed to have everything figured out. Beginning with finding a place to live once her rental agreement at her current place was up in ten days.

After her relatives left, Molly thanked Beckett and Sierra for hosting, hugged them both and walked outside into the balmy summer evening. Jase drove her back to the rental house she was staying in.

"How you holding up?" he asked as he made the turn off Salt Spray Lane and headed toward town.

"Okay. Just glad it's done."

He was silent a moment. "Do you want me to stay with you tonight?"

The offer surprised her. Though he'd been supportive and helpful at every turn since the night Carter died, she couldn't help but feel that he'd grown a bit distant from her. "I thought you and the guys were going out together?"

"I can skip it."

"That's sweet of you, but I'm okay. With most of the house packed up I don't have anywhere to put you anyway. Everything's in storage, even my sofas." In the morning, priority one was to find another rental to move into. Although ideally it would be something she could see herself and the baby living in long term, and eventually buy.

"Then you can come back to my place and sleep in the guest room." He glanced over at her. "I just don't want you to be alone tonight."

Molly smiled as warmth filled her chest. Maybe she'd been wrong about the distance she'd sensed from him. "I appreciate that, thank you, but I need to be alone for awhile. I'm going to have a hot bath, watch a movie, then crash."

His jaw tightened, but he nodded once. "Okay."

At the rental house he walked her to the door. And out of nowhere, the prospect of another long night alone suddenly triggered a flare of dread. Molly almost changed her mind about taking him up on his kind offer. He'd always been an amazing friend to her and Carter, so the new shift in their relationship bothered her.

"What about you?" she asked on the welcome mat, keys in hand. Stalling.

He frowned, the moonlight gilding the side of his face. It was strange seeing him clean-shaven. She was so used to seeing him and the others with beards or at least a few days' worth of growth on their faces. "What about me?"

"Are you okay?"

Something flared in his eyes for a moment, then he looked away. "Yeah, I'm okay."

He wasn't. Not really. But of course he would rather die than admit it.

Molly sighed. Stubborn-ass alpha males. They were all the same. And that's why she'd stayed with him this past Friday night—because he'd needed someone and would never have asked for help.

Ruefully shaking her head, she stepped forward and

wrapped her arms around his neck. He returned the embrace almost hesitantly, as though afraid to hold her too tight.

Molly rested her forehead on his sturdy shoulder for a moment, some part of her knitting back together with the embrace. Carter had been a huge bear of a man. Jase wasn't as tall as her ex-husband had been, and not quite as broad, but he still towered over her and was built of solid muscle.

It felt damn good to be held by someone who cared. "Thank you for everything," she murmured.

"You don't have to thank me, Moll. You know I'm always here for you," he said, and released her. He eyed the house, then her. "You sure about this?"

"Yes."

He nodded once in acceptance and stepped back. "Call me if you need anything, yeah?"

"I will."

He didn't look convinced. "Promise?"

"I promise." She unlocked the door and stepped inside, where a stack of packed moving boxes greeting her. Turning around, she stood there with one hand on the door and watched as Jase strode down the pathway.

Him leaving triggered two reactions. A sinking sensation in the pit of her stomach.

And the sudden weight of loneliness that threatened to suffocate her.

Chapter Three

"Well?" Mick asked through the phone's speaker.

Rafe passed a slower-moving car on the way out of town, checking his mirrors. He'd already made two circles to ensure he wasn't being followed, but the need to stay vigilant was long ingrained in him. "She's either clueless, or one of the best liars I've ever met."

His boss grunted. "Coming from you, that's saying something."

One side of Rafe's mouth curved up. "I know."

"So which do you think it is?"

"Not sure yet." Molly Boyd was a lot tougher than he'd thought she would be when he'd first started investigating her just days prior to her ex's death. Even at the funeral she'd been strong, not shedding one tear.

Maybe she'd hated the son of a bitch she'd divorced, Rafe wasn't sure. But if she had, then why had she been front and center at the service as the grieving widow, and why had Boyd kept her as beneficiary on his life insurance policy? Unless he hadn't had time to change everything before he killed himself. Rafe didn't believe for one second that it was an accident.

Either way, Molly clearly still had some feelings for

her ex. Feelings he could exploit to get what he wanted.

"Doesn't matter," Mick said. "That asshole owed us money. And she's his widow. She has to know something."

"I don't think she knows shit about any of it. I don't think anyone does."

Mick scoffed. "You said he wasn't close to the rest of his family."

"He wasn't. Or at least he wasn't when he died." Rafe made it a point to know about his targets' lives. Boyd had been all alone for the weeks prior to his death.

Mick's annoyed sigh gusted across the line. "The widow must know something. I don't care how you get it done. Just get the money."

"What if it was suicide? What if the life insurance policy doesn't pay out?" A hundred-and-twenty grand. Not an insignificant sum. And the way things were going, it looked like Rafe was going to need every penny of it, too.

"So what if it doesn't? He owes us the one-twenty, dead or not. She's the ex-wife. She'll pay."

"With what?" She was a nurse, and a renter. As far as Rafe could tell, the only thing she owned was her car and it wasn't worth anything. Squeezing her might not get him any of the money. That thought expanded the burning knot of anxiety deep in his belly. He needed to get all the money he could, and fast.

"With whatever she can get her hands on to settle the debt."

Desperate as he was, Rafe had his doubts about this one. It wasn't the first time he had gone after a dead man's widow to collect money, and it wouldn't be the last. The size of the debt Boyd had racked up with them meant it had to be recouped.

He'd been a desperate man. So desperate that he'd gambled away all his money, incurring crippling interest charges with the money he borrowed from them, and still came back for more. Certain in his crazed mind that his luck would magically change.

Rafe was becoming well acquainted with exactly how that kind of desperation felt. He was growing more and more frantic with each passing day. "She doesn't have much."

"She's an ER nurse," Mick said, papers crinkling in the background, his voice holding not a single ounce of concern. "She's got enough brains to figure something out."

"He beat her, you know. The night he died." Maybe guilt had made Boyd give the wheel a sharp turn as he'd rounded that final bend in the highway.

"Don't care. Just get the money."

Rafe's pulse drummed faster. What if there *was* no money? The dude had been seriously fucked up, and Rafe had dealt with a lot of whackos in his time. Had it been a coward's way out? Or the ultimate act of selflessness to leave his beloved wife something after he was gone?

If there was no money, Rafe was fucked.

"We done?" Mick said in an impatient tone.

"Yeah. I'm going." Rafe had to play this cool, not let his boss or anyone else see him sweat. Mick was the brains behind this arm of the organization, and Rafe the brawn. Mick handled the books and managed the other businesses the higher ups used as a front for their money laundering operation. Rafe enforced the terms of the agreements their clients signed: pay up or die.

"I'll let you know what I turn up," he said, and reached for the button to end the call.

"I heard she's pregnant."

Rafe paused, his finger an inch from the button. He could hear the smirk in Mick's voice. "Where'd you hear that?" He hadn't heard it, and he'd been keeping regular tabs on her these past couple of weeks.

"I got my sources too."

She hadn't looked pregnant. Was it Boyd's?

"Anyway, that should be useful to you."

Rafe narrowed his eyes as he made a turn at the next corner. His tail was still clear. "Meaning?"

Mick heaved another impatient sigh. "It's not just her life at stake, is it?"

A heavy, oily feeling coated the inside of his stomach. He'd tortured people to get money back. Even killed some of them, or their relatives. Sometimes he made it look like an accident. A slice to the brake lines in their car. A gas leak in their house.

And sometimes he used far more brutal and direct methods.

But he'd never targeted a pregnant woman before. Or a child. Not deliberately, anyway. Usually the threat of violence against them was enough to get the debtor to come up with a creative way to pay off the loan, with interest. Barring that, they either wound up working for Rafe and Mick until the debt was paid, or they met unpleasant ends.

In this case, it didn't matter. Carter Boyd was beyond the reach of threats and intimidation, but Rafe needed every last cent of the money Boyd owed.

"I'll call you tomorrow after my meeting," he told Mick in a clipped voice, and disconnected. He had an early morning flight to catch to Vegas.

He always got the money back, no matter what, even if it was from a dead man.

But this time, he had far more motivating him than protecting his perfect, ruthless reputation.

If he didn't get all the money he needed, he would wind up dead too.

****

After dropping Molly off, Jase headed home to change into jeans, dress shirt and his grandpa's bomber jacket before heading out to meet the guys. Today had been the first time he'd worn his Class A's in months. He'd worn them for Carter. The Army may have been his life for a long damn time, but that was all over now.

The Sea Hag stood in the middle of Front Street, a dark green, cedar-shingled building that had stood here since the founding of Crimson Point back in the 1890s. Since moving here he'd spent more than a few pleasant evenings at the Hag, having beers with Beckett and Noah, other guys from the company's construction crews. Carter too, at first.

As soon as Jase thought of him, the heaviness in his chest returned. Carter Boyd was the closest thing he had ever had to a real brother, and Jase was still grappling with his death. Along with an additional helping of guilt about wanting Carter's widow.

It had been damn hard to hide it from her since Carter died. So many times he'd been tempted to tell her how he felt, wanting to be more than just a friend through this whole mess. Thank God his saner judgment had prevailed. As far as he could tell, Molly was still completely in the dark about his feelings for her, and he'd pulled back a little to make sure she never guessed the truth.

Inside the Hag the air held the yeasty scent of beer and freshly baked bread. In the center stood the long bar, polished to a high gloss, with a large mirror reflecting the fading light that flooded in through the western-facing windows overlooking the beach.

In it he caught sight of Beckett, Mac and Noah over in the far corner, sitting with the other Army guys. Jase had served with most of them. Many of them were still active duty and had flown in from Fort Bragg for the funeral.

"Boys," Jase said as he approached the table.

"Weaver." Beckett waved him over to the end.

"Saved you a seat, wee man," Mac said in his Scottish burr.

Wee, because Jase was a whopping inch-and-a-half shorter than Mac. Jase took the chair beside Beckett and glanced at the half-empty bottles and rows of shot glasses on the table. "What? You guys started without me?"

"Nah, this is just the appetizer," Beckett said, passing a cold bottle of beer to him. "Finish this and we'll get started."

Jase drank it, dividing his attention between the stories being passed around the table and the view outside the long, wide windows overlooking the beach. It was beautiful here.

Crazy to think he'd wound up in a small town like this after he'd left the Army, but he loved it and was glad Beckett had asked him to come work for his renovation company when they'd both decided not to re-up their contracts after their last tour. And of course it also meant he was close to Molly, a double-edged sword most days.

"All right, let's do this," Beckett said and rose from his chair, his natural air of command and Captain's tone taking Jase right back to their days in the field together. Those had been some of the best and worst times of his life, and they had all forged bonds between them that would last forever.

Even beyond the grave.

Beckett raised a shot glass high. "It is foolish and wrong to mourn the men who died. Rather we should thank God that such men lived."

George S. Patton. A murmur of agreement came from the table. "Aye," Mac said with a nod.

Beckett paused, his dark gaze sweeping over the men assembled to say goodbye to Carter. "A toast, brothers. Raise your glasses to 'Absent Companions'."

"Absent Companions," they all chorused, and

knocked back the shot. A loud, hollow *thunk* sounded as nine shot glasses hit the table almost simultaneously.

The whiskey burned down Jase's throat, providing the only real internal warmth he'd felt all day. They'd lost too many friends and fellow warriors to these wars through PTSD, injury, combat and suicide. But none of the previous losses had hit Jase the way Carter's had.

Mac stood next, taking Jase by surprise. "Here's to honor," the Scot said, raising another shot into the air. "To getting honor. And not getting off her, until you get off on her."

Jase barked out a laugh at that as a raucous cheer rang out around him, drawing the attention of everyone else in the bar. Some people gave them curious looks, while others smiled. God, Carter would have loved that little speech. Jase could picture his wicked grin so clearly.

When the guys had quieted down, Jase pushed to his feet, his heart growing heavy once more. He was silent a moment before offering his toast. "The soldier, above all other people, prays for peace, for he must suffer and bear the deepest wounds and scars of war." Douglas MacArthur, and that ballsy bastard had known what he was talking about.

Everyone went quiet. They stared at him for a tension-laden moment, the gravity of what he'd said hanging in the air along with the stringent scent of alcohol.

Then Jase upped the ante. "May the brave soldier who never turned his back to the enemy never have a friend turn his back to him." He knocked back the shot as soon as the last word was out of his mouth, and somehow managed to get it down before his throat closed up. He'd looked up quotes about toasting a fallen friend last night, and that one had hit him like a knife to the chest.

The ugly truth was, he'd turned his back on Carter at the end. They all had. And now Carter was gone, maybe because of it.

The logical part of Jase knew it wasn't directly his fault. That despite his problems Carter had been a grown man and made his own choices. Jase hadn't driven that truck over the cliff, Carter had. Yet his conscience refused to let him off the hook regardless.

"Wow. That was heavy, wee man," Mac said at last, reaching out to clap a big hand on Jase's back.

Yeah, he was aware. But he'd needed to say it even if it made everyone else uncomfortable. He didn't have many regrets in life, but this was far and away the biggest.

With the tension broken the others chuckled, and within moments the other toasts began. Jase paid only partial attention, still wrestling with his thoughts. The life insurance company might be conducting its own investigation into Carter's death, but Jase already knew the truth.

Without a doubt Carter had deliberately wrenched the wheel of his pickup as he rounded that final bend on the highway outside of town. Why he'd done it wasn't as clear. If Molly didn't get the life insurance money, things were going to be really hard for her and the baby. It would be pretty damn hard to prove it hadn't been an accident, however, given the weather at the time of the crash and the winding stretch of road.

He stared down at the next shot of Jack that Mac had pressed into his hand as conversation buzzed around him. He'd seen and done a lot of shit in his time in the military, some of it so bad it had left permanent stains on his soul.

But that night. The terrible events of the night Carter died would haunt him for the rest of his life.

When he'd gone to confront Carter that night, he'd never dreamed his friend would race out of that bar and drive off a fucking cliff.

The guilt corroded his insides like sulphuric acid, a constant burn that never went away. He didn't regret the things he'd said or the punches, because he'd meant them, and because Carter had known he deserved them.

What he couldn't get past was being responsible for making Carter race out of there and get behind the wheel when his friend was clearly distraught. Ever since that night, Jase's personal demons had been out in full force to punish him for it, robbing him of sleep and haunting him even while he was awake.

"So, Weaver. You're a pencil pusher now, huh?" one of the other SF guys down the table said to him, a slight smirk on his face.

"Nah, man. Bean counter. That's what I heard," the guy next to him said.

"That's right," Jase answered them both. "Not a bad gig, except my boss can be a giant dick and the benefits kinda suck."

Everyone chuckled as Beckett sliced him a hard look. "My dick *is* giant," he allowed after a moment, and laughter broke out along the table.

"What about you, Mac?" the second guy, Glen, said to Aidan. "You got sucked into this sad little civilian operation Beck's got going on too?" He indicated Beckett and Jase with a sweep of his hand.

Mac shrugged good-naturedly. "Ach, it's not all bad. I was sweatin' my bollocks off in Florida anyhow. And as project manager I get to keep bossing folk around, which I'm fond of doing, so there's aye that."

"You must miss it, though," another guy said to them, looking from Jase to Mac, then Beckett. "The action."

"Nope," Beckett said.

"Me neither," Jase and Mac responded at the same time. It was mostly true. Jase sure didn't miss freezing his ass off or going hungry, or being shot at.

Glen's expression was skeptical. "Yeah? Think you'll stay out for good?" he asked them.

"Not sure," Beckett said. "I thought I would go nuts working a regular job, but I gotta say, it's growing on me.

It's got its perks."

"Yeah, meaning you get to go home and crawl into bed with Sierra every night," Jase said, and everyone laughed.

Beckett grinned, his hard face lighting up. "What can I say, I'm a lucky guy."

Yeah, he was. Jase was glad he realized that.

"Plus, this way you get to keep ordering our sorry arses around," Mac pointed out.

"Yeah, that doesn't hurt either," said Beckett.

Jase smiled. He'd wondered whether he could handle a desk job after over a decade in one of the Army's most elite units. Beckett's job offer had come at exactly the right time. After years of constant deployments to various hellholes all over South Asia and the Middle East, Jase had been flirting with burnout.

For now, a safe, nine-to-five accounting position was good enough. Even though a part of him was already restless, hungry for the challenge of something new, and at some point he would crave the adrenaline rush of living at the tip of the military spear again. That was simply part of who he was.

For the time being, however, he was content to stand down and relax, spending his days with his neatly-compiled spreadsheets with their columns of numbers. Tidy. Concise. Peaceful.

Keeping the job also meant he could stay close to Molly. Because whatever else happened from now on, he would be there for her and the baby.

"You guys have room for one more?"

Jase whipped around at the familiar, feminine voice behind him, a bittersweet sting spreading through him at the sight of Molly standing there. She wore a pale yellow summer dress that left her shoulders, arms and legs bare and made her light brown skin glow. Her tight, dark curls were pulled up into a clip at the back of her head, little spirals bouncing at her temples and the nape of her neck as she moved.

And the smile. It damn near broke his heart because it was so courageous and he hadn't seen her smile like that in so long. She was like a ray of sunshine breaking through the gloom.

"Of course," Beckett said before Jase could, rising from his chair.

The rest of them stood and Jase moved his seat over while Beckett pulled another chair from the next table over for her, placing it between them. Jase got a whiff of her light, fresh scent that always reminded him of springtime as she scooted in toward the table and mentally slammed the gate shut against the inevitable tide of yearning he always felt when she was near.

"What changed your mind?" he asked her.

"I decided I needed a change of scenery."

Good for her. "I'm glad you came." She needed to get out more—she'd barely left her rental house in the past month. Molly was a social animal, loved people and being in the thick of the action. She and Carter had always been the center of whatever gathering they came to. Jase would hate to see her lose that part of her personality.

She shot him a brave smile. "Me too."

Mac leaned toward her across the table. "What can I get you, bonnie lass?" His tone was friendly, nothing more, but even still the "bonnie lass" comment made Jase's hackles go up. It was a stupid and irrational reaction, but there it was. He was protective and borderline territorial when it came to Molly.

Jase sat back, enjoying the chance to watch Molly as she talked with the others, laughing at stories they told her. Some about Carter, some about Beckett and him.

God, he loved the sound of her laugh, husky and sultry as the air before a summer storm. But watching her was bittersweet in its own way too. He'd become used to the stab of pain he always felt when he saw her with Carter. Now it almost hurt more to see her pregnant and alone.

Jase remained quiet as he observed her, drinking in the sight of her smiles and the welcome sound of her laughter. Surrounded by a table full of warriors, she shone bright as the sun, and he would have to be content with the few rays that fell upon him.

He would stay in Crimson Point as long as she needed him. But if that ever changed, for his own sanity he needed to leave this town and put a few thousand miles between him and Molly Boyd.

Chapter Four

Sierra called the following Thursday night just as Molly climbed out of her car at the storage facility. "Hey," she answered with a grin. "I was just thinking about you."

"Aww, you were? Where are you now?"

"Just going through a few things in my storage unit," Molly replied, entering the passcode into the keypad.

"Did you find a place yet?"

"No. I looked at three apartments yesterday and one today. One of them wasn't too bad, but it was dark and depressing. Beggars can't be choosers and all that, but I can't handle a long, gray winter being cooped up in a dark house."

Finding something decent that she could afford on her salary was proving almost impossible. And she couldn't apply for a mortgage because she was unsure whether she was going to get any insurance money and didn't have enough for a down payment. Ideally, she wanted a rental with the option to buy, but they were hard to come by in her situation.

"Well, we've got a room all ready for you here if you need it."

"I love you guys. If I don't find anything in the next

couple days, I'll be moving in with you this weekend."

"Is it selfish of me to hope you don't find anything yet? It would be so cool to have you stay here. We could have girls' nights all the time."

Molly smiled. "I don't want you to get sick of me."

Sierra scoffed. "That would never happen."

"Beckett might feel differently."

"He'd adjust."

"But I love him enough to not put him through that." Her first shift back at the hospital was on Monday, so she intended to get as much done before then to get the rest of her life as settled as possible.

"You going to be at the storage place long?"

"For a while. I've been putting this off, and it's time."

"So, does this mean we're not going to yoga class tonight, then?"

Molly laughed under her breath at the hopeful note in her best friend's voice. "Of course we are."

"Oh."

She shook her head, smiling. "I thought you said you weren't hating it anymore. You told me last week that you might even have started to like it."

"No, that was Poppy."

"No, that was you. Dork."

Sierra laughed. "I must have been high on endorphins or something, because I do *not* remember saying any such thing."

"Liar. It's an hour a week, and it's good for you. Plus it helps me find my zen, which you gotta admit, I could use more of these days."

A loud sigh answered her. "Ouch, heap on the guilt, why don't you. Bitch," Sierra teased.

Molly smiled. "You know you love me."

"I do. And so I'll meet you at the damn yoga studio at six with Poppy."

"Good stuff. See you, doll." She ended the call and walked into the storage container.

She hadn't been here in almost a month. It had taken this long to finally summon up the courage to come here and start going through all her and Carter's stuff. With Sierra and Poppy's help she'd put aside some of his cherished personal items from his military service for Jase and Beckett, kept other sentimental things for the baby, then donated everything she didn't want to keep. Now there were only a few pieces of furniture and a dozen or so boxes remaining.

The box at the top of the second stack was marked *photos*. She'd been holding off going through it because she just hadn't been strong enough to face the memories inside it. But she couldn't avoid it any longer. If she wanted to truly put the past behind her and begin moving forward, this was a necessary step.

She dragged the box down and sat cross-legged in front of it to start going through the contents. The first album she found put an instant lump in her throat. *A Warrior's Journey*, she'd entitled the memory book she'd made.

Inside was the story of Carter's ordeal that began during his final deployment to Afghanistan. The first picture was of him standing in their kitchen in North Carolina wearing jeans and an olive drab T-shirt, his big grin visible in the midst of his heavy, dark beard.

She remembered the moment vividly. He'd been trying to coerce her into a final quickie before heading to the airport, and she'd made him pose for the picture first.

The next page contained some pictures he'd taken at camp in Helmand Province over the next few weeks. Most were of him being an ass, clowning around with the guys from his team. The vast majority were of him and Jase, causing trouble and mugging it up for the camera.

Jase had always been the straight man to Carter's comedic personality, more grounded and subdued. The two of them had been almost inseparable from the night she'd met them at the bar near base.

She turned the page, and the visceral clench of her stomach was all too familiar as she looked at the images of the destroyed Humvee Carter had been riding in when the IED went off. Jase had given them to her afterward.

The entire front half of the vehicle was missing. Both the driver and the front passenger had been killed in the blast. Carter had been knocked out with a skull fracture in the backseat, and the guy next to him had lost both a leg and an arm. Jase had been riding a few vehicles behind when the explosion happened. He'd been the one to pull Carter out of the wreckage.

The sight of the blackened, twisted metal sickened her, reminding her too much of the mangled mess of Carter's truck the night he'd died.

She quickly flipped to the next page, showing her dressed in scrubs at Carter's bedside at the hospital in Landstuhl, Germany. She'd flown there the night she'd gotten the call that he'd been injured, to be with him when he woke up post op.

In the shot she was bent over his bed, her head close to his, smiling at the camera with him. His head was wrapped up in bandages, his eyes blackened and swollen, but he was grinning, giving a thumbs-up to the nurse who had taken the picture for them.

The image hurt for a number of reasons. When he'd come out of the anesthetic, he'd been so happy to see her he'd held her to him so tight that her bones had ached.

Molly had thought it was a miracle that he'd survived without serious cognitive loss or permanent physical dysfunction. Neither of them had known the nightmare that was in store for them later on.

She flipped through the rest of the book, lost in

memory as the pictures and text chronicled Carter's recovery and eventual release from Walter Reed several months later.

There were more books in the box, and special framed photos. Their wedding album. A portrait of her and Carter. One of them with Jase, who was best man. A picture of her and Carter on the beach on their honeymoon in the Dominican Republic.

Bittersweet memories she didn't want to look at every day, but she couldn't bear to throw them away, either. And the baby deserved to know and see Carter as he had been.

After sorting through and organizing what remained in the storage locker, her energy level had plummeted and was hovering near zero. Tired and in need of a recharge, she locked up and drove over to Whale's Tale, her friend Poppy's bookstore/café in the heart of Front Street.

Poppy gave her a sunny smile when Molly stepped through the front door, the smell of baked goods and freshly brewed coffee filling the air. "Hey, this is a nice surprise." Golden blond hair up in a knot, she came out from behind the front counter wearing a frilly little half-apron around her waist and engulfed Molly in a warm hug. "You hungry?"

"*Starving*. What've you got in here today?" She sniffed the air. "I think I smell my favorite soup."

"You do. Come on." She tugged Molly to the counter and immediately went over to ladle a large serving of homemade tomato basil soup into a compostable takeout container. "Want some focaccia to go with it?"

She mentally checked in with her pregnancy stomach and got a thumbs down. "Got any of those cheese biscuits instead?"

"Sure."

Molly perused the pastry case as she waited. She shouldn't go nuts with the junk food, because gestational diabetes was no fun at all, but it'd been a hell of a few months, and she was growing a small human in her belly. She deserved treats.

"I'll take two peach tarts, and a couple apple turnovers, too. Oh, and couple sweetened iced teas as well." Not the sweet tea she'd grown up with, but pretty tasty and much better for her.

Poppy glanced at her with a teasing glint in her eyes. "You're eating for four now instead of two?"

"Ha, no. Some of it's for tomorrow."

Poppy bustled around getting the order together. "Sierra says we're still on for yoga tonight?"

"Lemme guess, she called you to see if you wanted to cancel."

"Yep." Poppy put the pastries into a white cardboard bakery box decorated with the Whale's Tale symbol of a humpback fluke on the top. "She's really looking forward to class tonight."

"No she's not."

Poppy laughed. "Okay, not even a little. But hey, she's going. And I'm looking forward to it, so that's something."

"Glad to hear it." Molly paid for her order and dropped a five-dollar bill into the tip jar over Poppy's protests. "You're the best. See you at class."

Outside in the parking lot, her phone rang. Jase. "Hey. What's up?"

"You busy right now?"

"Not at this moment, no. Why?"

"I need you to meet me somewhere." He gave her an address that was only a few blocks away.

She frowned. "Is everything okay?"

"Yeah, everything's good."

"Then why? What's going on?"

"Just come."

"Okay. I'm at Whale's Tale right now, so I'll be there

in two minutes."

"Perfect."

What was Jase up to?

She drove south on Front Street past all the pretty shops and businesses along the waterfront. September was the tail end of tourist season and the beach was fairly busy on this perfect, sunny afternoon, gentle waves rolling in endless curls onto the beach. Families with young children flew brightly-colored kites in the brilliant blue sky while gulls circled overhead, searching for an unwary tourist's food.

A wistful smile curved her lips as she thought of all the things she and her baby could do together in the coming years. Lord it was pretty here. In a completely different way than North Carolina's Outer Banks. Wilder. The ruggedness called to something inside her.

She arrived at the address four minutes later. A house. And not just any house—a gorgeous, new-looking Craftsman-style one. Jase's and Beckett's trucks were both parked out front.

Jase was there to pull her door open for her, a big grin on his face. "Well, whaddya think?"

"Of the house?"

"Yeah."

"It's gorgeous. But why are you showing it to me?"

"No reason. Come on." He grabbed her hand and started for the walkway to the front door, the scent of his leather bomber jacket so familiar, his strong fingers secure around hers.

She loved that he wore his grandfather's jacket. And that he adored all things WWII era including the music because it reminded him of his grandparents. An elite warrior he might be, but deep down he was a sentimental sap. She loved that about him too.

"Is this one of your latest projects?" The renovation company Beckett owned and ran specialized in fixing up heritage homes, but they did other projects as well.

"Yep."

"It's beautiful." Just the sight of it made her happy.

It had an almost East Coast feel, the wooden exterior boasting a fresh coat of smoky blue-gray paint and white trim. Black shutters framed the windows on both floors and the front door was painted a glossy, soft aqua. A tall redwood cedar stood in the tidily-landscaped front yard full of shrubs and other plants, and though she was blocks away from the beach here, she could smell the ocean on the breeze.

The sweet smell of sawdust hit her as she followed Jase up the walkway to the front porch, along with the whine of a power saw and the thud of hammers from inside. "You're being awfully mysterious right now," she said to him.

He shot her a grin and kept walking, then opened the front door and stood aside, motioning for her to enter. The first thing she noticed was the natural light flooding in, and the shiny hardwood floors.

She walked past the staircase and into a beautifully done kitchen with stone countertops, creamy cabinets and new appliances. "Wow." Large double windows above the sink looked out directly over the back deck and small backyard large enough for a swing set and maybe an above ground pool.

"You like it so far?" he asked from close behind her.

She couldn't stop looking around. "Are you kidding? What's not to like?"

"Here, check out the living room."

Molly followed him into the other part of the great room. There was so much character in the house, giving it a warm, cozy feeling. It even had her favorite color on the walls, a deep blue-green teal.

"There are three fireplaces, this one, one in the office here on the main floor, and one in the master bedroom.

All gas."

She stopped and faced him. He looked tired, with dark circles under his eyes. He'd recovered well from the flu, but the funeral and the late nights he must have been putting in here had taken their toll. She wanted to hug him, make those shadows disappear. "Jase. Why are you showing me all this?"

His aqua eyes were full of warmth. "Because it can be yours if you want it."

Her mouth fell open. "What?" He had to be kidding. "There's no way I could ever afford something like this—"

"It's got a fully separate suite downstairs. If you got a renter, that could pay for most of the mortgage every month." He raised a golden-brown eyebrow. "Wanna see the rest?"

She bit her lip, but couldn't hold back an excited smile. "*Yes*."

His answering grin made her heart flutter, catching her off guard. "Good."

Shoving aside her strange reaction, she toured the upstairs, which was just as great as the main floor. Two smaller bedrooms, a Jack-and-Jill bathroom, and the master suite. From the hammering and sawing going on in there, it wasn't done yet.

"We're almost finished in the master bathroom," Jase told her, leading the way into the master suite.

"Ohhh…" The room was bright and spacious. Again, the walls were that gorgeous, jewel-toned teal, with creamy white moldings and baseboards and oak hardwood floors. "Did you guys redo all of this?"

"No. It was in pretty good shape when we got it. We just refinished some things and updated some others." He nodded to the left. "Come see the master bath."

She didn't move, feeling a little awkward. The guys had gone to so much trouble for her, no doubt working after hours to get this done so Jase could show it to her. "I didn't even know you guys were working on this one."

"I wanted to surprise you. I knew you needed to find a new place, so when the owner decided to sell instead of completing the renos he'd hired us for a few weeks ago, the company bought it so we could fix it up for you."

She had no illusions that it had been his doing. He always seemed to go above and beyond to help her. "I can't believe you'd do all this for me."

He shrugged. "I want you to have a home you feel comfortable in. And I promised Carter a long time ago that I would take care of you."

What? "Oh." Her heart hitched. He'd never told her that before.

"Take a look at the walk-in closet. I just put more shelving up."

She walked over to it, unsure what to think. Taking all this on for her benefit was going way above and beyond, even if he'd made that promise to Carter.

Looking around at everything with new eyes, it suddenly hit her how well Jase knew her tastes, because it was reflected in the details. He'd obviously been paying a lot closer attention over the years than she'd realized.

Not just the overall style and feel of the house, which was reminiscent of the coastal region of North Carolina, but right down to the fixtures and paint colors. The teal on the walls. The glossy aqua on the front door.

"Jase, this is unreal," she said to him, stunned by all he'd done for her.

He shrugged like it was no big deal. "It's yours to rent if you want it. And it comes with the option to buy later on."

Damn, he knew her so well. "How much is the rent for the main part of the house?"

"Whatever you can afford comfortably every month."

No. This wasn't right. She couldn't take advantage of his or Beckett's generosity. As much as she appreciated his offer and the sheer amount of work he'd put into this, it stirred complicated feelings in her.

"I can't accept this." She shook her head, glanced around her. No way this was in her price range. "You could get a premium rent for this from someone else."

"Moll." His voice was low, calm. "It's yours if you want it. But you don't have to decide right now. I just wanted to show you around so you could get a feel for it. Go home and sleep on it."

She turned her attention back to him, and there was that undeniable tug of awareness again. She shook it off, unwilling to face or examine it. There were more important things to worry about right now, like where she was going to live. This place felt right. Jase had made it that way, for her and the baby.

She swallowed the lump forming in her throat. While she didn't like being on the receiving end of charity, she wasn't so stubborn that she would let an opportunity like this pass by. She couldn't afford to be prideful right now.

"I'd better go see the bathroom and say hi to the others," she said, mainly to change the subject and give her an excuse to put some space between her and Jase.

The hammering stopped as she entered the master bathroom, a bright, spacious, spa feel to it. Aidan was busy prepping the walls, his deep auburn hair, face and shoulders dusted with drywall dust, sweat stains on the chest of his shirt and under his arms. "Hey, gorgeous," he said to her in his deep Scottish burr.

"Hi." She switched her attention to Beckett, who was grouting the tile in the huge walk-in shower.

"Hey, Moll. What do you think of the place?" Beckett asked, trowel in hand as he stepping out of the shower enclosure.

"It's perfect."

Beckett's dark brown eyes gleamed with humor. "So you'll take it?"

She glanced at Jase, who stood in the bathroom doorway, the breadth of his shoulders all but filling the space. Why hadn't she ever noticed the way the fabric of his shirt clung to the muscles across his chest and shoulders before?

Realizing her gaze had lingered on him a little too long, she focused back on Beckett, feeling bad that the guys were working here in their spare time every day. "I'm seriously tempted."

"Glad to hear it."

"Why don't you take another look around and make note of anything you'd want changed. If you give me a list, I can do them, for you," Jase said behind her.

"It's already perfect," she murmured. "But yeah, I'd like to look around more."

Leaving them to continue their work, she did another tour, noting more details that Jase must have put in for her. Lantern-style pendant lights above the kitchen island. Chandeliers in the bathrooms.

She went back upstairs and into the hallway, looking for something to make herself useful with. A warm vanilla ice cream color had been put up on two walls, making the most of the natural light. A gallon of paint, tray and roller lay on the floor next to one of the remaining primed walls. She wasn't much of a handyman, but she could paint, and the guys had their hands full. Working on their own time, for her.

She pulled her hair back into a clip, rolled up her sleeves and poured some paint into the tray. Then she lifted the ladder away from the wall and opened it, loaded her brush in the paint, and climbed up to begin cutting in near the ceiling.

"What do you think you're doing?"

She started to turn her head just as Jase rushed over,

then gasped in surprise when his arms banded around her waist and lifted her to the floor. The strength and warmth of his hold penetrated her awareness, leaving her skin strangely sensitive. "Hey," she protested.

"Hey nothing." He spun her around and plucked the paintbrush from her hand. "I don't want you lifting a finger here, let alone up on a ladder and breathing in paint fumes right now." He carried the brush into the master bedroom.

"Jase." She followed him, annoyed. At his ridiculous overprotectiveness. At her body's unsettling reaction to the feel of his arms around her.

Her skin tingled where he'd touched her, the easy strength in his muscles making her heart flutter. Both things she didn't want to think about.

What was wrong with her? She was a pregnant widow and he'd been her husband's best friend. The very idea of her being attracted to Jase that way…it was ridiculous. "I'm pregnant, not helpless. I can roll some paint."

"I appreciate the offer, but no. We've got this," he said without looking at her.

He was ridiculous. She put her hands on her hips. "Seriously?"

That startling aqua gaze of his sliced over to her. "Seriously."

She stood there scowling at him, not really angry at him but for some reason she couldn't look away. Not even when he climbed back into the huge walk-in shower to resume grouting with Beckett.

Against her will her gaze slid over his shoulders and back, tracking the way the fabric of his shirt pulled taut along the ridges of muscle there.

Unbidden, an image flashed into her head. Of him standing in that same shower while the water sluiced over his naked skin, down the rock-hard slab of his chest and belly to his groin—

She mentally slapped that painfully vivid picture away, stunned and unsettled. Where the hell had that come from?

Molly tore her gaze from him, ashamed. Carter was barely cold in his grave, and here she was, fantasizing about his best friend.

She didn't know what to do with these strange, budding feelings for the man who up until now had simply been one of her closest and most dependable friends.

I gotta get outta here.

"I have to go," she called out.

Jase stopped and looked over at her. "Already?"

She nodded. "I have some things to take care of." Like sorting out her tumultuous thoughts.

He studied her a moment. "Okay. So you'll think about taking the place?"

"Yes," she promised. "Thanks for…everything." That was so lame in light of everything he and the others had done, but it was all she had.

"Sure. Have a good night."

"You too." She rushed downstairs, trying to sort out her racing thoughts.

She had always liked Jase. Loved him as a friend. But she hadn't ever pictured her friends naked in the shower before, and that was worrisome. Hopefully it was just pregnancy hormones making her temporarily insane, but whatever the case, her awareness of him as a desirable man was growing stronger every time she saw him, and she couldn't seem to shut it off.

This was bad. What would people think if they knew what was going on in her head? And she knew all too well the risks that came with getting involved with a Green Beret. Even if Jase was out of the military, it didn't mean his service hadn't affected him. Or that it wouldn't affect him later.

Still a little shaken, she got into her car and drove

back to the older rental she was staying in. Determined to push the unnerving thoughts and Jase from her mind, she packed up a few more moving boxes from her bedroom and closet, leaving only the most basic essentials until moving day.

Someone knocked on the front door as she was finishing up an hour later.

Pushing up from her kneeling position, she hurried to the front door. "Coming," she called.

There was no peephole and no side window to look out of, so she pulled the door open just a few inches to see who it was. A jolt of surprise hit her when she recognized the man who had approached her at the funeral standing on her doorstep.

"Hi, Molly," he said, giving her a confident smile that was right on the edge of oily. Today he was in jeans and a dress shirt, his dark brown hair styled perfectly, his sunglasses dangling from his fingertips.

"How did you find me?"

"I came by to visit Carter once. My name's John, by the way."

She didn't believe him. On either point.

She stayed where she was with the door partially ajar, refusing to open it more. What was he doing here? How had he found her? "What are you doing here?" Her tone was barely polite, her expression just on the unfriendly side of neutral.

"I was hoping we could talk for a few minutes."

"About what?" A thread of unease wound around her insides. No way she was letting him inside. Dense trees bordered three sides of this lot. No one would see or hear them. If she screamed for help, she doubted anyone would hear, much less help.

"I'd rather talk in private."

"Here's just fine."

He smiled thinly at her refusal, then sobered.

"You've been through a lot lately. I know this is a hard time and I don't want to add to your burden, but I get the feeling you aren't aware of the financial problems your husband was in when he died."

A sense of foreboding crept over her. "What do you mean?"

"His debt."

Debt? Her stomach shrank and she didn't correct him by saying ex-husband. That was none of his damn business.

"What kind of debt?" She and Carter had held separate bank accounts for almost two months before he died. She hadn't been able to access his banking information because she wasn't authorized on his new account. That's why dealing with all the financials before the funeral had been such a nightmare.

"John" gave her a pitying look. "You were living apart for a while before he died, right?"

She didn't like where this was going. Why had Carter been in debt? How much? What had he spent his money on? "So?"

"So you weren't aware of what he was involved in."

Involved in... She wanted to tell him to leave her the hell alone and slam the door in his face, but she couldn't move.

She'd wondered what Carter had done while they were apart. How he had supported himself and come up with the money to live on after those first few weeks, since Beckett had been forced to fire him and he hadn't had much in the way of savings.

Before Carter had left, most of what they earned went towards rent and the rest of their bills. Anything left over had gone into a joint savings account that he'd given to her when he'd moved out.

"Were you aware that he developed a gambling habit?"

Oh, shit.

A hole opened up in the bottom of her stomach. Carter had enjoyed gambling on occasion, but he was never irresponsible about it and he'd steered clear of it after his injury because he knew his brain wasn't functioning the same and hadn't trusted himself to be able to stop when he needed to.

"What kind of gambling?" she made herself ask.

He shrugged evasively. "Little of this, little of that. Unfortunately, he either got greedy or desperate. Bet everything he won, and lost it all. Then he came to us."

She swallowed, her mouth suddenly dry, afraid to ask who "us" was, because she was starting to get a good idea on her own. "How much?" she asked dully.

"He owes us a hundred-and-twenty with the interest."

Her eyes went wide. "A hundred twenty *thousand?*"

"Yep. Give or take a few." He put his hands in his jacket pockets, cocked his head. It was only then she realized how big he was. How powerful his build was. And how very alone she was. "I need the money back."

Her pulse hammered in her throat. "Well I can't help you. As you saw the other day, my ex-husband is dead and buried."

His hazel eyes turned hard, and the twist of his lips sent a frisson of warning through her. "That doesn't mean the debt is forgiven."

Cold crawled up her spine. "You need to leave. Now." She started to shut the door, barely stifled a gasp when he shot a hand out to grab the edge of the door to stop her. Their eyes locked and an icy trickle of fear slid through her veins.

The sound of an approaching vehicle made them both dart a look toward the driveway. Relief punched through her when she recognized Jase's white pickup coming toward the house. "Whatever Carter did has nothing to do with me," she snapped to "John".

He turned back to face her. "As you're no doubt aware, unfortunately life's not that simple."

The implied threat chilled her even more. "Go," she ground out. "Now. Or I'm calling the cops."

He held her gaze for another few heartbeats. Unflinching. And from his calm demeanor and total lack of concern for being seen by Jase, some part of her recognized that this man could be lethal when he chose to. "We'll talk soon," he murmured, and stepped back.

Molly couldn't answer, her throat was too tight.

She stood there rooted to the spot while he got in his car, quickly reversed and shot past Jase in the driveway. There was no time to grab her phone to take a picture of the plate. She was just glad he was gone, and even gladder that Jase was here.

Chapter Five

Jase couldn't see the Audi's driver clearly through the tinted windows but he saw enough to know it was a man. Who was it? He watched in the rearview mirror, unable to get the plate number because of the angle, and continued up to Molly's house.

Molly was waiting at the door when he pulled up. "Who was that?" he asked as he climbed out. "Someone from the insurance company?"

She shook her head. "No." She was visibly upset, immediately putting him on edge. And she'd taken off from the house abruptly. Something else was bothering her.

"Do you know him?"

"He was at the funeral. Said his name is John, but I trust him about as much as I can pick him up and throw him."

"What did he want?"

She hesitated, and that alone told him she was hiding something. Why? "Something about Carter."

Jase waited for her to elaborate, but she didn't. He swept his gaze over her, noting the way she had her arms wrapped around her waist. He also couldn't help but notice the changes in her because he noticed *everything* about Molly and always had. Her breasts were bigger now, and her belly showed a slight curve above the waistband of her jeans.

While it was hard to see the visible reminder of the baby Carter had left behind, the child was also part of Molly. Jase wanted to be there for her, wanted her *period* if she would only give him a chance.

No way in hell he was going to tell her how he felt, however, at least not yet. There was too much history between them for her to get past right now—and she was pregnant—but some part of him that refused to die hoped that in time she might change her mind and see him as more than just a friend.

If something—or someone named John—was bothering her, he wanted to know about it. "Moll, I want to help. But I can't if you won't talk to me."

She waved a hand, a frown knitting her eyebrows. "It's just—it's something to do with Carter. I don't even know if it's true." She turned and headed down the hallway before he could ask anything more. "Did you need something?"

I need you to stop and talk to me. "I was just on my way to the gym and wanted to come by and make sure you were okay. You seemed a little upset when you left the house earlier."

"No, I was just a little overwhelmed, that's all." She went into the kitchen. "You want some dinner? I've got some leftover casserole from last night."

"No, I'm good." The woman tied him into knots without even realizing it.

He'd secretly pined for her for years and that hadn't changed now that she was single. While he'd loved Carter like a brother, his best friend hadn't always treated her the way he should have. He hadn't been attentive or affectionate enough. Hadn't fully appreciated what he had in her. And though he and Molly had been happy enough prior to the TBI, even at his best Carter had been about as romantic as a rock.

To Jase's knowledge Molly had never complained about any of it, but then, she hadn't complained about anything, not even the frequent and lengthy deployments that must have worn on her.

All he knew was, if Molly had been his, he would have shown her each and every day how much he appreciated and cherished her. How lucky he was to have her. God, how he wanted that chance, but he didn't dare tell her.

Packed boxes filled the entryway and hall. "You about finished packing?" he asked, leaving the male visitor and Carter issue alone for now as he followed her into the kitchen. Pushing Molly would only make her retreat more.

"Pretty much. Just have the bare essentials to go."

He nodded. The counters were bare, all her knick-knacks and personal items gone. The space looked strangely bare and devoid of life without the colorful splashes that matched her personality decorating it. "If I overstepped by finding the house and springing the house on you like that, I apologize."

She stopped in the act of scooping some casserole onto a plate, her gaze lifting to his. "No. Really. I was just taken aback, that's all. I'm beyond touched that you would do all of that for me."

He shrugged. "It's no big deal."

"To me it is. I hope you and the others know how much I appreciate everything you've done."

"Of course we do." Jase was tired, he wasn't going to lie. He went into the office a couple hours early each morning so he could get all his work done by mid-afternoon, allowing him to get over to Molly's new place a few hours before everyone else.

He was always the first one there and usually the last to leave. Because while Beckett, Mac and some of the other guys from the crews were hard workers and wanted to help Molly by fixing up the place for her, for Jase it was personal. It gave him a deep satisfaction to work with his hands again, and he enjoyed working on something that would give Molly a sense of security and a fresh start in a place she loved.

But there was also a selfish reason for it. He wanted her to stay in Crimson Point rather than go home to North Carolina and raise the baby there.

She'd moved out here for Carter, leaving her entire life and family behind. Jase was thankful she was still here, but he realized that she could change her mind at any time. Even if he couldn't have her, losing her that way, not being able to see her, would have been too hard to bear.

He stuffed his hands in his pockets, watched her move around the bare kitchen while she heated up her dinner in the microwave. The vibe between them seemed a little strained all of a sudden. Did she feel uncomfortable about the house?

All he knew was, things between them were definitely not relaxed and comfortable at the moment. Actually, they hadn't been the same since the night Carter died. Did some part of her secretly blame him for it? Or maybe she was embarrassed that he'd been the one to find her hiding in the culvert that night?

Jase had no idea what was going on in her head, but clearly she wasn't up for company right now. At least, not his company. He should go, except he didn't want to, and he was still wondering about that guy who had just been here. Was she in some sort of danger? The thought made his hackles rise.

Wanting to ease the subtle tension between them, he slid onto one of the stools at the kitchen island. "How you holding up now, Moll?" She'd been so busy in the lead up to the funeral. Now that it was over, she had to be feeling the same kind of emotional crash he was.

She glanced at him. "I'm managing. You?"

"Same." He pushed out a breath. "You know, I keep meaning to talk to you about something, but there never seems to be a good time."

"Talk to me about what?" She sucked the tip of her thumb, and the sight of it disappearing between her lips put all kinds of X-rated ideas into his head.

"How you feel about the baby now."

"Oh." She looked away, watched her plate turn around and around in the microwave as it finished heating. "Much better. I'm even getting a little excited."

"That's good." It had been one hell of a sucker punch to get that news initially. Probably for her, too.

She hummed in agreement.

He waited for her to say something more. She didn't. Her silence weighed on him.

The Molly he used to know would sit down next to him and talk it through with him, telling him the entire story from her perspective. Or she'd start with that and change the subject so she wasn't the topic of conversation.

She'd never been uncomfortable talking to him about anything before, but she was now, and he didn't like it. He never wanted her to pull back or hide anything from him, especially if she was in any trouble.

"Will you stay and raise the baby here?" he finally asked, dreading her answer.

She carried her plate to the island and stood on the other side of it rather than come sit beside him. "I haven't decided yet."

A sinking sensation filled his gut, along with tiny tendrils of panic. "You've got lots of support here. People who love you." Her family could go screw themselves as far as he was concerned. They'd done jack for her since Carter was injured. Her mother hadn't even come out once to help her through the past few hellish months. He was surprised they'd bothered coming to the funeral, but they sure as hell hadn't wasted time in pressuring her to move back home "for the baby's sake".

She put on a smile, but it didn't reach her eyes. "I know. That's why I'm still here."

That was something, at least. "Good."

With the conversation over, Jase stood, his heart heavy. He was trying his best to accept that she would never be his and move on, but after so many years of wanting her it was like getting ready to amputate a limb with a dull, rusty knife. So far, he hadn't found the guts to make the first painful but necessary cut.

He rounded the island, sadness hitting him at the way her shoulders stiffened. It was subtle, but he saw it.

She watched him almost warily for some reason, those gold-green eyes fixed on his.

The part of him he was desperately trying to shut off wanted so badly to brush that tight spiral curl from her cheek, cradle the side of her face in his hand and lean in to settle his lips on hers. To comfort and reassure, chase away the shadows in her eyes. Pull her close, mold her curves to his body while he learned the taste and shape of her, find out what made her shiver and moan and melt.

"I'm here if you need me, okay?" he murmured instead.

She nodded, her smile grateful and a little sad. "I know. Thanks."

The sorrow in her eyes sliced him up inside. He wanted to make her smile, make her laugh again. God, her laugh was the sexiest thing about her, warm and sultry. She'd been so quick to smile before things had gone bad, so full of joy and confidence. Now it was as though someone had hit a dimmer switch inside her, muting her beautiful inner light.

He couldn't walk away like this. Not with this lingering awkwardness between them.

Steeling himself for possible rejection, he slid his arms around her back and gathered her into a hug. Sighing, she returned it instantly, triggering a bittersweet pain beneath his ribs as she rested her cheek on his chest, leaning on him.

She felt so damn right in his embrace. So damn perfect. Jase squeezed his eyes shut, wishing—

Wishing for the impossible. Exactly why he had to find a way to get over her. He couldn't keep living like this.

Molly squeezed him and let go, stepping back, her gaze on the floor. He was forgiven, but she was still holding back. "Well. I better eat and get out of here. I'm meeting the girls at yoga class in twenty minutes."

A polite but clear way of asking him to leave.

"I love the house," she added. "I'll sleep on it and let you know one way or the other tomorrow. Okay?"

"Sure. Have a good night."

"You too."

He drove back to his place deep in thought. It didn't matter that he knew he needed to figure out a way to move on.

No matter what logic told him, his heart wasn't going to get over Molly Boyd anytime soon. Only a major shakeup was going to help that.

Maybe the security contracting job he'd been contacted about and a cross country move to Virginia was the best thing for him. Although he was starting to think that nothing short of death would ever get her out of his system.

Chapter Six

Rafe crossed his arms and leaned against the wall as he faced his boss of the past three years, seated behind his antique desk in a private office overlooking the river in downtown Portland. Their little slice of the operation specialized in the darker side of business that other men didn't have the stomach to touch. It was why they were in such demand.

In his mid-forties, Mick leaned back in his leather office chair and took a sip of the bourbon he'd just poured. "You get what you were looking for at your meeting this morning?" His gray eyes gleamed with interest.

"Yep." A hundred-and-fifty grand from a trust fund junkie who couldn't quit his habit of hookers and blow.

"Did he make it interesting?"

"He tried." The kid had been stupid enough to try to run when Rafe had caught him a few blocks from the casino. Initial coercion during their meeting hadn't done the trick, so Rafe had taken a hammer and methodically broken the kid's kneecaps, then moved on to individual bones in his hands until he'd puked all over himself and agreed to hand over the money.

Forty minutes later one of Rafe's guys dragged the kid into his parents' mansion in the richest neighborhood in Vegas. Five minutes after that, Rafe had walked out with twelve grand in cash from the safe and the one-fifty transferred to an offshore account. They'd left the kid bleeding on his father's office floor, handcuffed and helpless. He had a lot of explaining to do when Daddy came home.

A solid morning's work, except that even with that extra twelve grand in cash, Rafe was still a long way from the total he needed. The organization had been lenient with him thus far while working to repay his debt. But that could change at any moment.

"What about the Boyd money?" Mick asked, almost as an afterthought.

"Insurance company hasn't made a decision yet." Rafe was already losing sleep because of it. The way things were going, that one-twenty could literally mean the difference between life and death for him.

Mick huffed in annoyance. "What the hell's taking so long? They figure a guy with that kind of training just suddenly loses control of his truck because of a rainstorm and drives over the side of a fucking cliff?"

"You and I both know it's bullshit. But that policy is about the only way we'll ever see any of that money again."

A loaded pause followed. "You'd better hope that's not true."

Rafe schooled his features, outwardly not reacting even as his abs contracted as if from an invisible blow. "I've got it covered." His debt.

"Yeah? I sure hope so, Rafe, because you're damn good at your job. Your real job, not the one that got you into this...predicament you're in."

Rafe longed to scrub the shitty-ass smirk off the bastard's face. With an industrial sander. "Don't worry." But *he* was worried. So worried it was a constant, grinding pain in the middle of his gut.

He'd grown up poor. So poor he knew what it was like to eat out of garbage cans just to keep from starving, and showing up to school filthy and in rags while the other kids made his school hours miserable. Years later, when he'd left the military and joined the organization, Rafe had vowed to make so much fucking money that he could buy whatever the hell he wanted for the rest of his life.

As Mick said, he was good at what he did. So much so that the bosses had given him more latitude to make business deals on his own when he'd approached them about branching out from straight enforcement work. Everything had been going fine and building momentum. He'd made a few million within the first two months before he made a mistake and took the gamble he now regretted.

The shipment of weapons and drugs worth three-point-eight million was caught at a port in L.A. The authorities had seized it, leaving the organization almost four million in the hole. Needless to say, the bosses were pissed and Rafe was on the hook for the full amount, plus interest.

He had sold his house, his cars and almost everything else he owned, emptied his bank accounts and investments to pay it back, and he was still nearly a million short. He had a few more people to collect from, but he needed Boyd's life insurance policy and everyone else he could squeeze money out of to have a prayer at covering the rest.

"Heard they named a deadline," Mick added casually.

Rafe barely kept from reacting, his fingers biting into his palms. "Yeah? I didn't."

Mick shot him a pointed look. "You surprised? Guy on the hook is always the last to know."

He hated being played with. "When is it?"

"October ninth."

Shit. Just over a month from now. Cold prickled across his scalp. What if they ruled Boyd's death a suicide? Where the fuck would Rafe get that chunk of money from then?

"You're a smart kid. I'm sure you'll figure it out. Where are you off to now?" Mick asked, leaning back casually in his seat.

"Another meeting." This one much closer to home, and far more personal.

"A collection meeting?"

"Tribiani."

"Ah, good. That son of a bitch has gotten off easy so far. Call me when you're done, I wanna hear all about how he pisses himself," Mick said and dismissed him with an impatient wave.

Rafe put Mick and the churning anxiety about the debt from his mind as he drove to his first stop, where everything was already in place. When he was on a job, he had to be totally focused, or fuckups happened.

Sometimes Mick annoyed the ever-living fuck out of him, but most of the time they worked well together. If he ever became too much of a pain in the ass to deal with, Rafe could always snuff him and make it look like an accident, then the organization would find someone else to handle the books. That's how this business worked.

After he had what he needed, he drove to the meeting location. Ten minutes later he arrived at the warehouse in an industrial area just south of Portland and parked behind the nondescript building. It was one o'clock in the afternoon on a Wednesday. Busy enough that his presence wouldn't stand out, and the borrowed vehicle ensured anyone trying to trace him would hit a dead end.

One of his low-level guys was waiting outside the back door. "He ready?" Rafe asked, and received a curt nod as the man opened the door for him.

It was dark inside, the noise from adjacent warehouses perfect to drown out any sounds that might occur during this "meeting". Rafe pulled off his sunglasses and tucked them into his jacket pocket. Two armed men stood guard outside a locked office in the back. One of them knocked sharply on the door twice as Rafe approached, taking off his jacket. He handed it to the other man, waited a few seconds for the door to open. Rafe's most valuable guy stood there, his face grim.

"Started to wonder if you were ever gonna show," Sam said.

"Had some loose ends to tie up." He rolled up his sleeves, noticing that the armpits of his shirt were damp. His heart rate was elevated too. "You got what I asked for?"

"It's all set up."

He nodded once. "Wait outside." Without pause he stepped into the darkened office and shut the door, the only light coming from a tablet set up on the desk. Tied to the metal chair chained to the floor, Tribiani stared up at him through one eye, the other one already swollen shut.

"I gave you plenty of chances," Rafe began in a disappointed tone. He needed this money bad. "Too many, because of our history together. You knew the risks, yet you thought you could steal money from us and get away with it." He shook his head, no longer angry, but resolved. He never did this kind of work when he was angry. Business was business, and had to be conducted with a clear head. Even the messy stuff.

"Rafe," the man croaked. "I swear I was gonna pay you back. I was in a tough spot, I needed the money to—"

"I don't care," he said quietly. "You understand that? I. Don't. Care." He crossed to the tablet.

"Please," Tribiani said. "Please just hear me out. I can get you the money. I've got some stocks."

"We're way past that now." He tapped the screen, loading the video he'd sent a few minutes ago. "And you know what happens to people who cross us."

"No, please, man. Please listen."

Rafe watched Tribiani's face as the video started. "Look familiar?" A house came on screen. Two-story American Dream kind of a house set in a cute little cul-de-sac. It even had a white picket fence out front next to where Tribiani's young wife was parked in the driveway.

"Oh, Christ," Tribiani moaned, terror lacing his voice. "You can't. You can't, man, she's not part of this."

"Shh. My favorite part's coming up," he said.

Silence filled the room for the next few seconds, his prisoner's tension rising palpably. Then an ear-splitting explosion ripped through the quiet as the house exploded. The camera Rafe had installed across the street shook with the force of the concussion, capturing every moment. The windows and front door blew out. A second later flames poured through the openings, engulfing the home.

"*No!*" Tribiani screamed. "Oh, fuck, *Natalie…*"

"Yeah, those gas leaks can be nasty," Rafe said. "Don't worry, though. She didn't know it was coming and wouldn't have felt a thing. Unfortunately, you're not going to be able to say the same."

Tribiani was sobbing now, his swollen eyes fixed on the tablet and the wreckage of his burning house, knowing his wife was being reduced to ash inside.

Rafe let the video keep playing, the crackle of flames and concerned shouting of the neighbors providing a hellish backdrop to what he was about to do. He picked up the spare T-shirt sitting on the desk and approached Tribiani. The man's head snapped up, sobs still wracking him as his gaze fixed on the shirt.

And then the coiled hose sitting on the floor.

Tribiani let out a garbled shout as Rafe tied the shirt securely around the man's face. "I've already arranged for a transfer of the insurance money from your account to one of ours," Rafe told him as he picked up the hose, ignoring his victim's protests and thrashing. "But now I've got to teach you firsthand what it's like to be on the receiving end of one of your favorite methods of persuasion."

He squeezed the trigger, allowing the rushing water to flow for a few seconds, heightening Tribiani's fear before he aimed the stream directly on the man's covered face. Tribiani twisted and bucked like a landed fish, but it did him no good. He was bound and helpless, and couldn't do a thing to avoid the horror of feeling suffocated.

Rafe made him pass out three times, reviving him with sharp backhands across the face.

"No more," Tribiani pleaded, his voice shredded. "I'll sign whatever you want, man. Just please, no more."

Rafe smiled thinly, even though Tribiani couldn't see it. "I don't need you to sign shit, asshole. I just need you to die."

He lifted the hose again, opened up the stream to full force and blasted it over the sodden T-shirt. Tribiani struggled for a few minutes, then finally went still. Rafe lowered the hose and opened the door to order his men to dispose of the body in the river. His mind was already on his next task.

Molly Boyd.

And how he could squeeze every last possible cent out of her.

****

The weapon felt so natural in his hands it was almost a part of him.

Lying prone on the cool grass of the field, Jase snugged the butt of the rifle against his shoulder and stared through the scope of the high-powered rifle at the metal target two hundred yards downrange. A lot closer than some of the targets he'd fired at, but it had been a while.

Exhaling, he paused a beat and squeezed the trigger.

Ping.

"Yeah, you're right, Weaver. You're rusty as hell," Noah Buchanan muttered dryly next to him, laughing under his breath. "All this time off's really played hell on your aim."

"I'll say," Beckett chimed in from Jase's left. "You didn't even hit center mass. That's just sad. You never would've made it through selection, shooting like that."

Jase tuned out their banter and racked another round. It had been way too damn long since they'd done this.

After thinking over his offer for a few days Molly had agreed to rent the newly renovated house. He and the others had spent the morning moving her stuff over there, getting her furniture in place, and then he'd hit the gym.

The exertion still hadn't burned away all his frustration about Molly. Shooting was cathartic for him, and one of the only things that seemed to stop his mind from spinning, made him stop thinking about all the shit in his head about her and Carter.

He focused on the target downrange, checked his alignment and the windage. The tops of the trees rustled slightly in the distance, indicating the breeze was less than five miles per hour.

Another exhalation. He squeezed the trigger again.

Ping.

"Get away wee man, is that all you Yanks do at the range? Fire at a stationary target so close my wee, ninety-two-year-old grannie could hit it with a rock? I say we see if he can still hit something that's moving," Mac put in.

Jase lowered the weapon and rolled to one elbow to look up at the Scotsman. "Who the hell invited you here again?"

"He did," Mac and Beckett said at the same time, pointing at Noah.

The sheriff shrugged, grinning. "I didn't know he was gonna be such a giant pain in the ass."

"Yeah you did," Jase said. Then to Mac, "Why don't you head down there and put an apple on your head? I'll see if I can shoot it off you as you run past."

Mac laughed. "After what I just saw? I've nae got a death wish."

Jase chuckled and got to his feet. "All right then, let's see what you've got," he said, inviting Mac to take a turn with a sweep of his arm.

"What I've got? I've got whatever it takes, laddie." He lowered himself to his belly behind the rifle.

This was a hell of a lot better than therapy. For all of them.

Jase tormented Mac along with the others as the Scot took his turn. Damn, he'd missed the camaraderie he'd felt in the military.

He liked the order and routine of his new civilian job and needed the break from operational work, but he missed his old life sometimes too. Not the danger or crappy conditions, but the guys. Being with them in the field, being part of something that gave them a sense of pride and purpose, and knowing the guy beside you had your back no matter what. Since his visit with Molly the other night, however, he was even more convinced that making a major change might be good for him.

Transitioning back into civilian life was way harder than he realized it would be, and Carter's death weighing on him made it that much worse. Remembering the good times and all the fun they'd shared helped only so much.

He rarely slept for more than four or five hours a night, and it was usually broken up by a nightmare or two. Sometimes they got mixed up with flashbacks, either about pulling Carter from the burning Humvee, or about the fight the night he died.

"You heading to Molly's place after we have a drink?" Beckett asked him.

"I'll stop by for a bit, clean up a few things." There were a handful of things left to finish in her space, then he could focus more on the downstairs suite. Another few days should do it, and then she could find someone to rent it and take the financial stress off her shoulders.

Instead of heading to the Sea Hag or Beckett's place for a beer after everyone took a turn on the rifle, Beckett suggested they go to the beach. In all the months he'd been here Jase hadn't yet experienced a beach bonfire, and the prospect sounded ideal.

The sun had just set when they arrived down on a wide, practically deserted strip of beach near town. Becket built the fire while the rest of them set up the chairs and got the food and drinks ready. They sat around talking shit for well over an hour, laughing and joking while they demolished the beer and s'mores fixings Beckett had supplied.

"Wish I could stay longer, but I need some sleep before my shift in the morning," Noah said, rising and stretching his arms over his head. "You boys have a good night."

"I'll go with you," Mac said, jumping up and dusting sand off his jeans.

Noah slanted him a dubious look. "You just want me to move my stuff out of the garage, don't you?"

Mac grinned, having moved into Noah's empty house soon after the sheriff had moved next door into Poppy's place. "That would be grand, thank you."

Jase and Beckett shared a comfortable silence for a while after the others left. Jase soaked in the soothing rush of the waves on the sand, the flames bathing his face and chest in warmth as a cool breeze whipped over him. "Twenty degrees warmer, and this would be paradise," he said finally.

"It already is."

Jase wasn't going to argue. He just preferred more tropical temperatures when he was at the beach.

"So, how's Molly doing with everything?" Beckett asked, tipping his beer bottle to his mouth.

He shrugged. "Okay. You know her, she'll soldier through anything put in her way."

Beckett nodded, lowered his beer and settled his dark gaze on Jase in a way that made him want to squirm. "When are you gonna tell her how you feel?"

The question threw him completely off guard. "What?"

Beckett snorted. "I heard what Carter said to you that day in the bar. I'd never noticed anything between you and Molly before, but after he said that, it was pretty damn obvious."

Embarrassed, Jase looked away, into the fire. He and Carter had had a major blow up about it a few days before he'd died. And those condemning words still pierced him like bullets.

You're still hung up on her, huh? Yeah, you are. That's so fucking sad, man.

Jase had been stunned. He'd never realized Carter had known how he felt about Molly. Sure as hell they'd never talked about it until that day.

You've always had a thing for her, but you couldn't have her because she chose me. And you hate that, don't you? You hate that she's my *wife.*

"I'm not gonna tell her," he finally answered.

"Ever?"

Jase shook his head. "Nope. No point."

"You sure about that?"

"I'm sure." He didn't want Molly to know. She was already acting a little uncomfortable around him. The last thing he wanted was for her to figure it out and risk that invisible wedge driving them farther apart.

Although it was getting harder and harder to keep his feelings locked down around her now that she was moving on from Carter's death, much less make them go away. And that put him in one hell of a dilemma.

The longer he stayed, the higher the chance he would let his feelings slip one day.

Chapter Seven

"This place is freaking fantastic," Sierra commented as Molly completed the tour of her part of the house.

"It really is, isn't it?" Molly had weighed the pros and cons about taking Jase up on his generous offer to rent it, and even though she was still a little uneasy about being indebted to him—not to mention her sudden and frankly disconcerting shift in perspective where he was concerned—she'd have been stupid to pass it up.

"Yes. It's so you," Poppy said.

Yeah, it was. Because Jase had made it that way. Which only made her love it more. "Thanks, I love it already."

Molly led the way back into the kitchen. She hadn't had a girls' night in too long. *Way* too long. The past few months had been nothing but stress that had ended with the funeral, and now this latest issue with some intimidating guy claiming Carter owed him a huge amount of money was weighing on her mind. She'd needed this time to unwind with her girlfriends.

The kitchen smelled heavenly. "I can't stand it anymore—I have to eat those pancakes you brought."

"Yeah, serve 'em up, Poppy," said Sierra. "Food

first, then unpacking and picture hanging later."

They chatted in the kitchen while they helped themselves to the feast Poppy had generously brought with her. "I know you guys are busy with your men, but we need to do more of this," Molly said, stuffing a bite of pancake into her mouth.

"I agree," Poppy said, helping herself to more pancakes. She made the best in the entire universe.

Today it was Hawaiian pancakes studded with chopped macadamia nuts, and each one contained a fresh pineapple ring. She'd made a ridiculous caramel-mac nut topping to go with them. And there was vanilla ice cream in addition to the whipped cream, too. Because Poppy was a goddess and knew what preggo mamas liked to eat.

Molly shook her head. "You're gonna make sure I put on all the weight I lost, aren't you?" Due to all the stress and chaos, she'd dropped almost fifteen pounds since first finding out she was pregnant. If she kept eating like this, she'd put it all back on and then some in no time.

"Yes, ma'am," Poppy replied, smiling as she transferred the last couple of pancakes from the hot griddle she'd brought with her to the serving platter. "If you don't, it's not for lack of effort on my part."

"I can't stop eating them," Sierra groaned, helping herself to two more and reaching for the little pitcher of warm caramel-mac nut sauce on the table between her and Molly.

"You guys have barely put a dent in the pile I gave you," Poppy said with a laugh.

"That's because you keep putting more on there," Molly mumbled around another mouthful. She swallowed, waved her fork at Sierra. "We'll have to watch her at Christmastime. She's one of those people who keeps refilling your Bailey's without you noticing, and then you end up drinking most of a bottle without a clue. Not that I'll be drinking this Christmas. Still, I'll keep an eye on her for you."

"You're the best, Moll. That's above and beyond, seriously."

"Just one of the perks that comes with being my bestie." She leaned back in her chair to smile over at Poppy. Both she and Sierra had been unbelievably good friends to Molly through this whole mess with Carter. They'd been nothing but supportive, and seemed excited about being honorary aunties next year. "That extends to you now too, you know. The bestie title," she added to Poppy.

Poppy looked up from the stove, a touched smile flashing across her face. She'd had a tough life back in her hometown, thanks to the small-minded bigots and bullies she'd been forced to interact with. Molly was glad she'd settled into the community and joined their circle. "Same."

"So, how's our baby doing today?" Sierra asked her.

She'd had another check up that morning. "Great. Everything looks the way it should. My hormone levels all look good, and baby's heart rate is perfect."

"Of course it is," she said, beaming like a proud aunt already.

"First ultrasound's not for a few weeks yet."

"Oh, that's so exciting," Poppy gushed. "Your first baby picture."

Molly smiled, a bittersweet pang hitting her. "Yeah." She'd always imagined that once she and Carter started a family, he would be with her at all the appointments. It still felt strange going through this alone.

"Do you want to know if it's a boy or a girl?" Sierra asked.

"I haven't decided yet. I'm torn."

"I would totally want to know," Sierra said, pouring more syrup over her pancakes. "I'm such a control freak."

"Yeah, you are," Molly agreed with a grin.

"Have you thought about names yet?" Poppy asked, joining them at the table.

"Some. Part of me thinks it should be something to honor Carter if it's a boy, but I'm not sure how I'll feel about that once I get close to term. Maybe for a middle name instead. I dunno yet. Haven't thought of a girl's name I love, either."

Sierra nodded. "You've got lots of time to make that decision."

"True." But it sure seemed like time was flying. She was already more than four months along.

"I'll go with you if you want. Just let me know."

"Thanks." Molly wasn't sure if she wanted someone with her or not. Maybe she'd ask Jase to be there, if he was comfortable with it. As her trusted friend and the closest living link to Carter, the thought of having him there felt right.

For a moment she thought about bringing up the situation with him, then thought better of it. She wasn't ready to talk about their changing relationship. Or her strange new feelings for him. Not even with her best friends.

She didn't know if she could trust her feelings anyway. She'd only been separated from Carter for a couple of months when he'd died, and even though she hadn't been in love with him anymore, she'd still had some grieving to do when he'd died. Even if she'd been living an emotional roller coaster a long time before that.

Was she growing more attached to Jase now simply because she was lonely and she'd become used to turning to him? Because she trusted him and he was always so good to her?

The heightened awareness and being attracted to him confused her. She couldn't pinpoint when it had begun, but somewhere along the way her feelings for him had shifted past friendship. It was a hard thing to face.

"Anyway, enough about me and the baby," she said, hating to be the center of attention, and she'd been that way too often over the past few months, for all the wrong reasons. "What's the latest with the wedding plans? Have we got dresses yet?" she said to Sierra.

The doorbell rang a few minutes later. "That must be the flower girl," Molly said, hurrying for the front door. "Hi, ya'll," she said to Ella and Tiana.

"Hey," Tiana replied, her fiery hair flowing loose around her shoulders. Sticking with her Boho-chic style, today she wore a long sage-green skirt that flowed around her as she walked, and a white peasant-style blouse with flowers embroidered around the bodice.

Behind her, Ella wore a big smile, her blond hair up in a ponytail. "I brought a special guest," she said, leading Walter in on his leash.

The ancient basset-spaniel mix waddled slowly behind her, eyes and ears drooping, his upper lip caught on one of the only remaining teeth in his floppy mouth, but his feathered tail was swishing back and forth across the hardwood floor.

He was the saddest-looking animal Molly had ever laid eyes on, his expression like someone had just run over his best friend in front of him. She had fallen in love with him on sight, and so did pretty much everyone else. He used his looks to his advantage that way.

"How's my handsome boy?" Sierra gushed as she got out of her chair and bent down to greet him. "Did you miss me? Huh? Did you miss your mommy?" She reached out to scratch Walter's soft ears and the little guy's tail moved faster, his red-rimmed, droopy eyes gazing up at his human with total adoration.

"Are you guys hungry? Poppy brought over some Hawaiian pancakes."

"I *love* pancakes," Ella said, and headed straight for the kitchen.

Tiana chuckled. "Now she's in heaven. It's the first time she's ever been a flower girl, so she's really excited."

In the kitchen, Ella was already piling pancakes onto a plate. "This is going to be the *best* wedding *ever*," she declared.

Molly's smile slipped a fraction. She loved Sierra and Beckett and wanted them to have a wonderful life together. But she no longer believed in happily ever after. Her own fairy tale had turned into a waking nightmare, and she would never put herself or the baby in that position ever again.

After Ella and Tiana ate, they talked more about the wedding plans and then the adults visited while Ella played with Walter. He retrieved the ball exactly three times before losing interest and flopping down on the floor in stubborn refusal, feigning exhaustion.

"Well, it's getting late," Tiana said two hours later, rising. "Ella, we should go, sweetie. It's a school night."

"Oh, but Walter's cuddling with me," she protested, turning big blue eyes up at her mom. Walter was passed out with his head in her lap, tongue lying on the floor, snoring like a champ.

"You wanna take him for a sleepover?" Sierra asked. "Poppy and I are going to pull an all-nighter helping Molly get unpacked. And we're not letting her lift anything heavier than a quart of milk, either," she finished with a warning look at Molly.

Ella's face lit up but she sliced a look at her mother. "Can I?"

Tiana shrugged. "Sure."

"I'll run over and get him before work in the morning," Sierra said.

Ella was already nodding and shaking Walter awake. "Come on, Walter. You're sleeping on my bed tonight."

"No, not on your bed," Tiana said with a laugh, and started for the door.

"I'll walk you out," Molly said. "The porch lights aren't up yet, so I've got a flashlight by the door." Jase was coming to install them tomorrow.

She grabbed the flashlight, turned it on and followed Tiana and Ella out into the driveway, a moment of clarity hitting her. She'd sort of been avoiding Jase for the past few days because her attraction to him unnerved her, but it wasn't something she was willing to lose his friendship over. She should invite him to dinner and smooth things over. If she felt that tug of awareness again, then she needed to seriously examine what it meant and what she was prepared to do about it.

The air was muggy and still, not even the breath of a breeze stirring the trees. Strange for the coast at this time of year, reminding her of summers back in North Carolina. Weirdly, it even made her a little homesick, and brought up another question she'd been pondering. She'd thought that staying here to raise the baby was the right decision, but was that really true?

"Would you be interested in coming to yoga class with us next week, see if you like it?" Molly asked Tiana as she walked them to their car.

Hand on Ella's shoulder, Tiana glanced over at her, seeming surprised by the invitation. "When is it?"

"We try to go on Thursday nights at six, but the day varies because of my shifts. The class is only an hour, and then we sometimes go out to eat after. You should come."

"Maybe, if I can find someone to watch Ella."

"Bring her along. She can join in if she wants."

"Oh, can I, Mom?" Ella said, clearly enchanted with the idea of being included.

A genuine smile tugged at her mouth, the first one Molly had seen in a long time. "We'll see."

Molly watched her open the car's back door for her daughter. Ella climbed in, coaxing Walter into the back. Tiana lifted him in. "He weighs a ton for his size," she said with a laugh, then waved and got behind the wheel.

Molly waved back and headed for the house, thinking. Now there was a woman who seemed to have figured out single parenthood while juggling a full-time job, and her kid was pretty damn awesome. If anyone understood the challenges Molly faced, it was Tiana.

Molly made a mental note to pull her aside after yoga this coming week to talk.

Chapter Eight

Bing Crosby's mellow voice filled the cab of Jase's truck when he pulled into his driveway the next evening after work. He liked listening to 40s music. Every night after dinner it had floated up the stairs of the farmhouse while he'd been in his room studying.

Normally he'd hit the gym but he needed to get the porch lights installed at Molly's place so he'd swung by to pick them up from his garage. As he was loading them into the back, he paused when he heard a faint voice calling out. He straightened, listening.

"Help," a woman said, her voice thin, weak.

Jase glanced around, frowning. What the hell? Had someone come onto his property and fallen somewhere?

He started around the side of his house to check the backyard.

"Help. Jase, please help."

It was coming from the next house.

Shit. "Mrs. Wong?" he called, breaking into a jog as he pushed through the cedars between their properties.

"At my…side door," she answered.

Jase ran faster, heading right to skirt the side of her house. His heart lurched when he saw her lying on the ground beside her wooden steps, her knit hat lying nearby and two bags of groceries spilled all over.

He knelt beside her, carefully unwrapping her scarf so he could check her for injury. "What happened?"

"I...slipped," she said, a grimace of pain tightening her wrinkled face. She grasped her right hip with both hands, her golden-toned face pale and damp with sweat. "I can't get up."

Hell. "How long have you been out here?"

"I don't know. I got home at just after one."

Jesus, it was almost three-thirty. "I'm not going to move you right now, just in case you've hurt your spine or your neck." He slipped off his bomber jacket and laid it over her to help keep her warm, then pulled out his phone to call for help.

She grabbed his wrist, shaking her head. "No, no. Don't bother them. I—"

"You need an ambulance." He made the call.

She continued to clutch at his arm, squeezing when a spasm of pain hit her. Jase kept talking to her, keeping her calm, promising help would be there soon. He took her wrist, pressed his fingers to the inside of it.

"Are you checking my pulse?" she asked. "Because with you here, it's going to be a lot faster than normal."

Jase smothered a laugh. "Mrs. Wong, are you seriously flirting with me right now while you're lying here broken?"

Her grin turned into a grimace as another spasm hit her. "If you have to ask, then I'm not doing it right."

"No, your flirting game is strong."

The firefighters arrived first, stabilizing her spine and moving her onto her back for transport. Jase stayed with her, talking to her to try and distract her from the pain. "It just so happens I've got a good friend who works in the emergency department," he told her. "Tell her you're my neighbor and she'll take extra special care of you."

SHATTERED VOWS

Mrs. Wong nodded distractedly, the pain and fatigue etched into her face. "What's her name?" she managed, trying to pay attention.

"Molly."

When the ambulance arrived, it was just a matter of putting her on a gurney and loading her into the back for the ride to the hospital.

Just before they left, Jase grasped her hand and leaned over her. "Is there anyone I can call for you?"

She shook her head tightly. "No." Her rheumy eyes fixed on him. "Will you come with me?"

He was supposed to say no to her when she had no one else?

He gave her a reassuring smile. "Of course."

****

"Three patients en route from an MVA. Husband, wife and young child, arriving by ambulance, ETA twelve minutes. Husband has possible fractured pelvis and facial injuries. Wife has head trauma but is conscious. Son has probable fractured clavicle, and lacerations on his face," Molly finished, then organized her team and everyone prepped for when the ambulances arrived.

The moment the paramedics pushed the gurneys into the ER, she and the others were ready. She oversaw the initial assessments and alerted the on-staff physician, tending first to the husband, who had the most serious injuries. While two other nurses got to work cleaning the mother's face, the radiologist did x-rays of the husband's pelvis and prepped the CT scan for the mother.

Finally, Molly moved to the little boy. Wesley, six years old. He laid on his back on the gurney, his face bleeding from a few lacerations along his cheekbone and jaw. His big brown eyes were filled with tears as he stared up at Molly.

"Hi, Wesley," she said, giving him a gentle smile. "Your mom and dad are both going to be all right. They're being taken care of right now, and I'm going to take care of you. Okay?"

"Kay," he whispered. His bloody jaw was trembling, a combination of shock and fear.

Molly kept her voice low and calm while speaking to the other staff members assisting her. They did a thorough assessment, checked his vitals and got him cleaned up for the doctor to come examine. The bleeding on his face had slowed to a trickle, but the wounds were deep and would need suturing.

"It's twenty minutes to shift change," the nurse opposite her said. "You don't have to stay, I've got this."

"Thanks, but I'll stay," she answered. Kids were different, and she'd promised to take care of him. No way would she leave a frightened little boy to another nurse's care just because he happened to come in at the tail end of her shift.

She kept tabs on the parents and stayed with Wesley while the doctor came and checked him. They closed the lacerations with steri-strips for the time being while they waited for the plastic surgeon on call to arrive.

She talked to him softly throughout, found a children's book in a basket at the nurse's station and read to him until the surgeon got there. She held Wesley's hand and continued reading as the specialist injected the freezing into the wounds and carefully stitched them up.

"Do I look like the monster in Frankenstein?" he finally asked her when the plastic surgeon was all done.

Molly gently applied an antibiotic ointment and covered the sutures with dry gauze. "No. Frankenstein's monster was scary-looking. You're handsome. And the doctor who just put the stitches in is so neat and tidy, you'll barely see the scars once they heal up."

Wesley seemed to perk up at that, and he was quite

content once Molly raised the head of his bed and tucked him underneath a warm blanket. "Now. What about a popsicle?" she asked him.

His eyes lit up. "You have popsicles here?"

"We don't give them out to just anyone. Only our bravest patients. What flavor do you like?"

"I like red or purple."

"Coming right up." She brought him one, then wheeled him down the hall to the room where his mother was being treated. Another nurse waited outside to take over. "Okay, buddy. This is my friend Trisha. She's going to stay with you for just a few more minutes and then you can go see your mom. The doctor is just putting her stitches in now." A few dozen more than Wesley had needed, but at least she would be okay.

"Can she have a popsicle too?"

"Only if she's as brave as you." She ruffled his dark hair gently, his crooked little smile making her heart squeeze. His dark hair and eyes reminded her of Carter's. Would her child look similar to this one day? "You take care, okay?"

"I will."

She was headed into the back to do her files when she was informed of another ambulance inbound.

"Eighty-three-year-old female, possible femoral or pelvic fracture due to a fall."

A few minutes later, Molly watched in astonishment when the ambulance arrived and Jase climbed out after the patient. "What are you doing here?" she blurted.

"She's my neighbor."

The woman flung back a hand to grab Jase's arm. "You're not leaving, are you?" She sounded almost panicked.

Jase walked alongside the gurney, the smile he gave the elderly woman turning Molly's heart over. "No ma'am."

The man had a serious thing about rescuing damsels in distress. How could she not love that about him?

The patient—Mrs. Elsie Wong—relaxed visibly, then switched her focus to Molly. "Are you his friend?"

"Yes," Molly answered. "And we're going to take good care of you." She shot Jase a little smile and hurried Mrs. Wong into a curtained room for examination. After an initial assessment she was sent off for x-rays. Molly went with her because the woman clung to her hand and wouldn't let go, and waited in the hall until she came out of the room.

"Oh, son of a bitch, that was awful," Mrs. Wong moaned as the tech wheeled her out. "Almost as bad as childbirth."

Molly's eyebrows went up. "*That* bad?"

"Yes. But of course, nothing hurts as much as pushing out a baby." She cast Molly a pleading look. "When do I get some drugs?"

"Soon as we get you back to the ER."

"Thank God. Make sure you give me the good stuff."

"I will."

Jase was waiting for them when they arrived, and Molly immediately began administering the pain relief the doctor had ordered. Within a minute, Mrs. Wong sighed. "Oh, God, *yessss*."

Molly smothered a laugh and met Jase's amused eyes. "Think that did the trick."

Mrs. Wong shot out a hand to grab the sleeve of Jase's bomber jacket. "You're still not leaving, right?"

"Wouldn't dream of it," he replied, deadpan. He was adorable.

"Good." She focused on Molly. "He told me that once I get better, he'll take me dancing to celebrate."

"Did he? Well color me jealous, because he's a fabulous dancer." She'd never met a man so at home on the dance floor. Jase was smooth and confident. Made a girl wonder if that translated to the bedroom. Molly was betting it did.

Mrs. Wong frowned at her, her eyes a little unfocused. "You're not just saying that?"

"No, it's the truth."

"Well now my pride is wounded," Jase said, rising from his chair. "I feel the need to defend it." He held out a hand to Molly. "Mind being my partner?"

Something quivered low in her belly at his low, intimate tone. "No, not at all." She took his hand, the shock of the connection shooting up her arm.

Her gasp got lost beneath a giggle as Jase tugged her close and spun her, smoothly turning her in an elegant circle there in the midst of the emergency ward, then reeling her back in and sliding a rock-hard forearm beneath her lower back to finish with a dramatic dip.

Slowly, Jase pulled her upright, all easy strength, and spoke to his neighbor. "Satisfied?"

"Not as much as her, I'll bet," she answered, grinning at Molly, obviously feeling no pain anymore. "But now I can't wait. Bring on my bionic hip."

Molly's heart beat erratically. Heat suffused her face even as she stepped away, grinning at Mrs. Wong. Holy. The way Jase had handled her just now with such ease was seriously sexy, and she'd enjoyed the feel of his hands on her way too much.

Hands on hips, Jase gave a satisfied nod. "Good." Then he turned his gaze on Molly, and a velvet shockwave rippled through her middle. "Isn't it past the end of your shift now?"

"Yes. I'm supposed to meet the girls at yoga."

He nodded. "Don't let us keep you. I'll sit with her awhile longer. I'll get to the porch lights tomorrow."

He was such a good guy. "Don't worry about them. You're needed here more." And how freaking endearing was it that he was taking care of his elderly neighbor?

Yeah. If she wasn't really damn careful, she could wind up in deep trouble where he was concerned.

Chapter Nine

She left the hospital tired but lighter inside than she'd felt in weeks. After rushing home to shower and change, she arrived at the yoga studio late. Class was already in session.

"Hey," she whispered as she quickly unrolled her mat next to her friends. "Sorry, got caught up at work." But worth it. So very worth it to see that side of Jase she'd never known about before.

Sierra wore a resigned expression, but Poppy and Tiana were bright-eyed. "Hey, glad you could make it," Molly said, patting Tiana's shoulder. The other woman gave her a smile. "Where's Ella?"

"She's with Beckett. And Walter." She tossed a grin at Sierra. "It was her doing."

"Well, you wouldn't have come otherwise." Sierra shrugged and stretched out on her yoga mat between Molly and Poppy. "And Beckett was happy to watch her for a couple hours. You know he loves her."

"Of course with Walter," Molly whispered back, shaking her head. "She's in love with that dog."

"I know," Tiana said with a sigh and a fond smile. "I thought for sure she would have lost interest by now and stopped wanting to spend time with him, but that hasn't happened at all."

Molly nodded. "I'm impressed with how responsible she is."

"I'm pretty proud of her," Tiana said and unrolled the yoga mat she'd borrowed from the basket in the corner. "So how advanced is this class, anyway? Is the teacher going to break me in gently?"

"I'd say it's a middle of the road class. Just do what you can. She's great, she'll adjust poses for you if she sees you're struggling."

As soon as she got into the poses, the tension she'd been carrying around in her neck and shoulders all week started to melt away. Yoga was one of the only things she'd ever found that helped managed her stress level. Now that she was coming out the other side of her personal trial by fire, she craved the sense of calm and relaxation it brought her.

Inner peace, however, was a different story.

She was still tangled up with conflicting emotions about Carter. Grief and loss and anger, bitterness and disappointment. Loneliness and uncertainty about the future. But on the whole, she was in a much better place now than she had been for the past few months.

Except now she was increasingly mesmerized by a man with pale turquoise eyes. She couldn't help notice how sexy his smile was. How he seemed to intuitively know what she needed and always watched out for her.

"Allow your breath to fill your body. Imagine it's a soft, white light filling you, bringing serenity and healing energy."

Eyes closed, Molly forced her concentration back to the instructor's voice. Even after practicing yoga for these past six months, her mind still had a habit of wandering during class.

Usually her thoughts centered around Carter and she

had to block them before they could undo the calming effect of the class. Tonight, her mind kept shifting between the guy Carter owed money to, and Jase. And rather than make her feel embarrassed or weird, in her relaxed state her mind focused on the way Jase made her feel when he was around.

Safe. Calm. Protected.

Aroused.

Her eyes flew open. *Oh, God...*

It took her a solid ten minutes to push the thought to the back of her mind and concentrate on the rest of the class. They finished more deep breathing and one final visualization exercise while in corpse pose.

"*Namaste*," the instructor murmured, signaling the end of class.

The lights around the room came on the dimmest setting. Molly didn't move, savoring the peacefulness. Her conflicted feelings about Jase and the worry about the guy who'd approached her were there on the periphery of her consciousness, but she was able to hold them at bay a little longer.

Sierra sighed beside her. "This is my favorite pose. Actually, I think it's the only one I like."

"You *would* like this one," Molly teased, eyes still closed. She didn't want to open her eyes. Didn't want to face the realization she'd just come to. She wanted to stay in this warm, safe place, remain in this state of relaxation with her friends surrounding her.

"I liked that last one too," Tiana said with a chuckle. "So, do we just...lie here for a while now?"

Molly opened her eyes and looked over at her. Tiana's mismatched eyes were totally alert, with none of the hazy sleepiness Molly always felt at the end of the class. She chuckled. "No. We're just being lazy. You can get up if you want."

"Great." Tiana jumped up and began rolling up her

mat.

"Somehow I feel like she didn't get into the same zen zone as the rest of us," Poppy said on Molly's left.

"It's her first time out. Sierra barely even closed her eyes the first time out. Now look at her."

Lying on her back, Sierra flapped a hand at them without opening her eyes. "It's been a long week. Leave me alone."

"So cranky," Molly teased. "You better stay for another class, mellow out some more."

"Oh God, if I did that, I'd spend the rest of the night right here on the floor."

"How you liking your new digs, Moll?" Poppy asked her.

"Loving it so far." After all the help from the guys, and Sierra and Poppy, it was starting to feel like home. The downstairs suite wasn't quite done yet, but it should be within the next week or two.

She also had four days off coming to her starting tomorrow. She couldn't wait to get everything else done at the house and then…

And then what?

She wasn't sure yet. But that was something she had to figure out quick, because it was just her now. Her and the baby she had to prepare for. That was the biggest reason she hoped the man following her never came back again.

As they were all leaving, Molly nudged Tiana gently and whispered, "Can I talk to you for a minute?"

Surprised, Tiana nodded. "Sure." She hung back with Molly as they left the building. "What's up? Everything okay?"

"Yeah, everything's good." And it was. Mostly. She was just trying to figure out what her new normal was supposed to be. "So, you know I'm pregnant, right?"

"Yes. When are you due?"

"February."

She nodded. "You feeling okay? You've been through a lot."

"Boy, don't I know it," Molly said with a wry grin. "No, physically everything's fine. I was sick at first but I'm good now. I just wanted to ask you about what comes after the baby's born, what to expect since I'm on my own. You seem to have everything all figured out, and Ella's bright, polite and extremely well adjusted. Got any words of wisdom you care to pass on to a fellow single mom?"

Tiana stopped walking and faced her, her expression suddenly tense. "Trust me, I don't have it nearly together as much as you think."

Molly blinked. "Well you sure seem like you do."

"I wish. But if that were true, I wouldn't keep picking losers or expose my daughter to a sexual deviant."

Ouch. Sierra had told Molly all about the incident with the guy Tiana had last dated.

The sick freak had exposed himself to Ella while the little girl was naked in the tub, and probably would have molested and raped her if Beckett hadn't got wind of it. But he had, and he'd marched straight over to smash the bastard's face in. Now the asshole had been charged and was awaiting trial.

"Hey, you didn't know he was a deviant," Molly said.

Tiana cringed. "No. But man, I sure know how to pick 'em. I'm not to be trusted with that, so I won't be trying to re-enter the dating waters for a looong time. Maybe ever."

Molly slung an arm around her shoulders and squeezed. "You're a great mom. Know how I know? Your kid loves you to bits. And look at how Ella's turned out. That's proof right there."

"She's only nine, so she hasn't 'turned out' yet. But

I really hope she stays the way she is." She met Molly's gaze, her face serious. "You can't imagine the depth of love you'll feel for your child until you have one. You think you know, but you don't. It's fierce. Primal. Unlike anything you've ever felt before. The night I found out what Brian did? It was like a switch got flipped inside me. If Noah hadn't been there to stop me, I would have attacked him. Maybe even shot him, if I could get my hands on a gun.

"And when that cougar cornered us in front of Poppy's place, I shoved Ella behind me without thinking. I was terrified, but it was instinctive. I didn't care what happened to me, I just knew that I was ready to die to defend my daughter, and that I would bite and claw and tear into that cat and do whatever it took to stop her from getting to Ella."

"Mama bear," Molly murmured with an approving smile. "That's the way it's supposed to be."

Tiana smiled back, but it was sad. "Yes. That's the way it should be. But it isn't always." She looked away and Molly lowered her arm, sensing something more was beneath the other woman's words. Then Tiana focused on her. "So how are you feeling about the whole thing? I mean, now that the funeral's over and everything."

"I'm looking forward to meeting the baby. I love that a piece of Carter is still here. I always thought I would have kids someday, I just never imagined I'd do it on my own. But here we are."

"Here we are," Tiana said with a grin. "And you'll figure it all out, trust me. Not gonna lie, though, there will be times when you'll be totally overwhelmed. Single motherhood isn't easy, or for the faint of heart. And the financial stress is tough."

Yeah. She'd been putting away whatever was left over at the end of each month, but it wasn't going to go far. Even though it made her feel a little selfish, she hoped she would get the insurance money from Carter's settlement. "Did you ever think you'd be a single mom?"

She shook her head vehemently. "Never. I was raised in a...strict family. Girls were supposed to graduate from high school, maybe go to college for a year or two, then get married and stay home with the kids. When I got pregnant without a wedding ring on my finger, my parents disowned me."

Molly winced. "Ouch. I'm sorry." That was so damn backwards. Families were complicated.

Tiana shrugged. "I wasn't surprised. I expected it. But there was no way I was getting rid of or giving up my baby. I felt like that little soul had been hand-picked for me, entrusted to me specifically to cherish and protect. You know what I mean?"

"I know *exactly* what you mean," Molly answered, her throat tightening. She'd been blindsided about finding herself pregnant at the start of a divorce, but she'd never once thought of ending it.

Tiana gave her a warm smile, then it faded slowly. "I thought the guy who got me pregnant was The One. I thought he would stand by me and the baby. He did for a while, but a few weeks after Ella was born, he couldn't take it. He took off one day and never came back. He's a musician." She rolled her eyes. "How cliché is that? Anyway, last I heard he was down in LA somewhere."

"He has no contact with you whatsoever?"

"None, and I've got full custody of Ella. If he ever tried to be part of her life now, I'd fight him tooth and nail in court, spend every penny I have trying to keep him away, even if it meant Ella and I winding up in a tent together. If she wants to establish contact and have a relationship with him once she's grown up, that's her decision. For now, I have to do what I think is best for her."

"Of course. But you'd never wind up in a tent. If the worst ever did happen, you could live with me, or Sierra or maybe even Jase." He had a huge heart, and a protective streak a mile wide. He would also be a fantastic dad someday. "None of us would let you guys wind up homeless, so don't you ever worry about that."

A proud smile spread across Tiana's pretty face. "You don't need any advice from me, but you can always call me for help if you want it. This baby is lucky to have you for its mama."

Molly sure hoped so.

She felt ten times better as she headed to her car, parked around the side of the building. But the relief and morale boost Tiana's words had given her evaporated the moment she saw the man leaning against her car.

She stopped moving, her feet stuck to the pavement. "John". He'd been following her.

Molly glanced around. The parking lot on this side was all but deserted, and this town was too damn small to warrant any kind of security cameras posted in this location.

"Hey," he said, straightening, hands in his jacket pockets. His tone was friendly. Too friendly.

She took a step back, ready to turn.

"I'm not gonna hurt you, Molly," he said with a soft laugh. As if she was being ridiculous.

It doubled her unease that he knew her name and she didn't know his. She stopped but didn't move any closer, believing no part of his charming and nice routine. "What do you want?"

"Just wanna talk to you. We've got a problem we need to settle."

"I already told you, I can't help you. I don't know anything about the money."

He shrugged, the motion relaxed, casual. "Doesn't matter if you do or not. I need what he borrowed back."

She made a disgusted sound. "You think I've got that kind of money?"

"He had a life insurance policy."

Shit, how much did he know about her and Carter? And how? "Which I may never see a penny of."

He shook his head, enough light hitting his face that she could see his expression. And the pity in it. "This isn't going away, no matter how much you want it to. If you can't get the life insurance money, then you'll need to find it somewhere else. A friend, family member, whatever. I don't care where it comes from, as long as you get it to me."

What the hell did he expect her to do? He was scaring her. This wasn't her doing, and not her problem. "How do I know you're not lying?"

"You want proof?"

"Have you got any?" She didn't know much about loansharking, but as far as she understood it, bookies kept meticulous records.

"I do. And let's just say that the people I work with aren't very…understanding. They don't care that you're a widow unconnected to the money or that you've gone through a hard time."

The veiled threat sent a shock of ice through her. She spun around and rushed for the yoga studio door. Her heart thudded along with the sound of her shoes hitting the sidewalk, half-expecting to hear him chasing after her.

She ripped open the door and hurried inside, risking a glance over her shoulder. The man was gone.

She stopped, scanned the parking lot and sidewalk, but there was no sign of him. That didn't mean he was gone, though. He might just be waiting for her to come back out, or follow her home.

She whipped out her phone and called Noah.

The sheriff arrived ten minutes later in uniform, and met her upstairs in the yoga studio. She gave him a description of "John" and detailed the past three dealings, but there was no video footage or anything else they could use to identify him with.

She also had no proof of any credible threat against her. Just a hard knot of foreboding in the pit of her churning stomach.

Noah's expression was troubled as he put his hands on her shoulders. "You're right to be suspicious and vigilant. But without hard evidence of a specific threat, I can't do anything other than give you ways to protect yourself if he shows up again. Have you got a security system at your new place yet?"

"It's wired in but not hooked up yet. Beckett and Jase were going to do that next week."

"I'll talk to them. You'll want a wireless camera system installed too, though I'm sure they've already planned on it."

Molly didn't like that there was nothing else to be done about this. Carter was continuing to wreak havoc on her life from the grave, and there was nothing anyone could do to stop it.

It seemed that as in everything else in her new life, she was on her own with this too.

Chapter Ten

When Jase got the call from Noah, he couldn't believe it. Couldn't believe that Carter, even in his chaotic mental state, had done something so stupid to put Molly in this position. And even more, he couldn't believe that Molly hadn't immediately called him for help.

It made no sense. Had she known something more about what was going on when he'd seen that guy leave her rental place? If so, why the hell would she hide any of it from him? He'd flat out asked her what was wrong. Had she been hoping the situation would just go away? Or did she not trust him enough to reach out to him for help this time?

That second possibility was too much. He was angry. Hell, he was hurt. He'd done everything in his power to be there for her since moving to Crimson Point. All she had to do was call, and he'd be there. Jesus. Didn't she know that by now?

He was in his truck and heading for her new place before he thought it through, driven by the need to protect her and find out exactly what the hell was going on. As well as confront her about why she hadn't reached out when her safety was threatened.

Noah was just heading from the porch back to his cruiser when Jase parked behind her car in the driveway. "Place is secure and no one tailed us here," Noah said. "But the guy's been following her, no doubt about it, so he probably knows where her new place is."

Jase nodded, already assuming that and ready to take the necessary precautions. "Thanks for checking it out. And for calling me." Man, it pissed him off that Molly hadn't.

"Of course. You staying with her tonight?"

He hadn't thought that far ahead yet, but yeah, that's exactly what he was going to do. "Yes. I'll call you if anything else comes up."

"Sure. Have a good night."

"You too." Jase didn't wait for Noah to get in his patrol car. He marched straight to the front door and hit the bell, waiting on the mat with his hands on his hips.

"Who is it?" Molly called out.

"Me."

She opened the door ten seconds later. "Hey," she murmured, and stepped back.

Ignoring the urge to grab her and hold her close, he walked in without answering, his frustration putting the edge to his temper. After taking off his boots he walked through to the gleaming kitchen she'd warmed up with her personal touches, the silence building between them as she followed.

Jase stopped at the island and leaned back against it, folding his arms across his chest in a posture that was meant to be intimidating. Molly's expression was decidedly sheepish, but he couldn't wait a second longer to confront her. "Why didn't you call me?"

She sighed and lifted her hands in a helpless gesture. "Because I had to call the cops right away, and then Noah took care of everything."

He kept staring at her. Of course, calling the cops

was the right thing to do. But right after that she should have called *him*.

"And I didn't want to bother you," she added. "You'd already spent hours sitting with Mrs. Wong, so…"

His temper snapped. "*Bother* me?" She winced at his tone but he didn't stop. "Tell me you're joking. Some shady asshole shows up not once, but three different times, cornering you while you were alone, and tells you he's basically a loan shark/bookie who works for God knows who and he wants the money Carter owed, and you don't call because you don't want to *bother* me? Jesus Christ, Molly. This guy is definitely dangerous!"

Her cheeks flushed a deep pink and her chin came up, a spark of temper lighting the depths of her eyes. "I'm *sorry*. Okay? I'm sorry. There's just been so much…shit going on everywhere I look, and I didn't want to add yet another rock to the pile I've already dumped on you."

Ah, hell. He shook his head, not knowing how to make this absolutely clear to her so that she never misunderstood this point again. "Moll. When it comes to your safety and wellbeing, I'd carry an entire mountain for you if necessary. Do you seriously not know that by now?"

She lowered her gaze. "Yes, I know it," she answered, and her voice seemed a little rough.

He unfolded his arms and rested his hands on the island-top, curling his fingers around the edge of it to keep from reaching for her. Because he wanted to so badly the muscles in his arms ached. "Who is this guy?"

"I don't know, and I don't know who he works for. But apparently Carter owed him a hundred-twenty grand when he died."

Jase clenched his back teeth together. *God damn you, Carter.* "A hundred-twenty grand? How in hell did he rack up that kind of a bill so fast? And what the hell was he spending it on?" Carter had been living in a damn hovel of an apartment just off the I-5 when he died. If he'd had any money, he sure as shit hadn't been spending it on housing.

"Gambling, the guy said. If it's true, I'm guessing he was desperate, got in over his head, made a few bad decisions and by then it was too late to dig himself out. It snowballed out of control."

Jase was silent for a few heartbeats, watching her. "Do you think, if it was intentional, was it because of the debt?" he asked, meaning the truck going over the cliff.

"Could be. Makes a lot of sense now."

Yeah, it did. And if the insurance company got wind of this, then they would no doubt come to the same conclusion.

"Maybe he thought if he died, this guy would forgive the loan. Or maybe he did it because he didn't know how else to protect me."

Jase heaved a heavy sigh. She was strong and didn't like asking for help, but tonight had to have shaken her. "Instead he dumped more of his shit on you."

Molly put her head in her hands, and all the fight went out of him. "Don't," she whispered. "He's gone. Let's just remember the good times. Remembering the rest won't help any of us move forward."

"I remember everything." There had been lots of good times, before Carter was wounded. Afterward was pretty much a shit show. "But I can't overlook the mess he's left you in." Even in his tortured mind, Carter should have known that his death wouldn't have solved anything. That he was merely dumping his problems onto Molly.

She exhaled wearily. "He wouldn't have done this to me intentionally."

"I don't care."

She narrowed her eyes at him. "Why can't you look past what happened at the end and forgive him? If I can, then you should too."

"Because he hurt you." And for Jase that was unforgivable. He could have forgiven Carter for hurting him, or Beckett. But never Molly. Once Carter had crossed that line, for Jase there was no going back.

"You know he didn't mean to."

"And yet he did it anyway." Didn't matter to Jase whether it had been unintentional or not. But there was no point in continuing this conversation because clearly she wasn't going to listen to his reasoning.

Straightening, he changed the subject. "You eaten yet?"

She frowned at the abrupt shift. "I grabbed something on my way to yoga class. You?"

"I'm good. Go sit down and put your feet up for a while," he said, nodding toward the living room.

A hint of annoyance flashed in her eyes, allowing him another glimpse of the spark he loved so much in her. She was her own person, a strong woman, and he loved that about her almost as much as he loved her huge heart. "Is that an order?"

"Only if you're going to argue."

Her lips twitched, then she turned and walked away from him. Jase followed, sitting on the other end of the couch from her, and patted his lap. "Gimme your feet."

She hesitated, giving him a strange look.

"Come on. You've been on your feet all day." He patted again. "Put 'em up here."

With a sigh she stretched out and set them in his lap. They were so dainty, her nails painted a bright, glossy pink. He took them in his hands. "You're freezing," he reprimanded her, rubbing gently to restore some warmth.

"Yeah, well, running into that guy didn't exactly leave me feeling all warm and cozy."

Jase slid his thumbs over the soft soles of her feet, surprised she was allowing the intimacy and glad for the chance to do something to take care of her. What he wouldn't give to be able to pick her up in his arms and carry her upstairs to bed where he could take her mind off everything, then hold her close throughout the night and make her feel safe.

"You know he's going to come back," he said quietly. He was going to make sure they were prepared for it.

She nodded. "Not sure what I'm supposed to do about it. If he thinks he can get the money from me, he's nuts. He did mention the life insurance policy, though."

Jase sliced her a sharp look. "What about it?"

"He knew Carter had one. Not sure how he found out about it." She reached up and rubbed the back of her neck with one hand, rolling her head from side to side. "Hard to say, since we don't know who we're dealing with. But he obviously thinks or knows I'm the beneficiary if the settlement comes through."

Who the hell was this guy? What connections did he have that he would be able to get that kind of information? Unease tightened Jase's insides. "Maybe Carter told him about it."

Molly frowned. "He wouldn't have done that."

"Wouldn't he? Moll, who the hell knew what he was thinking at the end?"

"Yeah. True," she mumbled. "The guy also said I should go to my friends and family for the money."

"Do you want to pay it? If it'll get this guy off your back and make it all go away, I'll pay it."

"Jase, no. That's crazy."

He shrugged. "If that's what it takes, I'll do it."

"You've already sunk all kinds of money into this place for me."

"I've got some investments. I could cash them in."

"No, that's your retirement savings. But thank you. I know you'd do that for me if it came down to it."

Damn right, he would. To keep her safe? He'd do anything.

She fell silent, lost in her own thoughts for a minute before focusing on him again. "What really happened between you and Carter that night, by the way?" she asked quietly. "You never did tell me the details."

Jase's hands paused on her foot. He'd always assumed she knew. That someone had told her. He'd never brought it up because he hadn't wanted to make everything harder than it already was. "I thought you knew."

"No. Just that you guys had had an argument. I didn't ask before because you were upset enough. I didn't want to make it worse."

"You don't know anything else? Not even from Sierra?" Beckett had been with Jase at the bar that night. His former CO was a tight-lipped bastard, but even he would have told his fiancée some of the details.

"Not even her." Molly removed her feet from his lap and sat up taller, pulling her knees up and wrapping her arms around them. "Will you tell me now?"

All of a sudden Jase felt tired. Soul-deep tired.

He sighed and looked away, out the French doors across the room, because he didn't have the guts to meet her eyes when he told her. But she had a right to know.

Through the French doors, a half-moon painted the trees in her backyard with a silvery-blue light. It was so quiet here. Peaceful. He hated to ruin that.

"I left you with Noah and Sierra and went looking for him with Beckett." Jase had been filled with rage. He'd wanted to teach Carter a lesson. To punish him for what he'd done to Molly.

"And you found him at a bar north of here," she said quietly.

Jase nodded. "I was already worked up, after seeing what he did to you." God, he'd never forget the moment he'd spotted her hiding in that culvert, or when he'd seen the damage Carter had done to her face. How sick and helpless he'd felt. "When I saw him sitting in that bar, I lost it."

Molly made a soft sound of empathy he wasn't sure he deserved.

It was all still so damn vivid in his mind. "I punched him." *Mother*fuck*er*, he'd shouted, slamming his fist into the face of the man he had served beside, stood up for at his wedding, and at one time would have died for.

You cowardly sonofabitch.

He pulled in a deep breath. No taking those damning words back now. "I think the worst part was, he never even tried to defend himself or throw a punch back. Because he knew he deserved the punishment."

Sadness etched Molly's face but she didn't say a word.

"Beckett pulled me off him. And then Carter looked at me and asked…" He paused, cleared his throat because it was suddenly clogged. "He asked, 'Is she okay?'."

What the fuck do you think? he'd snarled back.

Jase had been beyond apologies by then. Wanting only to hurt Carter for what he'd done to Molly, not giving a single shit about his former friend's suffering.

He shook his head, the memory of the devastation in those dark eyes as Jase had laid into him burned into his memory forever. Carter's expression had been full of shame and defeat. A broken man where once a proud warrior had stood.

"He stormed out a couple minutes later and took off in his truck. I never thought… Never thought he'd die that night. That's what I can't forgive myself for."

But he couldn't tell her the rest. The heavy, resentful undercurrent running between them the whole time. Because Carter had known that Jase was in love with Molly.

A soft, choked sound broke him from his thoughts. Molly was watching him, her green-and-gold eyes brimming with tears that spilled down her cheeks. Crying almost silently.

Shit.

Jase immediately turned and reached for her, his chest threatening to split apart as she went willingly into his arms. He pulled her close and held her to his chest, pressing his face against her springy curls. *Ah, angel.*

He hadn't been able to comfort her through her grief, not even at the funeral, where she'd been the epitome of strength and class throughout. Until this moment he hadn't realized how badly he'd needed to have her seek this kind of solace from him.

"You sorry I told you?" he murmured after a while. She smelled so damn good. Felt so incredibly perfect snuggled up to him as silent sobs jerked her shoulders. What he wouldn't give to be able to hold her like this anytime he felt like it, for the rest of his life.

With effort he shoved the tortuous thought aside.

Her curls rubbed against his lips as she shook her head. "No. I'm just...sad. For him, and you." She rested her head on his chest with a shuddering sigh, her arms looped around his ribs. "And it wasn't your fault. Even if he didn't drive over that cliff on purpose, I think we all knew that with the way things were going, losing him eventually was inevitable."

"Yeah," he said, his own voice rough.

Molly rubbed a hand up and down his back. As though he was the one in need of comfort. "We have to forgive him, Jase. He never meant to hurt any of us."

"I know that."

She withdrew and sat back, regarding him with damp eyes as she swiped the tearstains away from her face with the heels of her hands. "You don't think you can forgive him?"

"I don't know," he answered honestly. There was so much damage and resentment built up. It was going to take a long time to get past all of it.

"Why not?"

He swallowed the words ready to rush out of his mouth. Words he'd held in for years out of loyalty and respect for both her and Carter.

"Jase? Why not?" she prompted.

"Because the day he married you he promised to love, honor and cherish you, and in the end, he broke every single one of those vows." It had killed Jase, because he would have given anything for Molly to be his. Watching Carter destroy her happiness and then her safety had been gut-wrenching.

"But by then he wasn't really Carter anymore."

True. But that didn't change the facts or the end result. "You asked me why not. That's why. I couldn't stand how he hurt you."

For a moment she seemed to falter for a response. Jase stared at her in the lengthening silence. His heart was thudding against his ribs, the pressure beneath them building, building, the need to blurt out his feelings so powerful it was excruciating.

"But I knew he loved me," she insisted. "And until he was wounded, we were happy." Her expression turned wistful, a faraway look in her eyes. "Even at the end, deep down, I knew he still loved me. That's what made it so damn hard."

Frustration burned in his gut. He resented listening to her defend Carter, minimizing all the damage he'd done to her and everyone else around him in the months before his death. "If he loved you, then he should have stayed away. He should have at least protected you that much."

Her smile was so sad it cut him inside. "He tried, remember? He forced that pistol into my hands and told me to shoot him if he ever came at me."

Jase remembered how sick he'd felt when Molly had told him the story and asked him to take the weapon away. He still had it. It had been Carter's favorite.

Her voice was soft. "In his own tortured mind, he

tried."

It broke his heart to think of the hell that Carter must have suffered, but Christ. Molly was so goddamn beautiful, inside and out. She deserved so much better than what she'd gotten.

Jase made himself take a breath and shook his head again, aching inside, the powerful yearning for her searing his chest. "It wasn't near good enough. If you were mine, I'd—" He barely caught himself before blurting out something disastrous that would ruin everything.

She stilled, surprise on her face…along with a deep, burning curiosity in her eyes that threw him. "You'd what?" she prompted softly.

It took him a second to find his voice. "I'd…"

Show you every day how much I love you, and how much you mean to me. I'd hold you and kiss you and dance with you. Make you laugh. I'd protect you, always. I'd make every other woman in the world jealous of the way I treated you.

But he'd said too damn much already. Either his words or his expression had given away too fucking much, apparently, because the almost stricken look on her face made his lungs constrict.

A deafening, shocked silence spread between them, brittle as spun glass as the endless seconds stretched out. He waited for her to speak, his heart in his throat.

"We can't go there," she whispered finally, staring at him. "You were his best friend, and I'm pregnant, and…" She shook her head, confusion all over her face.

"I don't care about any of that," he rasped out. "I only care about you."

Her lips parted in surprise, and it was all he could do not to bury his hands in those thick, spiral curls and bring his mouth down on hers. Kiss her the way he'd imagined for so many years.

Claim her. Love her. Make her see what they could

have together if she'd just drop the guilt and loyalty to Carter for five seconds and give them a chance.

Not ready to withstand the rejection he knew was coming, he shoved to his feet abruptly and stalked for the staircase, unwilling—unable—to stay and hear all the reasons why she didn't want him.

"I'm staying in the suite tonight to make sure you're safe," he told her without looking back. "And every night until this whole thing is taken care of and I know you're safe."

First thing tomorrow morning, he was going to finish setting up her security system. For tonight and the foreseeable future, he would stand between her and anything or anyone who posed a threat to her.

Chapter Eleven

Molly was surprised to hear the drone of a lawnmower coming from her backyard as she stepped out of her car the following afternoon. Who was back there? She hadn't hired a lawn service.

Frowning, she gathered the bags of groceries from the trunk and headed for the front door. She put them on the kitchen counter then went straight to the French doors that led out onto the back deck. Stepping out into the sunshine onto the freshly-sealed wooden planks, she stopped dead at the sight that greeted her.

Jase was cutting the grass in her backyard—shirtless.

An unmistakable surge of heat suffused her as she stood there gawking at him in all his muscular glory. He'd been up and gone before she rolled out of bed at seven this morning. She'd been glad, because after the way things had ended last night, she'd hoped a little time might ease the lingering tension between them.

But this new development definitely wasn't helping the tension any.

She wasn't blind. She'd always been aware that Jase was good looking and in great shape. She just wasn't used to seeing his naked torso on full display—or reacting to it.

Her mouth went dry as she watched him, the almost forgotten, heady rush of arousal stirring in her blood. Something about watching Jase walk around her yard like this seemed almost forbidden.

God, the look on his face last night when he'd said those unforgettable words to her. *If you were mine, I'd...*

She'd been stunned, but also interested. Thankfully, he hadn't seemed to be able to tell.

Realizing she was still standing there gaping at him, she yanked her wayward thoughts into line and went down the wooden steps to the brick patio. He was facing away from her now, giving her an up-close view of the sculpted muscles across his broad shoulders and back, gleaming with a faint sheen of sweat.

Then he turned the mower and her gaze slipped down to the gleaming expanse of his well-defined chest and abs. His skin was a pale-honey tone with only a little golden-brown hair on his chest.

He stopped when he saw her and released the bar on the mower, the impact of that aqua gaze making her heart thud. The engine died, and suddenly there was nothing but silence between them.

He dragged a forearm across his forehead, his sweat-dampened hair a shade or two darker than when it was dry. "Hey. Didn't think you'd be back yet."

Meaning he would have made himself scarce if he'd known she would show up now? "I just got back from errands." She paused, struggling to keep her eyes on his face, not knowing what to do about the irresistible pull he exerted on her.

They couldn't cross that line. It would be a stupid risk to take that might result in losing him. What would people think of her if she jumped into a relationship with Jase so soon after burying Carter—while pregnant with his baby? "I didn't even know I had a mower."

"It's mine. I wanted to cut the grass before the rain

hits overnight. Your security system's all hooked up too, and I installed a couple more cameras. I'll run through it with you later."

"Oh. Thank you. I appreciate it."

He nodded once. "No problem."

She groped for something to say. Having a security system was great, but she felt a hell of a lot safer with him staying here. She knew exactly what kind of training and experience Jase had. He could protect her. "I bought some lemonade. You want some?"

"No, I'm good." He wiped his jaw with his bare shoulder, the bronze stubble there catching in the sunlight. "I'll be done and out of your hair in about twenty minutes."

A pang of sadness hit her. She hated that she'd hurt him last night. Hated the awkwardness between them even more. "You're not in my hair, Jase." This was dumb. They'd been friends too long to let something like this come between them. She couldn't lose him on top of everything else. Some days she felt like one more loss would crush her into dust.

Finally he shifted his gaze to hers, those gorgeous, clear eyes piercing her. "Okay. Good."

The invisible ball of tension in her stomach eased and she gave him a little smile. Maybe they could get past this and go on as if what he'd said last night hadn't happened. "Let me know if you change your mind about the lemonade."

"Sure." He reached for the mower handle, not exactly dismissing her, but it felt a lot like that. She stood there uncertainly on the patio while he yanked on the pull starter, all those incredibly sexy muscles bunching and shifting under her avid gaze.

The engine fired to life, breaking the spell, and when he walked away to cut another line in the grass she turned around and hurried up the steps. Inside as she put the groceries away, she couldn't get that picture of him out of her mind.

How long had he been attracted to her? He'd hidden his interest in her until last night. She hadn't known he'd had those kinds of feelings for her. And now…

And now she wasn't sure what her feelings toward him were anymore.

She was still wrestling with that new level of confusion on her way home from a meeting with her financial advisor late that afternoon. Molly had texted Noah about it in case "John" might follow her again. He'd told her it was fine, as long as she was vigilant. Until the decision came back about the life insurance settlement, she should be okay.

On the drive home she was distracted, her mind skipping back to Jase. And the more she thought about him, the more the ache in the center of her chest increased.

To feel less alone, she called Sierra. "Hey, girlfriend. Guess what? I just saved a puppy's life by removing a piece of Lego from its intestinal tract. That's a first."

"You're my hero."

Sierra laughed. "So, Beckett said Jase is moving into your rental suite."

Molly nodded. "That's the plan."

"Was it your idea?"

"No, his. He's doing it to help me out financially, and for security reasons."

"What's that supposed to mean?" Sierra asked.

Molly dodged the question. "I feel bad that he's putting himself out for me, but I definitely feel a lot safer with him there." Even with the added complication of him wanting her. And her wanting him right back.

Too bad it was wrong. So, so wrong, because this was Jase, and she was pregnant with his best friend's baby. What the hell kind of person did that make her, wanting Jase now?

Yet even that didn't stop her from wondering what it would be like. To be able to touch and kiss him, feel his strong arms around her, that hard body she'd seen this afternoon pinning her beneath him as he took her. The thought made her insides clench.

She hadn't loved Carter at the end. But it still felt like she was dishonoring his memory by thinking these things. And the added worry about "John" didn't help matters. Anxiety squirmed in her belly, so strong she had to consciously relax her tense muscles. Her rearview mirror was clear. No one was following her.

"What's going on?" Sierra pressed. "You sound really down."

Molly hesitated, then gave in. Sierra was her closest friend and she needed to get this off her chest. Molly told her about Carter's secret debt and the man who had been following her.

"Jesus," Sierra breathed. "And you didn't think to tell me any of this why?"

"Because I didn't want to worry you. Noah and Jase both know all about it, so I'm sure Beckett does too."

"That man." Sierra made a frustrated sound. "Sometimes I could strangle him, I swear. Is there anything I can do?"

"Just listening helps. I've hated keeping this from you and Poppy."

"I sort of understand. But not really."

"There's something else."

"Okaaay," Sierra said slowly.

"Jase basically let me know he's…interested in me. I don't think he meant to, but it kind of came out last night."

Silence answered her for a few beats. Then Sierra said, "I'm not all that surprised."

"*What*? Because I sure as hell am."

"Remember how he was the night he found you and brought you to our place? I've never seen him like that."

Molly didn't know what to say. How had Sierra seen it when she hadn't? Yes, he'd been interested in her initially, on the night she'd met him at the bar off base, but once she'd made it clear that she wanted Carter, Jase had stepped back and never so much as hinted at feeling anything more than friendship for her. There was no way he'd been carrying a torch for her all along.

"What did you say?" Sierra asked after a long pause.

Molly glanced toward the sea. The sun was almost on the edge of the water now, a brilliant coral ball spreading color across the waves and glistening across the damp sand. It was beautiful, but she hated this stretch of road. "I was shocked. I told him it couldn't happen." Actually, she didn't remember exactly what she'd said, because she'd been too blindsided and panicked.

"How'd he take it?" asked Sierra.

"He was embarrassed, I think. And hurt." This was crazy. How was she supposed to fix this?

She had to fix this. Because she couldn't stand to be estranged from Jase. "But the thing is…" She inhaled deeply, dug down deep for the courage to expose her innermost feelings and thoughts. Vulnerability always made her uncomfortable, and that went tenfold since she'd gone through all this shit with Carter.

"What?" Sierra prompted gently.

"If I'm honest, I'm not sure it's entirely one-sided," she admitted, her voice barely carrying over the sound of the engine. "And I feel like hell about that."

Sierra made a sympathetic sound. "Oh, Moll…"

"He was Carter's best friend, and a good friend to me all these years. We just buried Carter." She shook her head, angry and disgusted with herself. It was true that their marriage had been in name only for months, but still. "It's too soon. Even if it wasn't, it's wrong."

"Honey, I don't know what to say."

"You don't have to say anything. It helps that you're listening." She put her free hand on her belly, thinking of the baby. "I was so lonely for most of that last year," she finally admitted, an unexpected lump forming in her throat. So incredibly lonely.

"I know you were."

I'm still lonely now.

At times she'd felt like she was dying inside from the lack of affection and intimacy. The cocktail of meds Carter was on had not only interfered with his ability to perform physically, but his mental state had deteriorated to the point that he had killed all the love she'd once had for him. For her, the divorce was merely a formality.

"What are you going to do?" Sierra asked.

"I don't know." Jase was a great guy. She didn't want to hurt him, and was afraid that's exactly what might happen if they crossed the line.

He'd done so much for her, finding and fixing up a place for her, putting his finances behind her to help give her a fresh start. She'd initially thought it was out of a sense of obligation, but now she saw it was more than that. What should she do? She didn't want to feel indebted to him, or feel pressured into anything she wasn't ready for.

"Well, before you make up your mind, be sure you know what you're doing," Sierra said, mirroring her thoughts exactly. "If you want to be with him, make sure it's for the right reasons."

Meaning, not just because she was lonely and afraid to go through all this alone. "I know," she answered, the sting of the gentle reprimand fading beneath the truth of Sierra's words. It was good advice.

"I also think you feel guilty and you're scared about getting hurt again. After everything you've gone through, that's understandable. If Jase really loves you, he'll be patient and give you more time to sort through everything."

I hope so. "See, this is why I called you. You always know exactly what to say."

"Hey, it's all part of the bestie job description," Sierra said, making Molly smile.

They ended the call a few miles away from Crimson Point, leaving Molly to think more about what Sierra had said. It was true. Molly *had* been hurt badly. She'd thought she'd found the love of her life with Carter. Sure, things hadn't been perfect, but what marriage was? Then he'd been wounded and her life had come apart at the seams.

Her stomach tensed. Jase was a warrior just like Carter had been. He'd been through the same training and combat missions. He'd been riding a few vehicles behind Carter's the day the convoy had been attacked. With that many years in Special Forces, he'd have suffered significant exposure to concussive forces as well.

What if his brain began to deteriorate from the cumulative effect of them one day? He could be at risk for developing CTE as well. He might have it right now, but in a latent form. If that was true it might not show up for years yet, and then…

That scared her almost as much as her changing feelings for him.

She surfaced from her thoughts when the notorious S-curve in the highway came into view ahead. Three hundred yards of curving asphalt high atop a cliff that plunged down into the sea, where the waves crashed against the jagged rocks below.

As if pulled by a magnet her gaze locked onto the newly installed section of guardrail when it came into view, and the faint skid marks still marking the road where Carter had plunged to his gruesome death.

She swallowed and tightened her grip on the wheel. It was almost like a sign, sitting there lit up in glaring neon.

If she were smart, she would never get involved with a military man ever again.

Chapter Twelve

Molly checked her phone one more time before entering the grocery store and found that Jase had finally responded to her dinner invite.

Thanks, but I've got too much to get done tonight.

Disappointment washed through her. He'd been working late every night since their awkward conversation four days ago, finishing up things in the downstairs suite, where he was now living full time—to help her with the rent and to keep her safe.

You can't come upstairs for a dinner break? she was tempted to type back, then thought better of it. Clearly, he wanted to avoid her. It made her feel even shittier.

Deflated, she put her phone back in her purse and headed into the store. Guess she was only getting dinner ingredients for one, then.

She was in the middle of gathering ingredients for a chicken and pineapple stir-fry when she abruptly changed her mind. Jase planned to avoid her for lord knew how long?

To hell with that, she would make a big batch of dinner and take him some downstairs. He couldn't stay away from her forever, they lived in the same freaking house now, and it was high time they moved past this hurdle.

The distance between them hurt and she wanted to mend the rift before it became a canyon.

She turned her cart around to find a package of brown rice, and froze. "John" stood at the end of the aisle, dressed casually and wearing a ball cap as he perused the shelves, an empty basket in hand.

Her scalp prickled. Molly retreated a step, unsure if he'd noticed her. He didn't look her way, but something about his stance told her he was all too aware of her presence. And him just showing up here randomly in the same section as her was way too much of a coincidence.

He'd followed her here.

Her pulse quickened as she turned the corner with her cart and walked two aisles over. There were so many people around she was pretty sure he wouldn't confront her here. When she left, however, it could be a different story.

She pulled out her phone to call Jase, but when she looked back, "John" had vanished.

Not being able to see him was twice as unsettling. Keeping her phone in hand just in case, she checked around her and walked to the next aisle. He was nowhere to be seen.

Still creeped out, she grabbed the rice and hurried to the checkout, forgoing the rest of her shopping and subtly glanced around. No sign of him. But there was no way his being here at the same time as her was in any way random. Had he followed her from her house? She hadn't noticed anyone tailing her, and she'd made a point of being on the lookout.

"Do you need any help out today?" the woman at the checkout asked her, handing over the receipt.

"Yes, thank you." She could easily carry both bags of groceries in one hand but she wanted someone with her when she went to her car.

Glancing up, she barely stifled a gasp when she spotted "John" two checkouts over. He was in profile to her, wearing sunglasses, but she could feel him watching her. For a second she thought about trying to get a picture of him on her phone, then thought better of it. He'd see her, and it might escalate things.

"Just a moment." The woman called someone for assistance. A minute later a young man showed up and gave Molly a friendly smile. "John" was already exiting the store at a casual pace, a grocery bag in hand.

It threw her for a second, then she shook herself. *You're not crazy or paranoid. He followed you here.*

What did he hope to gain from trying to intimidate her in public? She didn't have the freaking money.

"Where are you parked?" the male employee asked as he picked up her bags for her.

"Out to the left," she said still on the lookout for "John", waiting a few more moments before heading for the automatic doors. On high alert, she scanned the lot as they walked. "John" was halfway up the sidewalk now, walking in the opposite direction as her. Did he intend to follow her now, hoping to catch her alone?

Not happening. She wouldn't leave here until she had someone else with or following her.

She used her keyfob to remotely unlock the doors and lift the rear hatch. The employee loaded her groceries for her and started to close the hatch, then stopped. "Uh oh…"

Molly had been so busy keeping an eye on "John", she hadn't been paying attention to anything else. When she followed the employee's gaze, the blood drained from her face.

All four of her tires were flat, the rims resting on the pavement.

"Whoa," the guy said, kneeling down by the left rear tire, then looked up at her with a worried expression.

"Looks like someone slashed them."

Crap. The slash was about five inches long and went straight through the sidewall in a clean cut. Whatever knife had been used, it was lethally sharp. A warning? Or a threat?

Looking at it, Molly felt sick. "Yeah. Looks that way."

"I'll call the police." He got to his feet.

"No, I'll do it. But if you could…just wait here with me." She hated this. Hated this sick stalking game.

"Of course."

He stayed next to her while she called Noah, who promised to be right over. She called Jase next, but he didn't pick up so she left a message. He might be hurt or even angry with her, but he wouldn't turn his back on her after something like this.

Noah arrived, took in the situation and listened to her account of what had happened. "He was in the store the entire time you were, and you saw him walking away when you came out?" he asked.

"Yes, that direction." She pointed. "I didn't see where he went, or if he got into a vehicle. This had to have been him."

"Yeah, or someone working with him. It's not a coincidence."

A knot of dread formed in her stomach. The sense of violation added to her growing anger. "I don't suppose there are security cameras out here in the lot that might have captured it?"

"There are some. I'll check everything out. Have you called your insurance company?"

"Not yet." Exactly what she'd wanted to do this afternoon—deal with this shit and another scare. "I'll be honest, I'll feel a lot better if you can get good footage and ID this guy."

"You and me both. I've got a tow truck on the way.

Have you got a ride home?"

"No, but I can—" She broke off when she spotted Jase's truck coming toward them, a bittersweet sting lancing her chest. He'd rather avoid her at the moment, but still showed up when she needed him. The rush of relief made her throat tighten.

Jase parked near them, got out and took in the scene with a single sweeping glance before focusing on her. "What the hell?"

"Just my luck, huh?" she said with a pained smile.

"I'm going in to check with the store's security," Noah said to him. "Can you give her a lift home? Tow truck's on its way."

"Yeah, sure." Jase circled her car, his frown deepening when he saw the slashes on all four tires. Then he stopped and faced her, his aqua eyes assessing. "You okay?"

Rattled but trying not to be, and she was sorely tempted to crawl into his arms right now. "Just pissed off." She opened the hatch and reached in but Jase gently pushed her aside and grabbed the groceries for her.

"Come on," he said as he pulled the bags out. "I'll take you home."

"Thanks," she murmured, following him to his truck. He opened her door, set the bags at her feet and shut it behind her. "Sorry to interrupt your work day," she said when he got in his seat.

He shot her a hard look. "Don't ever say that. Or think it. Not when it comes to your safety." He was quiet as he steered out of the lot, his jaw tense. "I don't like this. I don't like it at all."

She wasn't sure if he meant the stalker/tire slasher bit, the damage to their relationship, or both. Either way, she agreed. "Me neither. I need to call my insurance company and explain all this."

She was still on the phone with them when Jase carried her groceries into the kitchen and began putting them away.

By the time she was done he was leaning against her island, watching her, his sculpted arms folded across his broad chest. Strong and capable and steadfast.

As well as impossibly masculine and sexy.

Even as she tried to remember the reasons why she needed to keep her distance, it was impossible not to be drawn to him.

"All taken care of?" he asked.

"Think so." God, she wished she could still drink alcohol. She would kill for a glass of wine or two right now.

His stare was somber. "Until this whole thing is taken care of, we need to take more precautions."

She frowned at him. "Like me going home for a while?" She'd thought about it already.

"Maybe. In the meantime, I'll drive you to and from work, or the store or wherever. And when you're home alone, you make sure you've got the security system armed."

"All right," she agreed reluctantly. What he said only made sense. She didn't need proof to know that the tire slashing was connected to "John".

"Have you heard anything from the insurance company yet?"

"I called them yesterday. They still haven't made a decision." Though she was starting to hope they would deny the claim, because if she was awarded that money, her problems could get infinitely worse.

Jase kept watching her, his expression unreadable. What was he thinking about? Her current situation? Them? She couldn't undo how she'd reacted the other night, and was sorry she'd hurt him. But she also couldn't stand the way things were between them now, especially after this scare. "Jase—"

He shook his head, dropped his arms and beckoned to her with one hand. "Come here."

Grateful that he was extending the olive branch, she closed the distance between them and went into his embrace, biting back a groan at the feel of those strong, caring arms wrapping around her.

A powerful surge of relief hit her as she leaned her weight on him, her cheek on his chest and his clean, slightly spicy scent surrounding her with comfort…and something more she still wasn't ready to face.

"It's gonna be okay," he said quietly, his breath fanning her temple. "It'll be fine. We'll handle this together."

Together. She nodded and stayed where she was, his caring warmth chasing away the chill inside her. Part of her wished she could stay cuddled up against him forever.

Jase rubbed his cheek on her hair, the curls catching on his stubble. A subtle tension formed between them, like the crackle of a low-level electrical field.

She let out a nervous chuckle. "Sorry. They're clingy." Raising her head, her laughter instantly died away. His intense stare made her mind go blank, a heady rush of anticipation sweeping through her.

Jase brushed en errant curl away from her cheek and cupped her face in his hand, the latent tension growing heavier. Her heart gave a hard thud against her ribs as his gaze dropped to her lips and the seconds stretched out between them.

She had plenty of time to stop him. She *should* have stopped him, but the tender, almost possessive way he held her face set off a swarm of butterflies in her belly and she'd wondered how it would feel to kiss him.

Then it was too late to stop it because his lips were on hers, and for the life of her, she couldn't pull away.

Her fingers curled into his shoulders. A shocking wave of heat shot through her, tightening her nipples and making her insides quiver.

Dear God. She'd imagined this. Had secretly longed to know how it would feel, and now...

His lips were warm and firm on hers, his confident hold and the heat pulsing inside her too perfect to interrupt. He kissed her like he had every right to. Like he'd wanted to kiss her forever and was finally staking his claim. She melted into him. Wanting to crawl inside him so that he'd never let her go.

Jase. I'm kissing Jase and it feels...

Way too good.

So good she didn't want to stop. So good she wanted to keep going until they were skin to skin and he was sliding into her, easing the throb he'd created in her core.

The thought was like a bucket of ice water dumped over her, immediately dousing the fire. Molly pulled away and ducked her head, shaken. But wanting more. Craving it until she ached all over.

Oh my God...

Jase wordlessly slid a thumb across her cheekbone and lowered his hand, allowing her to step back even as her body cried out in protest.

It took her a moment to find her voice, and longer still to find the courage to meet his eyes. When she did, the look on his face was so intent, so full of naked yearning it pushed the air from her lungs. He'd hinted the other night that he wanted her, but she'd never imagined his feelings ran so deep.

She struggled to find her voice. "Jase, what...?" She couldn't finish the thought.

He shook his head, his gorgeous eyes burning with frustration and a hunger that made her heart pound. "I've wanted you *forever*, Moll. Since the first time I saw you."

She sucked in a breath at his hoarse admission. He had? Even though she'd been married? To his best friend? Her thoughts were a chaotic jumble, shuffling back over the years since she'd known him, trying to find something she'd missed. But no, he'd never once shown his real feelings for her.

She floundered for something that would allow her to make sense of it. "But you were Carter's best man, you—"

"Stood up there like a good soldier and watched you pledge yourself to my best friend for better or worse and in sickness and in health? Yeah. I did. And even though I was happy for you both, I hated every fucking moment of it."

Holy... Molly was too shocked to answer. Though she understood why he never said anything, why he'd hidden it so well. Well enough that she'd never noticed it.

She put a hand to her forehead, her mind spinning. "Oh, God, this is so wrong." They couldn't take this any farther. It was too soon, they were friends, and she didn't want to screw that up.

There was the baby to think of. She couldn't lose Jase, and continuing down this path would risk everything she had with him.

Jase gave a slow, deliberate shake of his head, his eyes searching hers. "He's gone, Moll, and he's not coming back. You deserve to be happy again. So it's only wrong if you don't want me."

The unspoken hurt in his quiet words sliced through her like a blade. Because she *did* want him. She wanted him so much it scared her. But he was cornering her, pushing her into a place she wasn't prepared to go.

"I can't risk losing you," she whispered back, tormented. "I can't, Jase, so don't ask me to."

He took her face in his hands, his gaze steady and clear, full of emotion that tore at her heart. "Hey. I know you've been through a lot. But I'm not going anywhere. And the only way you'd ever lose me is if you shut me out and walk away."

Panic flared. She shook her head, gave him a pleading look. "Jase, no." He didn't understand what he was saying. How disastrous it would be if something went wrong.

"Moll, I know you're scared. But I won't hurt you. I would never hurt you, you know that."

She'd never dreamed Carter would, either. And yet he had.

The panic sharpened. Stabbed through her like a blade. "*No*." She shoved his hands away and stepped back, feeling sick. "I can't. Please understand, it's never going to happen. I *can't*."

His expression tightened. He studied her for a few awful, tense seconds, then nodded once, his jaw flexing. "Okay. Fair enough."

Molly stared after him helplessly, on the verge of tears as she bit down on the inside of her cheek to keep from calling him back. She felt like she was being torn in half.

She wanted him. Couldn't bear losing him. But she wasn't willing to take that plunge, and he was talking like it was all or nothing now. Couldn't he see how hard this was for her?

When his footsteps faded on the stairs leading to his suite, tears pricked the backs of her eyes. She sat on a stool at the island and put her head in her hands, more confused than ever. Guilt and worry pummeled her, corroding her insides.

This couldn't go on, this push-pull, this constantly feeling pressured and torn and uncertain, and now they were living in the same freaking house. If she didn't get out of here for a while, take some time to think, she would lose what was left of her sanity.

Sitting up, she drew in a shaky breath. In light of the escalating threat against her and this awful situation with Jase, for her own well-being she had to put some distance between them.

Exhaling, she drew out her phone and booked a flight home in the morning.

Chapter Thirteen

Jase arrived home early the next evening, desperate to see Molly but not wanting to push her after yesterday. He regretted the way he'd handled things last night, and intended to apologize face to face. But he didn't regret that kiss. He would never regret it. She'd been as sweet and perfect as he'd known she would be. Except now that he'd gotten a taste, he craved her even more.

If she'd stopped him or seemed turned off, it would have been easier. But she hadn't stopped him. No, she'd kissed him back, her eyes full of heat, giving him a tiny taste of what he knew it would be like between them. It had freaked her out. Her reaction to him, or the thought of them together, he wasn't sure. And rather than face or own up to it, she'd shoved him away and run.

He shouldn't have pushed her so hard. Shouldn't have put that kind of pressure on her. Since he didn't seem capable of keeping his mouth shut about his feelings anymore, he should have expressed himself in a subtler way and then backed off to let her process everything.

Now he was paying the price for his rash decision. He'd walked around all day feeling as though there was an anvil sitting on his chest, his heart ripped to shreds.

He'd thought about texting her to check in earlier but

had held off because he didn't know what the hell to say, because he'd said it all last night.

Her car wasn't out front because it was still in the shop. He let himself into the downstairs suite, disarmed the security system, then put his laptop and keys on the counter and went to the door that led to Molly's space.

Giving her space was probably the smartest thing, but he needed to see her. At least take the first step in trying to repair the damage to their relationship, and make sure she was okay after the latest update from Noah earlier.

The quiet registered as soon as he opened the door to the rest of the house. She usually left music on, even if she was out, and there were no tempting scents in the air. "Moll? You home?"

Five seconds after he reached the main level, he knew she wasn't there. The house was too still, too quiet.

He pulled out his phone, wondering if he'd somehow missed a text or call from her. Noah had reviewed the security camera footage from the grocery store yesterday but the images it had captured of that John guy hadn't been too clear, and his sunglasses and hat concealed enough of his face to make identifying him tough.

A camera posted on the exterior of the building had captured another man approaching Molly's car. Mid-twenties to mid-thirties, also wearing a hat and shades. A truck parked alongside Molly's car had hidden him from view when he punctured the front tires, but the camera had caught him crouching at the back of her vehicle and making a slashing motion.

Where was she?

Worry began to take hold until he spotted the note on the corner of her gleaming granite island.

Dear Jase. Going home for a while. Thought it was for the best right now. Not sure when I'll be back, but I didn't want you to worry. I can't give you what you want.

I don't want to lose you, but I don't want to hurt you either. I hope you'll forgive me. Molly.

Loss speared through him, a hot coal in the center of his chest that he couldn't ease. Fuck, this was all his fault. He'd been stupid and pushed too hard, too fast, but dammit, seeing her so scared and vulnerable had triggered everything he'd felt for her and he could no more keep his mouth shut and his distance than he could stop breathing.

Now she was gone. Not only that, once she got to North Carolina there was a chance her mom and grandmother would convince her to move back permanently to raise the baby there.

The paper crumpled in his fist as he crushed it into a ball. He sank onto one of the stools at the island and sat there for a long time as the silence surrounded him, unsure what the hell he was going to do now.

And even though her response had cut him in two, at least now he had his answer.

In a way, he should be grateful. A bullet to the head was way better than taking six to the chest and bleeding out.

"Oh, Christ," he whispered to the empty room, a ripple of panic licking up his spine. He was so goddamn stupid, and facing the prospect of a future without Molly in it completely gutted him.

In taking the risk of finally showing her how he felt, he may have lost her forever.

****

Even after ten days back home, it was strange staying in her old room. Her mom had cleaned a lot of the teenage clutter out after Molly had left for college, but the furniture hadn't changed and the walls were still the same vivid, peacock blue she'd chosen when she was sixteen.

She stared out her childhood bedroom window, deep

in thought. So far, the time and distance she'd wanted hadn't helped clear the turmoil in her mind. She'd thought coming home was the best thing for her, but now that she'd had time to process everything, she was unhappier than ever.

Jase was on her mind constantly. She even dreamed of him.

Vivid, poignant dreams of being tangled together in bed. Of his gorgeous aqua eyes staring into hers as he pinned her beneath him, his hands in her hair, his body buried deep inside hers. Dreams that left her aching and lonely and empty inside with the sound of his low, impassioned voice echoing in her mind.

You're mine, Moll. Mine.

She'd received a text from him the moment she'd switched her phone back on after stepping off the plane in Charlotte.

Let me know when you arrive safely.

She'd responded but kept it brief, impersonal, because she didn't know what else to say and didn't want to give him false hope. She hadn't told Sierra or Poppy what had happened between them either.

Have a good time, he'd replied. *You okay if I keep my old Ford in the garage?*

That's what things had come to between them. Horribly polite exchanges over insignificant things. They texted back and forth every day, mostly him just checking in with her, but it hadn't eased the strain between them one bit.

To this point, she'd had the opposite of a good time here. Her stalker situation also hadn't improved in her absence. Noah had been unable to identify "John" or his accomplice, but at least now if either of them or anyone else was looking for her, they would know that she was gone.

That made her mad too. Burying Carter was supposed to mark the start of a new beginning for her. She'd known it wouldn't be easy, but she'd also thought everything would improve from that point.

Her work had given her an extended leave of absence, but finances were already tight. She only had a little money in her savings, otherwise it was pretty much paycheck to paycheck. The life insurance company was dragging its feet with its decision about Carter's settlement.

She was about to be a single mom; she couldn't afford to wait any longer to get her finances in order. She'd just have to go on assuming she wouldn't collect a penny from the policy and save whatever she could from her salary.

The only bright spot of the past ten days had been this afternoon when she'd gone in for her ultrasound. A maternity doc at the hospital Molly used to work at had set it all up.

She'd gone alone, and while she'd been overjoyed at seeing the images of a healthy baby on screen, the experience was diminished because Jase wasn't there. For two hours after the appointment she'd agonized about whether to send him the pictures or not, then finally sent them anyway, as well as to Sierra and Poppy.

Jase's response had been immediate. *Everything okay? Do you know if it's a boy or girl?*

She'd assured him that everything was fine and that she'd elected not to find out. That had been the end of their communication. She kept hoping he would thaw a bit, reach out more, but the painful truth was, it wasn't going to happen. She'd overreacted that night when he'd pressured her, and she'd hurt him badly.

"Molly? Dinner's ready," her mom called from downstairs.

She sat up and rubbed at the back of her neck. "Okay, be right down." Her mom and grandmother were both ecstatic to have her home—mostly because Carter wasn't here. They weren't sad he was gone.

They'd never liked him. Well, not him so much as his lifestyle, and her being the wife of a Special Forces soldier, left behind whenever he deployed.

It hadn't been an easy life but Molly had known what she'd signed up for. She'd never complained, never regretted her decision to marry him. Until the after effects of the TBI. Then it seemed like her lifelong support system back here had suddenly disappeared.

The tantalizing scent of fried food reached her when she got to the top of the stairs, making her stomach rumble. She'd been sleeping better since her arrival but hadn't had much appetite. Much to her mother's consternation.

In the kitchen, she found her grandmother already at the table and her mom frying up something in a cast iron skillet. "Fried green tomatoes," she announced proudly, her teeth startling white against her brown skin, spatula in hand. "Your favorite."

Molly smiled. Nobody made them like her mother. "Thanks, Mama." She leaned down to kiss her mom's smooth cheek. "Can I help with anything?"

"Yes, you can eat everything I put on your plate, and then some. I won't have you starving my grandchild."

"I'm gaining weight every week. He or she is not starving."

"Wouldn't know it to look at you. You're skin and bones."

Molly huffed out a laugh and carried the plates and silverware to the table to set it all out. When they were all seated, they joined hands around the table to say grace. "And may blessed Jesus watch over my unborn grandson or daughter," her mom finished. "Amen."

"Amen." Molly dished out some black-eyed peas onto her grandmother's plate.

"So, have you put any more thought into moving home for good?" her mom asked, sliding four slices of fried tomato onto Molly's plate.

Molly hesitated, wishing they could have discussed this somewhere other than at the dinner table. She loved her mom and grandmother, but... This wasn't home anymore. She didn't belong here, and that was more evident than ever. "I can't, Mama."

Her mom stilled, platter in hand, and looked at her. "Can't? Why ever not? You've been through such a hard time, and we can both see how sad you are." She set the platter down, reached for Molly's hand. "You still miss him."

Such a complicated, loaded statement. "The old Carter, yes. But he's been gone a long time."

"Then why go back there? Nothing but an empty house and painful memories waiting for you."

Not an empty house. Jase was there, and she missed him so much it was a constant ache in her heart. He would never move out while she was at risk, so they would have to figure out a way to make the best of things. She would pay him rent until the insurance company came back with a decision. If she got the money, she could buy him out. If not, she'd find another place to live.

"My job and closest friends are there. And there's also someone I..."

Her grandmother's fork hit her plate with a clatter. "Oh, dear lord in heaven. It's another man," she said in distress and adjusted her glasses, the red plastic frames a stark contrast to her dark brown skin.

Her mother looked at Molly sharply, a frown tugging at her forehead. "Is it?"

She pressed her lips together, fighting the tide of emotion rising within her. "Yes. He's a friend. A good friend. Except now he's...something more, maybe, I don't know." She wanted him to be, and yet she didn't. "I've made a mess of everything."

A shocked silence filled the pause. "Do we know

him?"

Molly nodded and braced for the fallout. "Jase Weaver."

Their gasps were perfectly synchronized. "But he's…"

"Another former soldier? Yes. He is."

Her mom's lips pursed. "You would really risk going through all that again?"

Her secret fear stirred, the one that warned her Jase was too high risk. "He's an accountant now."

"An accountant," her grandma repeated.

"Are things…serious between you two?" her mother pressed.

"No. But they could be if I let him in."

"Is that smart? Given your condition? You've got the baby to think of. Wouldn't it be better to raise your child here, with family around? Who's going to help you back in Oregon? Who's going to be there for you if things don't work out with him? Who's going to be there if he decides he can't handle the responsibility of being a father and takes off one day?"

Sympathy welled up inside her as understanding hit. Molly's father had taken off when she was a baby, leaving her and her mom poor and ostracized from their friends and family, who had been scandalized that she'd gotten pregnant out of wedlock, and never approved of him in the first place.

Her mother made no bones about what a disastrous mistake her relationship with him had been, and how much she regretted it, except for having Molly.

"Mama, not all men are like that," she said quietly. "You and I both got hurt, but they're not all like that."

Her mom didn't look convinced. "You've been through enough. I just don't want to see you make the same mistakes I did."

She pulled in a breath before answering. "Mom.

Grandma. I love you both, you know I do. But my home is in Crimson Point now. That's where my future is, and that's where I want to raise my child."

A sheen of tears filled her mom's eyes. "But that means we'll barely see you or the baby."

"I'll still come back to visit. And I'd love it if both of you came out to visit us. We'll all have to put in a little more effort, that's all."

A brittle pause followed her words. "I see. Your mind's made up, then?"

She couldn't stay here any longer. She needed to get back to work and face everything, including trying to mend the damage between her and Jase. "Yes."

Molly's mom shared a look with her own mother, then gathered her plate and stood. "Well. I seem to have lost my appetite. You two finish up. Please excuse me."

"No, I'm not hungry either," her grandmother said, and left the table as well.

Alone, Molly forced a few bites of dinner down her throat. Once again it was more about her mother's feelings than any consideration for her.

She shook her head. Her mom and grandmother were both angry now, but they had to see the truth as plain as she did. They might not like her decision, but this was her life and she had to do what she felt was best for her and her baby.

Later, up in her room, she checked her phone. Sierra and Poppy had both texted her, excited about the ultrasound pictures and checking in to see how things were going.

Could be better, she answered. *Just broke the news that I'm coming back home to OR. They weren't happy.*

But they would get over it. They had to, otherwise they wouldn't have a relationship with her or her child.

They can deal. When are you coming back? Please say you'll be here for the author event Friday night,

Poppy said.

Right, the book signing with Zoe Renard. Poppy organized so many events for the shop, Molly had forgotten all about it. Poppy and Sierra were both insanely excited about it.

And I need to get you into the bridal dress shop, Sierra added. *Time's ticking.*

Yes, it sure was. The wedding was coming up fast. Molly smiled and messaged back. *All right, I'll book my flight tonight and let you guys know the details.*

She found a flight for the next afternoon and booked it. Outside the window, storm clouds were gathering on the horizon. Within a few hours the heavens would open up and the thunder and lightning would begin. A good storm used to excite her. Now it only reminded her of that terrible night Carter had snapped.

She'd also never forget how wonderful Jase had been to her. How incredibly safe she'd felt the moment he'd arrived.

Picking up her phone, her heart began to pound as she stared at the screen. It seemed only fair to warn him that she was coming back.

Rather than texting him, she called, unsurprised and a little relieved when it went straight to voicemail. "Jase, it's me. Just calling to tell you I'm coming home. My flight arrives in Portland tomorrow night."

She paused. See you soon? No, she had to be careful with her wording. She didn't want him to read anything into this. "Bye."

She set the phone down and put a hand on her belly where her little one was nestled all safe and sound. *Life goes on.* "Well, little one. Time to go home and face the music."

Chapter Fourteen

"What do you mean, you can't find her? Where is she?"

Rafe didn't react to Mick's annoyed tone coming through the phone as he steered down the curving highway. "Somewhere near Charlotte." He was still trying to find an exact address.

"Is she coming back?"

"Dunno. Haven't found anything telling me that one way or the other." He gripped the steering wheel tighter, his palm damp.

"And what about the insurance policy?"

"Still waiting." He purposely kept his answers clipped because he didn't want to talk. He had shit to do and not much time to get it done. Only a few days remained for him to come up with the rest of the money. He'd do whatever it took to make that happen.

A beat of silence passed, and Rafe could feel the coldness of it through the phone. "That bitch better pay up."

"She will." One way or the other. The organizations had connections all across the country. He was more concerned about the insurance company dragging its feet. Without the settlement, he would be hard pressed to get much from her anyway. Definitely not enough to pay off the remainder of his debt.

He shoved the uneasy thought aside. He'd lost too much sleep in the past few weeks. He had to focus, stay sharp. Until the life insurance policy came through, there was nothing more he could do.

"Get on it," his boss growled.

"Mick. Have I ever not gotten you the money?" he finally said with tried patience. "I'll handle it." Just as he handled everyone who owed them money. They always paid in the end, because of the ruthless reputation Rafe had earned. People who tried to run learned they could never run far or fast enough to outrun him and the organization.

And those few who didn't pay paid with their life, or the life of someone they cared about.

"Where are you right now?" his boss demanded.

"Just on my way to pay Eli another visit."

Mick grunted. "That's tonight?"

"Yep. Money should be in the account by midnight." That would put a pretty dent in what Rafe owed the organization, but still not enough. Not goddamn enough.

"Good. Let me know when you're done. Then I want you to double up on Molly Boyd. You're not getting soft on her because she's a pregnant widow, are you?"

Rafe snorted. "Not likely. I'll get the money." He disconnected before Mick could say anything else and pressed harder on the accelerator. The Audi responded immediately with a smooth purr that pushed him back into the plush leather seat.

This stretch of road was all but deserted this time of night. To his left the ocean sparkled beneath a half-moon, the waves exploding into sheets of foam where they crashed against the rocks.

His target was eleven miles to the northeast, in a sleepy little bedroom community tucked away at the edge of a large forest. He parked three blocks from the house and gathered his tools from the passenger seat. The upper middle class neighborhood was quiet, only a few people out walking their dogs as he made his way to the three-story brick home on the middle of the street.

Eli tended not to set the alarm when he was home, and a quick check proved that tonight was no different. Only Eli's car was in the double garage. Rafe pulled on his gloves and slipped inside the back door, cutting the wires that connected the security cameras to the main system.

The downstairs was quiet and dark. An elderly dog appeared at the foot of the stairs. Some black and white fluffy lap breed. It stared at Rafe a moment then let out a growl.

Rafe lunged forward and zapped the animal with his baton stun gun before it could make another sound. The dog jerked and hit the floor, unmoving as Rafe continued past up the carpeted staircase.

All was quiet upstairs, but a faint, flickering line of light coming from under the master bedroom door told him Eli was inside watching TV.

Rafe paused at the door a moment, making sure he was undetected, then burst into the room.

Eli jumped a foot in his bed, where he reclined naked, the blonde beside him that was definitely not his wife screaming.

Rafe stopped just inside the doorway and raised his pistol. "Don't. Fucking. Move."

Eli sat frozen, his pale blue eyes huge in his pale face while the blonde cowered in the bed and drew the blankets up over her naked body. "What are you doing here?" he blurted stupidly.

He knew why. And this wasn't the first time he'd tried to screw them out of money he owed. That had dire consequences. Rafe shook his head. "I came for my money, Eli. I'm tired of waiting." He spared a glance around. "Where is it? Somewhere close by, I hope. For your sake. I'm kind of in a hurry."

Eli gulped at him. "I t-told you, I don't—"

Rafe advanced on him. The blonde stifled a shriek and scrambled to the far side of the bed while Eli cowered against the tufted headboard. "Where's my money, Eli? I'm not gonna ask again."

The man shook his head, his throat working as he swallowed. "I—I don't have it here, b-but I'll get it. I'll get it, I swear, I..." He broke off when Rafe stalked toward him, shoving the pistol into the back of his jeans and pulling a KA-BAR knife from the sheath strapped around his ribs.

Custom made, the lethally sharp blade was matte black.

Eli's eyes bulged. "W-what are you doing?"

Rafe shot out his free hand to wrap around the back of Eli's neck and slammed him face first into the bedside table. The woman screamed almost as loud as Eli as his nose exploded on impact and sat there, frozen with fear.

Rafe let him go and stood by while Eli covered his face and began crying. Blubbering like a fucking little girl and begging. Rafe pulled in a breath, fighting for what little patience he still had. "The money, Eli. Where is it? Give it to me now, because if you think that was bad, you *really* won't like what's coming next."

Eli shook his head and kept babbling, tears and snot mixing with the blood pouring down his face.

Fuck this. There was only one way this was gonna end, because everyone knew what happened if he had to chase people down to collect the money. "Don't you fucking move. Hear me? You so much as twitch, and I'll kill the girl."

Eli froze and went quiet.

Rafe reached across the bed and dragged the blonde

across the covers by her hair. She shrieked and grabbed hold of his wrist to keep him from yanking her hair out. Rafe quickly bound her wrists behind her with zap straps, then secured her ankles and gagged her with duct tape. Once she was trussed up, he picked up her squirming form and dumped her in a chair in the corner before securing her hands to the frame.

Then he turned back to Eli. The man was still on his knees in the middle of the king-sized bed, his face wet with tears and blood. "Don't," he rasped as Rafe advanced on him.

"Last chance," Rafe warned, knife back in hand.

Eli shook his head, eyes wild, and lunged for the other side of the bed.

Rafe seized him by the hair just as he had the blonde, and sliced the knife across Eli's ribs. The man squealed like a stuck pig and instinctively flashed a hand out to staunch the line of blood streaming down his side.

Rafe caught his wrist and wrenched it up and back. The crunch of snapping bone was lost under another ear-piercing scream. But Rafe wasn't done yet.

He waited for Eli to settle slightly. Waited for those pale blue eyes to open and settle on him, blind and hazy with pain. Before Eli could draw another breath Rafe sliced the blade through the base of Eli's index finger.

Eli's eyes all but popped out of his skull, his mouth opening on a scream of agony and horror as his finger hit the snow-white coverlet. "Jesus *Christ!*" he bawled, trying and failing to wrench his hand free of Rafe's unrelenting grip.

Rafe wrenched his bleeding hand up to Eli's face. "I'm gonna keep going, Eli," he warned. "One finger at a time, and when they're all gone, I'll slice off your balls. And then your dick." He raised the knife again, as if to cut off another digit.

"Okay! Okay, Jesus fucking Christ, I'll give you the

money!" Eli sobbed. The blonde was crying behind them, great jerky sobs that didn't affect Rafe in the slightest.

"Where is it?"

"I—I'll transfer it. All of it. Just…" He broke down crying, his pudgy body shuddering. "No more. Please, no more."

Rafe released the bloody hand but didn't move so much as a step away from the bed as he pulled out his cell phone and called Mick. "Give me the account number," he said to Eli.

The man cried through the entire transaction, but within ten minutes the money was being transferred to the first of the accounts Mick would run it through, to clean and hide it. Eventually it would land in one of their offshore accounts.

Rafe put his phone away, wiped the bloody knife over the coverlet to clean it, and slid it back into its sheath. "You know what happens if you call the cops, yeah?" he said in a bored tone. His work here was done; he wanted to get working on the next job.

Eli's head bobbed up and down as he huddled there on his knees, cradling his bleeding hand to his chest, the severed finger lying inches from his knee. "Y-yes. I won't. I swear."

No, he wouldn't.

Rafe paused in the doorway to look back at him. Eli was gawking at him. So was the blonde.

He stared back at the man long enough to see the relief bleed from that pale face, and fear and resignation to creep back into his eyes. Rafe gave him a lopsided smile. "Yeah. You know how it works." Utter ruthlessness had propelled Rafe to the position he enjoyed now. The only way to keep it was to maintain that reputation.

He drew his silenced pistol and fired a single shot, hitting Eli directly between the eyes.

The woman screamed beneath the gag as Eli toppled

over, dead before he hit the bed.

Rafe turned on her. She was a cute little thing with huge brown eyes. Pleading eyes. Rafe almost felt bad for her. She might be a slut willing to fuck Eli while his wife was away, but she had nothing to do with his debt. She was simply in the wrong place at the wrong time.

Unfortunately, she'd seen and heard too much.

The carpet made Rafe's footsteps silent as he crossed to her. She shook her head, tears streaking down her cheeks as she stared up at him. Rafe's heart squeezed. He hated this part of the job.

"Close your eyes," he murmured, brushing a lock of hair away from her tearstained cheek. "I don't want you to see me leave."

She was so afraid she was shaking, but he could see the faint hope in her eyes. Hope that he would walk away and let her live.

But that's not the way this worked. Although he was willing to let her believe it could. She wasn't his intended target. The least he could do was try to lessen her fear and make this as easy as possible on her.

"Close them," he said again, even softer as he took a step away, letting her think he was just going to leave.

Her lashes fluttered, and her lids lowered.

The instant they did, Rafe put a round through her temple. An instant, quick kill. No suffering. She wouldn't have even felt it.

Holstering his weapon, Rafe jogged downstairs. The dog was still lying where he'd stunned it, ironic considering he'd meant to let it live. He let himself out the way he'd come and went back to his car, his mind already on the next job.

Molly Boyd.

A text came in from an associate. *Molly Boyd booked flight to Portland tomorrow.*

Rafe smiled. "Perfect." He would get the money

from her somehow. Whether or not she lived was entirely up to her.

Chapter Fifteen

"We should go dancing sometime."

Jase looked up from his menu at the woman across the table. "Sorry?"

"Dancing." Lauren pushed her long, shiny brown hair over one shoulder and gave him a soft smile. She was a successful investment banker a few years younger than him, with an impressive resume and a great personality. "I love to dance, but none of the guys I've ever dated have wanted to."

"Really? None?"

"Nope."

"Well that's just not right."

"I know, so we should fix that."

He smiled back. Since he'd already canceled on her once the night he was sick, and in light of the way things had gone with Molly, he'd seen no reason to hold off on going out with Lauren.

Molly rejecting him outright and going back to North Carolina had been a major wakeup call. So much so that in a bid to try and cope with the pain, he'd pulled the trigger and asked Lauren if she wanted to meet up because it was time he forced himself to move on. He'd made it clear again that he wasn't interested in anything romantic, and she'd seemed okay with it, even if he still got the sense she was hoping for more.

They'd gone for coffee the other day and things had gone well enough that he'd asked her to dinner tonight. He liked her and enjoyed her company. She was attractive, seemed sweet, was independent and at the top of her field.

On paper she was everything he was looking for. There was only one thing missing, and so far, it was proving impossible to get past.

She wasn't Molly.

"Sure, that would be fun," he said. And it might, if he could forget that she wasn't Molly for a few hours. He was working on that, determined to push himself into a different state of mind. The only way to do that was to forge ahead and see what happened.

Lauren shot him a skeptical look over the top of her wineglass. "Did you really take ballroom dance lessons?"

"I did."

"Not to seem judgmental, but you don't look like the type of guy to take up ballroom dancing."

He raised an eyebrow. "Why's that?"

"Oh, come on. Have you seen you?" Her green gaze swept over him, and he didn't miss the female appreciation there. His bruised and battered ego appreciated the boost.

"Actually, I took lessons for my grandma."

"Your grandma?" she said, her expression intrigued.

He nodded. "They raised me after my dad died. She and my grandpa loved to go dancing at the Legion or wherever. After my grandpa died, she stopped going out, lost touch with her friends and started to shut down. I took a few lessons and surprised her by taking her out dancing one Friday night."

Lauren made a soft, eager sound. "That is the sweetest thing ever."

He shrugged, not wanting to make a big deal out of it. "It turned out to be fun. I'll never forget the way she lit up when I got her out on the dance floor."

She put a hand to her heart. "Aww…"

Jase smiled as he remembered that night. "It was pretty great."

"Is she still alive?"

The smile faded. "No. She passed away a few years ago." He missed them both, but he had tons of great memories to carry with him.

"I'm so sorry."

"Thank you. I've got lots of things to remember them by, like this jacket." He stroked a hand over the front of the dark brown leather, lined with sheepskin. "My grandpa was navigator on a B-17 during World War II."

Her eyes widened. "A Flying Fortress?"

Jase blinked, surprised. "Yeah. How did you know that?"

She waved a hand. "Everyone knows that."

"Not everyone," he said with a shake of his head. He put the menu down and gave her his full attention, growing more interested by the minute. "Are you a history buff?"

"Sort of."

After that he started to really get into the conversation, surprised at how much they had in common. She came from a military family and had once considered enlisting herself.

They were chatting away over their main course when his phone vibrated in his pocket. He ignored it, waited until Lauren excused herself from the table while waiting for dessert to check it. When he saw the message, his abs clenched like someone had just sucker punched him.

Molly.

Flight was delayed in Denver but Sierra's driving me

back from Portland now. You home?

Jase stared at the message, torn. On the one hand he was glad that she was reaching out to him. On the other, he was dreading the first time he saw her and grappling with the finality that they would never be more than friends—and that was going to be hard enough for him after what had happened.

He couldn't go back to being her buddy yet and hanging out like they had before, it hurt too damn much. He needed time to come to terms with everything and was trying his damndest to but it wasn't any easier now than it had been the day she'd left.

I'm out right now, he typed back. *When will you be home?*

Around ten?

There was still a threat against her. If she was coming home, he needed to be there when she arrived to make sure she was safe. *I'll be there. Drive safe.*

He slid the phone back into his pocket just as Lauren got back to the table. Needing to be home for Molly gave him the perfect excuse to cut the night short. "That was fast," he said, standing.

"Well, I had plenty of incentive to hurry with you here waiting for me." Her smile was sweet with a flirtatious edge, and he recognized the invitation there.

Everything about her appealed to him, but he wasn't ready to date anyone yet.

You and Molly are never happening. Accept it.

He was trying, dammit. He would remain living in the downstairs suite until the threat against her was gone for good. Until that happened, he would have to suck up the pain and take it like a man.

With effort he pushed her from his mind and enjoyed Lauren's company over dessert. She was charming and witty and clearly interested in him despite his warning about this not being romantic. "The weather's supposed to be gorgeous this coming week," she said after the waiter brought their bill, which they split at her insistence. "Any way I could interest you in a hike?"

He'd have to check with Molly about her schedule first. Her safety was his priority no matter how badly he was hurting. "I'd love that. I'm busy Saturday, but might be free Sunday." Wedding-related things with Beckett.

Her eyes sparkled with anticipation. "Sunday works."

He drove her home, the conversation between them easy, and she even made him laugh by telling him a story about her and her older brother while growing up. When he pulled up in front of her house half an hour later, she undid her seatbelt and shifted to face him in the passenger seat rather than get out.

"I had a really good time," she said.

"Me too." Under different circumstances he would be totally into her.

She held eye contact with him, the moment stretching out. She wanted him to kiss her, and it wouldn't exactly be a hardship.

But he couldn't do it. Flat out couldn't stomach the thought of kissing anyone other than Molly.

She turned you down and left to get away from you. Get over it and move on.

Way easier said than done, unfortunately.

He gave Lauren a smile, wishing he could feel differently. He honestly liked her. Maybe he'd change his mind about them over time. He hoped so, because he was tired of being alone, wishing for something that was never going to happen. "What are you doing next weekend?" he asked.

She watched him for a moment. "Nothing important." She pulled out her phone to check her calendar. "You free Saturday the seventh?"

"I'm in a friend's wedding party." Beckett and Sierra

had included a guest on his invitation, but he couldn't bring Lauren when Molly would be there. "The reception's supposed to wrap up pretty early, though, because the groom told me they're leaving at just after nine. Are you free after that?"

Her delighted smile answered before her words did. "It's a date."

****

Molly rapped on the door to Jase's suite the following Friday night and waited, her stomach muscles pulling taut. Her heart kicked against her ribs when he answered, looking good enough to eat wearing a button-down, plaid flannel shirt and jeans.

Damn, her physical response to him hadn't lessened at all during their time apart. If anything, it was even sharper now that she'd had a taste of him. God help her, she wanted another. "Hey."

That alert aqua gaze scanned the length of her, a frown tugging at his eyebrows. "You going out?"

She'd dressed up in leggings, boots and a form-fitting top that stretched over the mound of her belly. "With Sierra. There's a book signing thing at Whale's Tale with Sierra's favorite author."

He nodded, his expression closed. "You coming back here after?"

"Yes. I figure I'll be home by between ten and eleven. If I'm going to be late, I'll text you." She could have texted him everything else too, but she'd wanted to see him. Since arriving home they didn't see each other often, even though they talked on the phone or texted each day and lived in the same house. He was always home when she was, and she was all too aware it was to make sure she stayed safe.

"Okay. Have a good time."

She forced a smile. It was the weekend and he was stuck home alone. Because he was trying to protect her.

She appreciated him looking out for her, but she also felt bad. She wished they could go back to being friends again. This constant strain between them was tying her in knots. Since coming home she'd gone back and forth about whether she was willing or ready to try a relationship with him. Twice she'd almost told him she was, provided they took things slow.

Except she had a feeling that if they ever crossed that line from friends to lovers, things would move anything but slow.

"I will. Thanks," she said.

A horn honked out front. She hurried to the front door and dashed off the front porch holding her jacket over her head to shield her from the rain as she raced to Sierra's car. She was tired, but needed to get out of the house.

"Hey, look at you, a true Pacific Northwesterner already, braving the elements without an umbrella," her friend said in approval as Molly hopped into the passenger seat.

"Umbrellas don't help when the rain comes in sideways or from the ground up," she pointed out.

"True." Sierra reversed and steered down the driveway. "So, you ready to meet a famous author?" Excitement radiated off her.

"Ready as I'll ever be." The truth was, she'd been in a crap mood since she got back from her trip the other night.

Tonight, she was determined to shake off her funk and enjoy herself. So Jase had made a point of avoiding her whenever possible since she'd been home. And maybe they would never be able to repair their friendship to the level it had been before she left. So what? She'd live. God knew she'd weathered a lot worse to this point.

Whale's Tale café and bookshop was all lit up when they parked out front, warm yellow light flooding through the front windows and glistening on the wet sidewalk and street.

"Wow, looks like Poppy's got a good turnout," Molly said. Every parking spot along the street was taken up on both sides and she could see a crowd of people filling the café portion.

"Well yeah, this is Zoe Renard we're talking about." Sierra grabbed her hand and all but towed her inside, bypassing the café and heading straight for the bookshop area. "Come on, I don't wanna get stuck at the back."

A buzz of conversation and laughter filled the air as they stepped inside the bookshop. They spotted Poppy at the back of the room, who waved and shot them a huge smile from the table that had been set up.

Dozens of women stood around holding books and bags, chatting to each other, some of them wearing Zoe Renard T-shirts. One woman Molly spotted even had a Zoe Renard-themed tattoo on her arm.

"Wow, that's hardcore," she murmured to Sierra. She hadn't known readers did that sort of thing.

"Right? But I get it. Zoe's fantastic." She was all but bouncing on the balls of her feet as they waited for the guest of honor to appear.

Poppy disappeared for a moment into the back office, and then an expectant hush filled the room, spreading from back to front. Excited murmurs broke out as Poppy came back in, escorting a woman who could only be the famous romantic horror author herself.

Zoe Renard certainly made both a statement and an entrance. Molly liked reading well enough, but romantic horror wasn't her thing. Actually, no romance appealed to her at the moment, because she was upset about the way things had turned out with Jase.

The guest of honor wore a long, ruffled black skirt

and a black Victorian-style riding jacket. Startling bright blue streaks colored the front of her otherwise dark hair that was twisted into a knot at the nape of her neck. Blood-red lipstick made her smile blindingly white, and the heavy, smoky eye makeup made her golden eyes stand out even from where Molly stood.

"Holy," she whispered to Sierra, who seemed speechless. The woman rocked the Goth look.

"I know," Sierra answered, her eyes glued to the woman.

She stood by while Sierra finally got her turn to meet the author, got an autograph and some pictures with her. Sierra was practically giddy as she walked away to find a seat for the question and answer session.

Afterward, Poppy brought the author over to introduce her personally. Zoe approached them with a big smile. "So, Poppy tells me you're expecting?" she said to Molly, the edge of a southern drawl in her voice. Different than her own. A little slower, heavier. Deep South.

"Yes, I'm over the halfway mark now," Molly answered, patting her stomach. She liked to touch it, rub it. And feeling the baby move always filled her with awe.

"Congratulations. I had my daughter last year." Zoe's gorgeous eyes lit up as she pulled out a phone decorated with a case that looked like a bat, all covered in black rhinestones. "This is Libby. Since she started walking she's like a human tornado, but we love her anyway."

Molly studied the picture of the dark-haired, blue-eyed toddler held by a gorgeous, powerfully built man. "Is that your husband?" He was huge, Carter's size, with a chiseled jaw, dark hair and blue, blue eyes.

Zoe grinned. "Yes. Clay."

Molly exchanged a look with Sierra before focusing on Zoe again. "Well, wow."

She laughed, a sultry, husky sound that suited her personality perfectly. "Yeah, I'm a lucky girl, right? But the best part is, he's a lot softer on the inside than he looks."

Sierra sighed and put a hand to her heart. "Oh, I love a big, tough guy with a squishy center. Mine's like that too."

"They're the best," Zoe agreed, then turned her attention back to Molly. "By the way, if you ever want to know what childbirth's *really* like, call me. I'll tell you the truth no one else will."

Molly laughed, surprised and warmed by how personable and down to earth she seemed. Molly hadn't expected that from a famous author. "I appreciate that."

"Molly's an ER nurse," Sierra put in, "so she's seen it all. Childbirth isn't going to faze her at all."

Zoe nodded, gave Molly a sympathetic smile even as humor danced in her golden eyes, and patted her arm. "Yeah. Still call me." Before Molly could answer, she found herself engulfed in a musky, floral-scented hug. "I'm serious. Anything you want to know, just call."

Molly patted her back, grinning at Sierra. Apparently, Zoe was a hugger. "I will."

"Oh my gosh, that was insanely awesome," Sierra gushed as they left just over an hour later. "I got a hug from Zoe Renard. And her husband? Holy shit. Don't tell Beckett I said that, by the way. I'll deny it."

They arrived back at Molly's place to find Jase working on his car in the garage. He stopped to talk to them a minute, though it still felt a bit strained. And she couldn't tear her gaze from him, the ache inside her so strong she thought she might burst. "I put a letter on the kitchen island for you," he said to her. "It's from the insurance company."

"Oh. Thanks." She went inside and straight into the kitchen, Sierra following her. The couriered envelope made her heart pound.

She ripped it open, torn about what she wanted the

letter to say. If they weren't going to pay the settlement, it meant not being able to afford this house. If they did pay, it meant she was in greater danger from the people Carter owed money to.

She began reading while Sierra hovered nearby. The invisible cables around her ribs eased their grip even as her stomach tightened. "They've ruled it an accidental death. I'm getting the money."

"Well that's good news, right?" Sierra said, wrapping an arm around her. "Will you get the full amount?"

"Looks like." A quarter million dollars.

People had been known to kill for a lot less than that.

"John's" face appeared in her mind, sending a shiver ripping down her spine.

"Then you can make a down payment and apply for a mortgage now?" Sierra asked, trying to keep things positive.

"Yes." She should have been thrilled. Once she paid him out, it would help the situation with Jase. "What if the people Carter owed money to know about this? They knew about the policy. If they know I'm getting this much money, they'll come after me."

Sierra shook her head, her expression firm. "That's not going to happen. My brother will find out who these assholes are and take care of it. And in the meantime, Jase is here to make sure you're safe, and Beckett too."

Yes, Jase was here. Because he felt obligated.

That familiar sinking feeling took hold again. "I haven't seen much of Jase since I got back." She'd have to tell him about the money, so he was aware of the possible threat.

"Oh?" Sierra said casually as she headed for the fridge.

Too casually. And they'd just eaten all kinds of food at Whale's Tale. No way Sierra could possibly be hungry.

Molly frowned at her friend's back. "Have you seen

him much?"

"The other day while you were at work. And a couple of times while you were away."

"Did he…say anything about me?" She hadn't told Sierra what had happened.

"While you were away? He asked if I'd heard from you."

Oh. "Nothing else?"

Sierra stopped in the act of pulling the fridge open to look over her shoulder at Molly with a sharp look. "No. Why? What's going on?"

Molly hesitated. Maybe she shouldn't say anything more. Maybe Jase didn't want anyone else to know.

Sierra stared at her. "Oh, man, I thought things were a little weird between you guys earlier. If something happened, you'd better tell me."

"He kissed me. The night before I left."

Sierra's blue eyes widened in shock. "Why didn't you tell me?"

"Because I panicked. I was embarrassed and confused."

"Embarrassed? Why?"

"Because of…everything." She made a helpless gesture toward her rounded belly. "I'm not sure what I feel and I was afraid of what you and everyone else would think."

"Aww, Moll, no." Sierra came over to take her by the shoulders, her deep blue eyes searching Molly's. "Sweetie, Carter's gone. There's no reason for you to punish yourself about moving on. And screw what anybody else thinks, you deserve to be happy. I know you care about Jase. If you want him, then don't push him away because of whatever reasons you've made up in your head."

She looked away. "I hurt him. Turned him down pretty harshly. He walked out, and then I booked my flight home and left before we could...resolve it." Although how could they resolve *that*? To his credit he hadn't tried to talk to her about it or change her mind since, so he'd obviously taken her decision to heart.

The problem was, she *did* want him. Couldn't stop wanting him. She thought of him constantly, dreamed of him every night.

"Then you need to talk to him," Sierra said.

"He's been doing his best to avoid me."

"Well he's been...busy, that's all."

Something in her friend's tone struck her as odd. She raised an eyebrow. "Busy with work, you mean? Or something else?"

Sierra grimaced. "Okay, I didn't want to be the one to tell you because I wasn't sure how you'd left things between you two, but I think he's seeing someone."

The news was like a gut punch, taking her completely off guard. How could he be seeing someone already? "Oh."

"I think they've gone out a couple times since you left." Sierra gave her a sympathetic look. "Are you upset?"

"No," she blurted. But hell yes, she was upset. How could he kiss her like that, say all those things and then go out with someone else right after?

"Are you sure? Because you look and sound upset to me."

"No, of course not." She tried to convince herself that this searing pain in her chest wasn't the remnants of her heart breaking. He hadn't done anything wrong. She'd told him they were never going to happen. What had she expected him to do, sit around pining for her the rest of his life? This was her own damn fault.

God, the irony. She'd been ready to consider putting her fears aside and following her heart to see if she could let him in the way he wanted, but not if he was seeing someone. She groped for a silver lining to ease the pain. Maybe they weren't meant to be. Maybe now they could go back to being friends. Someday.

"I want him to be happy." She truly did. But it still hurt like a bitch. At some point since the night he'd kissed her she had begun to allow herself to picture them together. She'd been nursing a spark of hope that things might work out if she could find the courage to risk her heart again.

Sierra watched her doubtfully. "Moll, if you have feelings for him, then you need to tell him. Don't let him go."

She shook her head, put on a brave smile even though it felt like her face might crack from the strain. Things happened for a reason, right? If he'd already asked another woman out, then clearly he wasn't that into *her*. "It's okay. My life's only going to get more complicated as time goes on. It's for the best that we both move on with our lives now."

But even as she said them, the words filled her with a terrible, empty hollowness.

Her phone rang. Her heart jumped, a spark of hope fading when she saw Noah's number instead of Jase's. "Hi, Noah."

"Hey, Moll. I've got some news I need to share with you."

He didn't sound too happy. "Is it good news, or bad news? Because I could really use some good news."

A pause followed. "It's not good."

Hell. "Okay, so it's bad. I should tell you first then, that the insurance company made their decision. I'm getting the money."

He groaned. "Okay, I reached out to an FBI contact of mine about your case and as a favor to me he had his people run 'John's' pictures we got from the security footage through their facial recognition software."

"All right. And…?"

"His real name is Rafe Baxter. And he's an enforcer with ties to the Russian mafia."

Chapter Sixteen

Aidan rapped twice on Jase's open office door and waited for him to look up from the computer screen in front of him. "You busy, wee man?" It was past dinnertime on Thursday night, and everyone else had gone home.

"You gotta stop calling me that. I'm barely an inch shorter than you. That doesn't make me wee." His pal had dark circles under his eyes, as though he hadn't been sleeping much.

Could be good or bad, depending on what was keeping him up—a willing woman, or personal demons. Aidan hoped it was the first one.

"In height, maybe no'. In personality and other important areas where size matters, trust me, you're much shorter."

Jase snorted and leaned back in his chair. "Remind me again why I thought I liked you?"

"Because I'm a charming bastard and I'm handy with a rifle when things get a wee bit dicey."

"Yeah, I'll give you the second thing. What's up?"

"I was thinking of hitting the pub for a pint before we get fitted for our glad rags. You in?"

"I've got some more things to finish up on this year

end, and then I'm heading home to finish sealing the kitchen counters in my suite."

"Away, man! Is that what you consider a good time now?" He scoffed. "That and working on that auld car in your garage?"

"Pretty much, yeah."

Something was up with their CFO, and Aidan wasn't sure what. Normally Jase was the social one in their management team, but lately the grim-faced and hard-edged Beckett had seemed more fun than him. That was all kinds of wrong.

"Molly doesn't get off work until seven, and she's staying at my place again tonight." Now that she was getting the insurance money, Jase and Beckett had taken all possible precautions to make sure she was safe from the people Carter owed money to. They'd been moving her around to keep her location secret, and increasing everyone's vigilance. She'd been staying with Aidan for the past two nights.

"You're picking her up, right?"

"Aye, of course." He might not have the personal connection to Molly that the others did, but he wasn't going to let her go anywhere unescorted when there was a Russian mafia enforcer after her.

The set of Jase's shoulders relaxed visibly at that. "Good."

The lad was wound up tighter than a grandfather clock. He needed to let loose a bit. "One pint," Aidan coaxed. "We'll be in and out in twenty minutes."

Jase glanced at his watch, frowning. "I guess I could go for a quick beer."

"Aye, you can. Let's go. I'll drive." He headed down to his SUV, Jase a minute behind him.

The Sea Hag was quiet now that fall was here, and while it didn't have the same kind of atmosphere that a proper pub back in Edinburgh did, it wasn't bad.

Mostly just locals were there when he and Jase walked in and took a seat at the end of the bar overlooking the water. The view was bonnie. Beckett had told him it was beautiful here, but Aidan hadn't expected to be so impressed. Not that he'd ever tell Beckett that.

Aidan ordered them each a beer—a disgusting watered-down American brand Jase liked, and a proper dark stout for him. "*Slàinte mhath*," he said in Gaelic.

"Cheers." They tapped bottles.

"So. How are things going with your new lady?" Aidan asked. He was nosy. Couldn't help it.

Surprise flitted across his buddy's face. "Lauren? We're just friends."

"Oh, aye?" He didn't believe it for a second. A man didn't hang out that often with a single woman unless there was more to it than friendship.

Jase nodded.

"You met her online?"

"No, at the gym."

"Ah. So, no worries about a case of false advertising then." Happened in the online dating world all the time.

Jase huffed out a laugh. "No, she's great."

"Glad to hear it. I've had some real nightmares, myself, meeting women online." He gave a mock shudder.

Jase smirked. "I'll bet. You're not doing that anymore?"

Aidan shot him a disbelieving look. "'Course I am. How else am I going to meet a woman livin' in this wee town? Naw, it's all a matter of knowing how to vet the profiles properly."

"Is that right," Jase said, deadpan. "Well if I ever dive into those shark infested waters, I'll run everything past you first."

He grinned. "Offer's always there." He slapped Jase's shoulder. "I got your back, wee man."

Jase shook his head and took another sip of beer.

"You're seeing someone around here already?"

"Seeing?" He shrugged. "I've been on a few dates since I moved here. Nothing serious, and that's the way I like it. I'm done with commitment until I'm at least sixty. Aye, seventy."

Jase raised an eyebrow. "Really. Something tells me there's one helluva story there. You know, given that you're the expert when it comes to IDing the wrong kind of women."

Aidan raised an eyebrow back at him. "How do you think I became an expert?" Having your heart broken—aye, stabbed, cut in half, ripped out of your chest and then set on fire while you watched—tends to make a lasting impression on a man. What's the American saying? Been there, done that, got the T-shirt.

"What happened?" Jase was all ears now, not at all distracted and down like he had been so often lately.

Aidan shrugged. "Classic tale of unrequited love."

"For real?" Jase's eyes widened. "Wait, not that girl you were hung up on back in—where was she from? Ben Dover?"

Ha. "Glasgow. And aye, that's the one."

Jase waited a beat, then made a *go on* motion with his hand. "You gonna make me drag it out of you, or what?"

He sighed. "Ach, fine, you nosy bastard. The short version is, I saw what I wanted to see, rather than what was actually there, ken?"

Jase frowned. "But weren't you guys engaged during that last deployment?"

"Promised. Not engaged." It still cut surprisingly deep to think about it, even two years later. "When I got home, she was gone. She did leave a letter, though, apologizing. That was good of her," he said wryly.

Except it wasn't funny, even now.

At some point during that deployment, or maybe before, he would never know, Ginny had decided she was tired of only having him for a few months a year. Tired of steady and safe when he was home, apparently, and she'd found someone who was home more and was more "fun".

He couldn't really blame her for the waiting bit, but he sure wished she'd been honest with him when her feelings had begun to change, rather than let him walk into an empty apartment carrying a dozen roses and a diamond ring in his pocket. And that second bit was pure shite.

More fun than him? He mentally snorted at the thought. *No one* was more fun than him, in the right setting.

"Sorry, man." Jase shook his head. "I didn't know. Is that why you took that contracting job in Florida?"

"Aye." After Ginny left, he couldn't get there fast enough. Though Scotland would always be home, and he missed it. "I needed the distance to make a fresh start. You ken?"

A shadow passed over Jase's expression. "Yeah. I get it."

A text message popped up on his phone. "That's the boss. We're to meet him at the suit hire place in twenty." Aidan wasn't technically in the bridal party but Beckett had asked him to wear a tux so he could act as an usher or whatnot, and Aidan loved the gruff son of a bitch enough to do it.

"What, you're not wearing a kilt?" Jase asked in astonishment twenty minutes later when Aidan walked out of the changing room in the tux. "I thought that was an unwritten law or something. That Scotsmen always wear kilts to formal events."

Aidan tugged at his bowtie to straighten it. "I would, but I don't want to steal the spotlight from the groom. And besides, if I wore a kilt, every woman within a two-mile radius would be after me, trying to find out if I wear anything under it." He met Jase's eyes in the three-way mirror and smirked. "So really, I'm doing you both a favor by wearing this penguin suit instead."

"Monkey suits," Jase said with a laugh. "And thank you. I think."

"We appreciate the sacrifice," Beckett remarked from the other side of the room where the woman was busy trying to find a jacket wide enough for his shoulders.

"Maybe you'd best lay off the 'roids for a while, big man," Aidan said to him. "Or you'll rip those seams on the big day."

Beckett's hard mouth twisted into a grudging grin. "Always the comedian."

"Aye. It's a thankless job, but none of the rest of you bastards are fit for it."

Beckett called out to him. "Mac, you got any plans for the night?"

"I'm picking Molly up after her shift, why?"

"I'm driving Jase to his truck. Can you do me a favor and swing by my place to take Walter out for a quick walk?"

"Quick? That dog is so old he doesnae go more than a hundred meters an hour. At most."

Beckett grinned. "True. So, will you? I called my little neighbor to see if she could do it, but I haven't heard back and I've got a ton of shit to do yet tonight."

"Awright. I will dutifully walk your wee beastie for you."

"Thanks." Beckett slapped him on the shoulder. "See you tomorrow at the place on Lighthouse Point Drive."

"Aye." Aidan wasn't really an animal person, but he didn't mind doing this. The drive over to Beckett and Sierra's was certainly no hardship. To the west the sun was just sinking into the sea, filling the sky with an incredible splash of color.

He parked in the driveway and started to climb out of his SUV, but stopped when a little blond girl appeared around the side of the house leading Walter on his leash.

She stopped, her almost preternatural stillness and unblinking stare telegraphing her unease at finding him there.

"Hello," he said, giving her a smile and staying right where he was to put her at ease. "I'm Aidan, a friend of Beckett's. He asked me to come walk Walter for him, but I see you've already beat me to it."

She stared up at him with haunted blue eyes, her hand tightening on the leash. It bothered him. He had teenage nieces back home he adored and the thought of anyone frightening this little one put all his protective instincts on high alert. "He texted my mom about Walter, so I came over to get him," she mumbled.

"It's all right, no harm done." He shifted his gaze to the dog. "Well, Walter, it looks like you're in good hands." The dog feebly wagged the end of his tail, his long nose twitching as he sniffed the air and his tongue dangling out the side of his mouth at a ridiculous angle. He looked like something a cartoon artist would dream up.

The little girl cocked her head at Aidan and frowned. "You talk different."

"Different bad?"

"No, I like it. It sounds neat."

"I'm from Scotland. Do you know where that is?"

"Yes." She ran her gaze over him. "The men wear kilts there. And play bagpipes."

He suppressed a laugh. "Aye, sometimes they do. But only the braw ones."

"Braw?"

He tried to come up with a relatable translation. "Awesome." Her tentative smile tugged at his rusty heartstrings. "What's your name, lass?"

"Ella. I live down the road." She pointed toward the

end of the lane.

He nodded. It was getting dark, and even if she lived on this street, he'd heard all about the cougar incident when Poppy had first moved into the area. He didn't like the thought of her walking out here alone. Where was her mother? "What if we walked Walter together down to your house, and then I'll walk him back home. Save you a trip."

Ella drew Walter closer to her, watching Aidan warily.

Smart lass. He liked that she was being cautious. "Hang on." He pulled out his phone and dialed Beckett. "I'm here with your neighbor, Ella," he said on speaker. "Can you verify who I am for her?"

"Sure. Hey, Ella," Beckett said, and Ella visibly brightened at the sound of his voice.

"Hi, Mr. Beckett."

"This is my friend Aidan. You're safe with him, I promise. Okay?"

Ella's shoulders relaxed and her sigh seemed full of relief. "Okay."

"Thanks, mate. We'll take care of Walter." Aidan ended the call, already charmed by the lass. "Well then, what do you think? Can I walk with you and Walter down to your place?"

"Yes," she said softly, and led Walter toward him.

Aidan made sure to keep a careful distance from her as they walked down the lane. Walter took his sweet time, his long, low-rider body waddling with each step.

"I think I just saw a slug pass us," Aidan said a few minutes later.

Ella looked up at him in surprise, then burst into laughter, making him smile. "It must have been a really fast one."

"No, I'm sure this one was just a regular slug. Do you have racing slugs here?"

"Not that I know of."

"Ah. We do in Scotland." He nodded at Walter. "I never knew a dog could walk this slowly."

A happy tinkle of laughter answered him. "You're funny, Mr. Aidan."

Ah, damn. No wonder this wee one had Beckett curled right around her finger. "Aidan's fine. Or Mac."

"Mac?"

"My last name's MacIntyre. People shorten it to Mac."

"Well, do you like Mac better, or Aidan?"

He had to smile. "I like both. You decide what you'd like to call me."

"Okay."

After the longest mile he'd ever walked, even longer than when he'd carried an eighty-pound rucksack through the Hindu Kush Mountains in the middle of winter, they finally reached the craftsman-style bungalow set into a wooded lot at the end of the lane. "At last. I can't believe we made it."

Ella giggled and started up the wooden steps to the porch, then stopped and turned to hand him Walter's leash. A good thing, since the animal had put on the emergency brake at the bottom of them, his red-rimmed eyes staring up at Aidan in defiance. "Maybe he'll be faster on the way back," she said, her eyes twinkling in the porch light. "Maybe he'll pass the slug this time."

"I wouldnae get your hopes up, Ella. It's uphill."

She laughed again, breaking off when the front door swung open.

The smile froze on Aidan's face and his mind went completely, utterly blank.

A woman with fiery red hair that flowed in waves around her shoulders stood there wearing a loose-fitting, flowy white dress. She looked like an angel, illuminated by the lantern hanging from the porch—

Except for the cold look on her face. Her gaze sliced right to him, her mismatched eyes locking on his face, one hazel, the other green as the Highland hills.

Beautiful and unique. And clearly not happy to see him on her doorstep.

He shook himself out of his stupor and opened his mouth to introduce himself, but the woman darted out a hand to grab Ella's shoulder and dragged her inside, bodily placing herself between him and her daughter. "Can I help you?" she said, her expression and tone frosty.

Her meaning couldn't be clearer. *To get near my daughter again you'll have to come through me.*

"He's Mac," Ella said before he could get a word out. "He's friends with Mr. Beckett. Mr. Beckett asked him to come walk Walter because he didn't hear back from you in time."

"Oh." Her expression thawed slightly, but only a bit. It was clear she didn't trust him.

"Aidan," he said, offering his hand.

"Tiana," she answered, refusing the gesture by wrapping her arms about her middle and retreating back to her doorway where she stood there like a sentinel guarding her daughter. Everything about her stance broadcasted defensiveness and protectiveness. And that told him something really bad must have made her this way. "You're walking Walter back, then?"

"Aye. It took us a while to get down here because of Walter's short legs."

"Mac said he saw a slug pass us on the way," Ella said with a giggle.

Tiana smiled at the sound of her daughter's laughter, but it faded as she faced him again. "Well. Thank you for seeing her home safely. Good night." She started to close the door.

Her dismissal damn near made him grin, but he managed to mask it. "Of course. Good night, Ella."

"Good night, Mac."

Tiana was still watching him warily through the gap between the door and the jamb. "Nice to meet you, Tiana," he said.

"You too." Polite but cool. She ushered Ella back a step and swung the door shut without a backward glance. Before Aidan had even turned around, the deadbolt slid home in the lock.

He dragged an extremely reluctant Walter back up the lane, thinking about Tiana's reaction to seeing him with Ella. There was a story there, he was certain of it. A bad one.

One more thing he was sure of: Beckett had been holding out on him. With a neighbor like that living just down the street, Aidan intended to find a lot more excuses to hang out at Beckett's place in the near future.

Chapter Seventeen

Jase rode shotgun in an armor-plated Humvee, fifth in line in the convoy headed north to Kandahar. A familiar sense of dread filled him as he took in their surroundings. Small villages full of mud brick buildings in the same, flat dun color as everything else out here in the southern part of Afghanistan.

In the dream, he was aware of an intensifying feeling of foreboding as they drove along. A sense that he knew what was about to happen. Something terrible he needed to stop.

The streets were empty. Normally they traveled at night, because the daytime was far more dangerous. He couldn't see anyone watching them from the windows or walls they passed, but he could feel them, and they were definitely watching.

Up ahead, the road curved slightly, following a shallow drainage ditch.

Stop.

The command was loud and urgent in his head. If they didn't stop something awful was going to happen.

They drove closer, the warning turning into a scream in his mind. "Stop!" he shouted to the driver.

Too late.

A remote-detonated IED exploded a few vehicles ahead. Jase grunted as the concussive wave ripped through his body. Up the convoy, the damaged Humvee was on fire.

Carter.

No! He threw open his door and ran, his M4 in his hands. Men were screaming as they burned in the flames. The heat seared his face as he neared it, his heart in his throat.

Carter was trapped in the back. He was unconscious, his face and chest covered in blood.

Jase wrenched the bent back door open and reached in, grabbing his best friend. "Carter. Carter, man, wake up."

Jase dragged him out, away from the flames, and settled him a safe distance away, his weapon at the ready as he got on the radio to call for a medevac. Blood leaked out of Carter's nose, signaling a facial or skull fracture. When Jase looked up, Beckett was running toward them.

Jase ripped off his gloves and checked Carter's vitals, fighting back the anguish inside him. "Hey. Come on, you big bastard, open your eyes and look at me."

He jumped when those nearly black eyes popped open to stare up at him. Not groggy or blank with confusion and pain.

No, they burned with rage and accusation that seared him to the bone.

"You turned your back on me," Carter rasped out while blood ran down his face into his thick, dark beard. "You deserted me and left me to die alone. And then you stole my wife." He bared his teeth, smeared with blood. "You swore to me you'd look after her, but instead you stole her because I'm dead and you couldn't have her when I was alive!"

Jase jerked awake, his heart thundering in his chest and his skin coated in a film of sweat. "Shit," he breathed, dragging a hand over his damp face. He'd been so wiped he'd given in and taken a nap. Bad idea.

He couldn't get Carter's face out of his head. Or those damning words.

Didn't matter if it had only been a dream or that Jase definitely hadn't stolen Molly. The sentiment behind them was true enough.

If he could have stolen her, he would have. Instead, they'd barely had a handful of conversations over two minutes long since she'd been back. And when they did cross paths, it was almost always small talk or something about the house or her security situation.

Shit. Was this ever going to get any easier?

His conscience continued to torture him about the fight he and Carter had had the night he died, and now that she was getting the money, the new intel about Molly's stalker made Jase's blood run cold. How Carter had gotten tangled up with the Russian fucking mafia Jase would never know, and one of its most lethal enforcers was after Molly to get the money back.

Jase was sick about it, and thankful that Beckett, Noah and Aidan had stepped up to help him guard her. She had protection everywhere she went, even work, because she was surrounded by people. Sometimes he thought it would be better to have her just hand over the money to make this all go away, but that was dangerous in its own right. If she paid it, other people might come looking for money too.

For the moment the only actions they could take were increased vigilance and more precautions. She couldn't stay here at the house anymore, even with him here. There was too high a chance someone could have tracked her here.

As a result, right now she was shuttling back and forth between Beckett's, Noah's and Aidan's places in the hopes of keeping her location hidden in case anyone came looking for her again, and he and the guys were taking turns driving her wherever she needed to go. Even though they still talked every day on the phone, Jase missed her like hell, but there was no help for it.

He stumbled to the bathroom for a long, hot shower, ate, and then texted Mac to invite him over. He'd wanted to see Jase's baby and Jase wanted to work on her for a few hours before they had to leave for the rehearsal. And after that nightmare he needed someone else around to help take his mind off it.

"You're sure that thing is gonna run when you're finished with it?" Mac asked in the garage twenty minutes later.

One hand braced on the opposite side of the old hood, Jase tightened a bolt on the engine block, not bothered by Mac's skeptical tone. "Positive. Can you hand me that 3/8 inch?"

The wrench landed in his upturned palm a second later. "Thanks. Hey, you're pretty handy to have around."

"I try." Mac leaned his hands on the other side of the hood to take a look at what Jase was doing. "I never knew you were into restoring old cars."

"For years. Just barely ever get the time to work on this old gal." That was one perk of being home a lot recently. He'd been spending more and more time on her over the past few weeks, since Molly had left for North Carolina. With the house all finished up, he'd needed a project to keep him busy, otherwise it gave him too much time to think.

The house felt empty without Molly here, but her safety was the most important thing and the current situation gave him more time to heal up.

"How old is she?" Mac asked.

"Rolled off the assembly line in '32."

"She looks it."

"She'll look brand new once I'm done with her." Jase

handed the wrench back and grabbed a rag from his hip pocket to wipe his hands. "Had this baby shipped out from Nebraska when I moved here."

"She's sentimental for you."

"Yep. Belonged to my grandpa. We used to work on it together on the weekends whenever I was back home between deployments. Built this beauty from the frame up."

Mac eyed the car doubtfully. "Brilliant." He straightened. "So, this is what you do in your spare time, then?"

"When I can. She's getting closer to being ready to hit the road. The engine's nearly done. All she needs is some new brakes and lines, some detail work, and a pretty paint job."

"Ah, you're as talented with cars as you are with weapons and spreadsheets, then. Good to know. Tell me the truth, though. Do you miss it? Because I do."

Jase didn't pretend to misunderstand that he meant the Army. "Sometimes. As messed up as that sounds."

"Naw, I get it." He shook his head. "Never thought I'd miss it, to be honest. At the end of my last tour I swore I was done with that life forever. But it gets in a man's blood. The lifestyle. The brotherhood."

"I know." The brotherhood especially. "That's why I'm here with Beck, pushing papers around on a desk instead of hunting insurgents and freezing my ass off in the mountains overseas somewhere."

"You ever think of going back? As a contractor?"

"I've thought about it." He was seriously contemplating it right now, the job offer with the security company back east still on the table. "I'm good where I am for now, but I'm not sure if I can do this long term." The job, the living situation, and constantly being around Molly.

"Aye. We miss the action."

Jase nodded. "Yeah. And the money in private contracting's hard to pass up."

"It is."

"Why'd you quit? I thought you were going to do it until you retired."

He made a face. "Burned out, plain and simple. I saw too many screw-ups on jobs. People got hurt or killed when they didn't have to. Beckett's offer came at the perfect moment."

Jase nodded, thinking about his own situation. Did he really want to go back to that life and take a job as a security contractor? Dignitary protection and security details in dangerous parts of third world countries. In places he never wanted to set foot in again.

Or was he considering it merely as a way to finally get free of Molly and the hold she had over him? "You planning to stay here long term?"

"Not sure. My work visa's up in April. I've applied for an extension, but no guarantees it'll go through. No point staying here if I can't work. I've been offered a security contract overseas by a mate of mine if I can't get the extension."

Jase understood completely. But he'd hate to see Mac go.

"Well, you'd best get cleaned up and wash that grease off your hands. Don't want to be getting that all over the tea sandwiches," Mac said.

Jase glanced at his watch, surprised to see that it was getting close to the time he needed to leave for the rehearsal dinner at Beckett and Sierra's. "Right."

Mac followed him there and walked up to the house with him. "You bringing a date to the wedding, by the way?" he asked.

"No, but I'm going out with Lauren after." Bringing her to a wedding might make things seem more serious than they were, and he didn't want that. But he needed a shove to push him forward, and he liked Lauren. "You?"

"Had one lined up, but she canceled." He glanced at

Jase, his warm brown eyes glinting with humor. "I'm looking forward to meeting this *friend* of yours. Think she has a thing for Scotsmen?"

He chuckled. "She might."

Mac lifted an eyebrow, and Jase realized he'd given the answer easily and without thinking—or feeling even a twinge of jealousy or territoriality about another guy potentially honing in on her.

So much for getting over Molly anytime soon.

A row of cars was parked up and down Salt Spray Lane when they arrived. The moment they walked in the door, Poppy bustled by with a tray in her hand. "Sausage pinwheel?"

"I'll take some of those," Jase said, snagging four and putting them on a napkin, bracing for the moment when he saw Molly.

"Hey, leave some for the rest of us," Mac complained, snatching a few from the tray before they were all gone.

Jase felt Molly's presence before he saw her. A subtle change in the air that sent a prickle of awareness through him. He glanced over his shoulder, his abs contracting as though to protect himself from an invisible blow.

She was more beautiful than ever in a simple knee-length dress that outlined the swell of her breasts and the mound of her growing belly.

If he'd thought more time away from her would do anything to change his feelings or attraction to her, he was sadly fucking mistaken. The yearning that punched through him was so strong it pushed the breath from his lungs and made his heart seize.

Look at me. God dammit, look at me the way you did that night.

The night he'd tasted those sweet lips and felt the imprint of her lush body against his. The night when, for just a few moments, all his dreams still might have come true. They were seared into his memory for all time.

As if she felt the weight of his stare, she looked over. Their gazes locked from across the room, and for the life of him he couldn't look away.

The tentative smile she gave him cut deep, reminding him of the invisible wall standing between them. A wall that in that moment, despite everything, he still wanted to obliterate.

Jase was aware of the all-too familiar pain spreading beneath his ribs. He didn't want this. Wished he'd never given into the desperate need eating him alive and kissed her, pushed her to give him what he wanted. It would have been better to leave things as they used to be, back when she'd been oblivious to the depth of his feelings.

Except the damage was done and there was no going back, for either of them. There was only forward.

Dammit. He'd sworn to Carter that he would look after her. He couldn't take having her wary and uncomfortable around him. And she was staying with Beckett and Sierra again tonight, so he wouldn't get to see her.

He forced a smile and broke eye contact, chewed the suddenly tasteless mouthful of sausage pinwheel and forced it down his tight throat. He would always love her. That was his cross to bear.

****

Rafe kept his hat and his fake glasses on as he walked into the administration office at the hospital, making sure he didn't look directly into the security cameras mounted along the hallway. He'd changed clothes before coming here, since his previous appointment had gotten messy at the end. But he'd secured the money, and that was all that mattered, because he was now a desperate man.

Only five more days remained until the deadline.

And he was still two-hundred grand short, after squeezing every dime he could from anyone he could. He either found the remainder by next week, or died.

It was just near the end of business hours. Some of the admin staff had already left for the weekend. He smiled at the woman seated behind the reception desk, confident with his disguise. "Is Janet still here?"

"Yes, she's in her office. Let me page her for you."

He stopped her as she reached for her handset. "No need. I know the way and she's expecting me."

His attempts to locate Molly Boyd had gone nowhere since she'd left for North Carolina. Even when he'd found out she'd flown back, she'd been frustratingly elusive, and he'd been too busy taking care of other cases to expend the time for an intensive surveillance. The easiest place to take her was when she arrived at the hospital for her next shift.

The rest of the cubicles were deserted as he headed for the office at the back. He knocked once and pushed it open. Janet spun around in her chair, a bright smile lighting up her face when she saw him. "Oh, it's you."

"It's me." She thought he was the guy she'd met on an online dating site ten days ago.

He shut the door behind him, slid his hands into his pockets. "I know we said we'd talk over the phone, but I was in the area and thought I'd stop by in person instead. Hope that's okay."

Her smile turned shy. And hopeful. "Of course. You look just like your picture."

She wasn't the brightest bulb. That's why he'd chosen her. "You look even better."

She flushed. "Are you here about your cousin's schedule?"

"Yes. And to find out if you're busy next weekend."

"Oh." She flashed him a sweet smile. "The updated schedule just went out this afternoon, and no, I'm not busy next weekend."

"Good." He put on his most charming smile.

Still blushing, Janet cleared her throat and typed in a few commands on her computer. "I'm just pulling it up, give me two seconds."

"Great." The security on the system was surprisingly formidable for such a small hospital. Rafe could have had one of his tech guys break in after hours to try and access what he needed, but he'd thought this would be easier and he'd been right.

He'd fed Janet a bullshit story about how his late grandfather had credited Molly Boyd's care after his heart attack to his survival, and how the family wanted to thank her by delivering a gift in person. Janet had eaten it up without any questions. "I'd rather surprise her at home than at work, but if this is the best I can do, I'll take it."

She shot him another smile. "I'd love to help you with that, but when I looked up her info on payroll, there was no address listed. She must have moved after her husband died."

"A terrible thing for such a good person," Rafe said.

"Yes. Okay, here's the schedule." She clicked on a screen and scanned it. "She's working ER, so… Here," she said, turning the monitor so he could see it and pointing to the schedule. "She's booked to start her next shift cycle on Monday night, starting at seven."

Perfect. Monday it was. "I can't wait to see her."

"She's going to be so surprised," Janet gushed.

"Oh, I sure hope so." He straightened and rocked back on his heels, watching her for a moment until that blush started up again. "Do you like Italian, Janet?"

"It's my favorite."

"Fantastic. I'll take you out to a great place I know next Saturday night. I'll call you during the week to set it up."

"Okay." She looked so hopeful he almost felt sad for

her.

She'd never hear from him again, and when the police questioned her later to find out what had happened to Molly, his disguise and fake online ID would throw them off the trail. He'd done it before. He'd no doubt do it another hundred or more times. "Thanks for your help."

"Anytime." Her voice was slightly breathless.

Rafe let himself out and walked out a different exit, making sure to avoid the cameras as best he could. He had only a few days left to close this file. He was prepared to do whatever it took to get that insurance money. He would never again feel the shame and helplessness and the pinch of hunger in his belly.

Now, he was the master of his own fate. Once this debt was paid off, he was free to start making money again, enough for him to live the lifestyle he deserved instead of the one that had been forced on him as a kid.

Except for his own, most mothers had an inherent weak spot when it came to protecting their children. That was something he could exploit.

On Monday night Molly Boyd would either pay with the insurance settlement, or her unborn child's life.

Chapter Eighteen

Sierra and Beckett's wedding day dawned bright and beautiful. The fine mist covering the ground that formed a blanket on the sea slowly burned away beneath the early October sun, turning the yellow, red and orange leaves into panes of stained glass made all the more vivid with the backdrop of dark evergreens surrounding them.

"I made pancakes," Poppy announced on her way in the side door of the Victorian house, carrying a big basket in both hands. "I do know how to make other things, but I know these are your favorite."

"You're the best," Sierra gushed, rushing over to help her.

"I'll get the plates," Molly said, and hurried to the cabinet.

She'd been staying here for the past three nights. It was bad timing with the wedding, but it was for her own safety and her friends didn't mind putting her up. While Beckett and Sierra were on their honeymoon this coming week, she would split her time between Poppy and Noah's, and Aidan's.

It sucked that she couldn't go home, but her baby's security was paramount, and given the way things were with Jase, she didn't want to be back at her house right now anyway.

She chatted with Poppy and Sierra over pancakes at the sun-drenched kitchen table while the stylists did their hair and makeup. Ella arrived partway through and was treated to having her own makeover before putting on her flower girl's dress.

Walter watched it all from his position spread out flat on the floor nearby, his protruding tongue trailing across the hardwood and those droopy, red-rimmed eyes staring up at them. He wore a snazzy black and white tuxedo vest that was completely at odds with his perpetually mournful expression.

Time passed in a blur of activity, and when Molly zipped Sierra into her gown and stepped back to see her friend in the full-length cheval mirror in the corner of the master bedroom, she got choked up. "Damn, look at you, girlfriend."

Sierra's smile was pure radiance. Her thick brown hair was done in a sophisticated updo with just a few elegant tendrils framing her face and neck. The off-white dress was organza, the cap sleeves framing a sweetheart neckline and a formfitting bodice that belled out into a beautiful, full skirt. "Right? I clean up pretty good." She fiddled with a fold of the veil that fell past her shoulders.

"Your bouquet just arrived, fresh from my garden—ohhh," Poppy breathed, pausing in the doorway to stare, one hand pressed to her chest. Then she grinned. "I can't *wait* to see Beckett's face when he lays eyes on you." She handed over the mixed bouquet of sunflowers and roses.

"Me too," said Sierra, accepting the flowers. "These are gorgeous, but the thing I love most is that we all helped plant them when they were babies."

Finally, it was time to go. "You ready?" Molly asked Sierra with a smile as she helped the bride down the stairs, carrying the back of her friend's train.

"*So* ready."

"Wait!" Ella cried, running from the kitchen. She came back in thirty seconds later holding something. "We almost forgot Walter's bowtie." The dog was sitting patiently by the side door, watching all the commotion with a completely disinterested expression.

"Oh, we couldn't forget that," Sierra said, bending to play with the dog's long, floppy ears. She helped Ella put the bright red plaid bowtie on him and clipped the leash to the ring on the back of the tuxedo vest. "He's going to steal the show, I just know it."

"You're so handsome, Walter," Ella gushed, coaxing him up on his stubby legs. The dog groaned and climbed to his feet with a weary sigh, pausing to look back at Sierra with a *why are you doing this to me* expression.

Molly helped adjust Sierra's veil and stepped back. "You look so beautiful," Molly said, her voice a little hoarse.

Sierra made a sound of distress and whacked her arm. "Stop it! How dare you make me cry ten minutes before my wedding." They both laughed as Sierra pulled her into a hug. "I love you."

"Love you too. Now let's go get you hitched."

"Let's." She accepted her bouquet from Poppy and together they headed out of the house and up the path that led to the lighthouse perched atop the cliff.

Molly carried the back of Sierra's train so it wouldn't drag on the dew-damp ground and Ella led Walter in their comically slow procession up the path.

"Walter, you're gonna make us late," Ella complained, clicking her tongue and trying to make the basset-mix move faster.

A salty tang filled the air. The breeze picked up along with the sound of the waves as they finally neared the cliff where everything was set up, and the closer they got, the more Molly's insides tightened. She still hadn't talked to

Jase.

During the rehearsal and dinner everyone had been busy, and he'd stayed well clear of her whenever he could, making it impossible for her to talk to him. When it finished, he'd already been on his way out the door talking on his phone, so she hadn't bothered going after him. Maybe today things would start to change for the better between them. She hoped.

They paused at a group of mixed evergreen and colorful deciduous trees that hid the wedding site from view. Sierra's father was waiting there for her, dressed in his tux.

Mr. Buchanan's eyes grew damp when he saw his daughter. "Well, baby girl, you look gorgeous," he said, drawing her into a gentle hug. "Sure you want to be given away? You know I love Beckett, but I'd rather keep you as my little girl forever."

Sierra laughed. "I'm sure, Dad." She put on a mock frown. "Wait, he showed up, right?"

"They had to drag him the last fifty yards or so up to the altar, but yeah, he's here, waiting for you."

Sierra's face turned all sappy. "I waited a long time for him, but it was worth it."

Molly shared a smile with Poppy, who bit her lip, her eyes glistening. Then Mr. Buchanan disappeared around the screen of trees for a moment and the strains of a violin carried on the early autumn air. He came back to get Sierra, smiling down at her as he offered his arm and tucked her hand into the crook of his elbow.

With an excited smile, the bride turned to Poppy and Molly and gave a nod. *Let's do this, ladies.*

Poppy held her bouquet at waist level and started the slow walk down the aisle, a strip of trimmed grass that led down the center of the outcropping where an arbor had been set up with the old lighthouse framed in the background. The view was spectacular, but Molly only had a moment to take it in as she followed a few seconds behind Poppy, because her gaze slid past Beckett and Noah and locked directly on Jase.

He stood beside Noah, hands folded in front of him, and the sight of him in his tailored tux took her breath away. Then his aqua gaze shifted from Poppy to her and for a moment Molly felt like time stood still. Every emotion she'd been fighting to suppress hit her all at once as she stared back at him for those endless few seconds—loss and regret and a yearning so strong it made her whole chest ache.

She turned her gaze straight ahead, afraid he would read everything she was feeling, and continued up the aisle to stand across from Noah on the other side of the arbor. Knowing he was seeing someone was eating away at her insides.

The violinist began the bridal march. Molly faced back the way she'd come.

A ripple of laughter rose from the guests when Ella stepped out at the end of the aisle leading Walter in his little tux and bowtie, the saddest ring bearer that ever bore a ring. She'd looped the end of the leash around the same wrist that held the basket, and tossed petals as she walked, a big smile on her sweet little face.

Walter, of course, didn't seem quite as happy about the whole thing, but he did wag his tail a few times. When Molly glanced at Beckett, his lopsided grin told her he liked his surprise.

Then it was the bride's turn.

Molly bit the inside of her cheek and swallowed past the lump that formed in her throat as Sierra appeared from behind the trees. A murmur rose up from the guests and when Molly glanced over at Beckett, the proud smile on his hard face almost did her in.

Sierra all but floated down the grassy aisle to stand in front of the man she was about to marry. Beckett reached for Sierra's hand, symbolically taking her from her father.

He bent his head and murmured something to Sierra too low for Molly to catch, but it made her friend's smile grow even more. Together they faced the minister, hands joined, and the ceremony began.

Molly studiously kept her gaze on them as she listened to the vows, avoiding looking at Jase and thinking of all the years and tragedies that had shaped Sierra and Beckett's love story, but her mind floated back to her own wedding.

Though it had been an elopement it had been such a happy day, so full of promise. Jase had stood beside Carter throughout the ceremony, and she'd been completely oblivious of his feelings for her. She was afraid to look at him now.

"I now pronounce you husband and wife," the minister announced at last. "You may kiss the bride."

Molly stifled a laugh as Sierra gleefully threw her arms around Beckett's wide shoulders. The guests whistled and yelled in encouragement as Beckett slid one hand into Sierra's hair and wound an arm around her waist to dip her backward as he kissed her...and kissed her.

Molly laughed too, overjoyed for her friends, and surprised. Beckett wasn't one for public displays of affection, but he seemed to be relishing this moment, and it was heartening to see. Finally, he righted Sierra and lifted his head, his lipstick-marked grin telling everyone how pleased he was with himself.

The violinist played for them as they proceeded up the aisle. She spared a quick smile for Noah as he offered her his arm, but the entire walk to the end, she was conscious of Jase standing right behind him with Poppy.

The receiving line was next, followed by pictures. Molly put on her best smile and posed with the bridal party for all the shots, aware with every heartbeat of exactly where Jase was, and how he barely looked at her. She got that he was hurt, but his distance felt like a punishment.

It hurt. Hurt so much she wasn't sure she could stand it. She glanced around, hoping no one else was noticing the strain between them, but everyone's attention seemed to be occupied elsewhere.

She'd been agonizing over their kiss and wrestling with her feelings for weeks, but knowing he was seeing someone made her wish she'd found the courage to get over her fears and take a chance with him earlier. Even now the thought of losing Jase was unbearable, and she was…okay, she was miserable and jealous.

What choice did her current position leave her? She'd already fallen in love with a Green Beret she had trusted with her whole heart, and it had all gone to hell. She was afraid. Afraid of what people would think or say. Afraid what might happen if she gave into her feelings.

And even more afraid of what would happen if she didn't. That it might already be too late for them.

She breathed a sigh of relief when the photographer finally dismissed them and they all walked back to Beckett and Sierra's house for the reception.

You're halfway there.

All she had to do was make it through the next few hours with a smile on her face, and then she could go upstairs and hole up in the guestroom for the rest of the night, alone.

****

Weddings weren't Tiana's thing. The idea that you could find and marry your "soul mate" then entrust your heart and dreams to them for a lifetime was nothing but an illusion.

As well as a surefire way to get your heart and life destroyed.

She was totally out of place here. She wouldn't have come at all except she adored Beckett and Sierra, and her daughter loved them even more.

The ceremony had been gorgeous and the dinner lovely, but it was hard to like weddings when you no longer believed in fairytales and happily ever afters. Tiana was far better acquainted with stark reality and the perils of letting a man into her life. Ella was her whole world now, and that was enough.

She scanned the buffet area and spotted her daughter's blond hair as she fed Walter a few treats from a platter of cold cuts on the table. Tiana couldn't help but smile. That girl was an animal nut and it wouldn't surprise Tiana in the least if she wound up being a veterinarian like Sierra someday. Lord knows she worshipped Sierra, and Beckett too.

"What are you doing over here all by yourself?"

She twisted around as Molly walked up and sat next to her in Ella's empty seat, the pale violet fabric of her dress pulled taut over the growing mound of her belly. "Just taking it all in," she said with a smile.

"Don't know too many people here?" Molly asked.

"The ones I do know are really busy." The bride and groom were making the rounds and Poppy was running around ensuring none of the food platters ever got close to empty.

"Well, I know Beckett and Sierra are happy you came. They're seriously in love with Ella."

Tiana smiled and looked back at her daughter. "I know. And it's mutual."

"She's sure attached to Walter."

"Tell me about it. She asks me every day when she can get a dog of her own."

"Any chance?"

"I'm softening, but don't you dare tell her that."

Molly held up a hand. "Cross my heart."

Tiana turned toward her more. "How are you feeling these days? Any heartburn yet?"

"Oh my God, yes," Molly said with a roll of her eyes. "I hate it."

"Just wait until the third trimester when your stomach's shoved halfway up your throat," Tiana teased. "You'll be popping antacids like candy."

"Can't wait," Molly said dryly. "Right now, sleep is the thing bothering me most. Or the lack thereof. I can't remember the last time I slept through until morning, and it's not because of my bladder."

"I think it's nature's way of prepping us for the sleep deprivation of having a newborn."

"Could be." Molly leaned back in the chair and put a hand to her adorable baby bump.

Tiana secretly envied her. She'd loved being able to rub her pregnant belly and feel the baby moving inside her.

"How are you doing, anyway? Last time we talked, you were pretty hard on yourself."

She shrugged, her insides tightening. "I'm okay." She deserved to be hard on herself after what she put Ella through. Didn't matter if it was unintentional or not, fact was, it was her responsibility to protect Ella, and her daughter had suffered because of Tiana's poor decisions.

"You know what?" Molly said, settling a comforting arm across Tiana's stiff shoulders. "As someone who is also way too hard on herself, I don't believe that for a second. And you know what I've decided? At some point we've got to learn to give ourselves some slack."

Tiana huffed out a grudging laugh. "You're not wrong. I—" She broke off, her entire body tensing when she spotted that big auburn-haired Scottish guy from the other night walking away with Ella. They were deep in conversation about something as they wandered away from the party together, around the far side of the house.

Tiana jumped up without thinking and hurried after her daughter. "Ella," she called out sharply, her heart drumming in her ears. People nearby had stopped talking and were staring at her but she didn't care, her only concern for Ella.

Her daughter stopped near the far corner of the house and looked back at her with a puzzled look on her face. "What, Mama?" The man—Aidan or Mac or whatever the hell his name was—was staring at her too, his expression unreadable.

"Where are you going?" she asked Ella, pushing down the fear rising inside her.

"I was bored, so we were just going to get Walter and take him for a walk up the road."

Tiana shook her head, willing her heart to slow down. "You and I can walk him together in a little bit. Come back to the table, we're going to eat dessert soon."

"But I want to—"

"*Now*, Ella."

"Do as your mother says, Ella," Mac/Aidan said quietly, watching Tiana as he urged Ella forward with a gentle hand on her back. Tiana wanted to rush over and slap his hand away, hating that he'd touched her daughter. "This is my fault, I should have checked with her first."

Damn right you should have, because I would have said no way. She stared right back at him, chin raised, telling him without words that as far as he was concerned, her daughter was off-limits, charming accent and being a friend of Beckett's or not.

"Good girl," she said as Ella came to her, relief hitting her as she turned around and walked back to their table. She could feel Mac/Aidan's eyes on her the whole time but she dismissed him, not caring what he thought.

Molly was watching them too, mild shock on her

face. "Everything okay?" she asked when Tiana sat down and pulled Ella into her lap.

"Yes, fine," she answered, her cheeks starting to warm. Okay, maybe she'd overreacted. Maybe she'd just made an ass of herself and caused a mini scene with Beckett's friend, but too bad.

She'd made too many mistakes already because she was a terrible judge of men. For Ella's sake, she was going to ensure she never made another.

Chapter Nineteen

Molly barely ate anything at dinner. By the time the speeches and toasts were done, she was feeling emotionally fragile and half desperate to escape into the house and up to her room. But she couldn't leave yet, not until the dancing was done, the garter was thrown, and the bride and groom left for their hotel.

Jase had barely said two words to her the entire day, speaking to her only when necessary. The tension between them was worse than ever, and she was near her breaking point.

Had anyone noticed? Sierra and Beckett seemed too lost in each other to pick up on it, and Molly hoped they hadn't. She didn't want anything to put a damper on their day, and she was good enough at hiding her feelings that hopefully no one had sensed any discomfort or tension between her and Jase.

It was driving her crazy, constantly on her mind. She missed the connection they used to have. Yearned for more of what that kiss had promised. She missed *him*.

Glancing down at the mound of her almost six-month belly, she thought about the life she and her child would have together. A life without Jase, at least without him being one of her closest and most trusted friends.

The future seemed duller, colder because of that. Not to mention lonely.

She stole a glance down the head table where Jase was seated at the end beside Noah. To her knowledge he'd avoided looking at her since the reception began.

She secretly drank in the strong lines of his profile, hungry for the sight of him after wrestling with her feelings all day long. He was the kind of man to stand by his commitments, and he'd made his feelings for her clear before. He would be an incredible father one day and there was nobody she trusted more, alongside Beckett and Sierra.

Much as it scared her, Molly wanted him. And she didn't want to be alone anymore, she'd been that way for too long. Somehow, she had to find the courage to risk her heart again, risk losing Jase forever if things didn't work out between them, and tell him how she felt. It was time she needed to learn to live again, woman up and take a chance.

She clapped along with everyone else as Beckett and Sierra cut the cake and shared another kiss, her pulse beating faster now that she'd decided to settle things between her and Jase one way or another. But just as she pushed her seat back to go over and talk to him, the DJ announced the first dance.

Beckett led Sierra out onto the center of the lawn, lit up by strands of lights and lanterns hanging from the trees. The first notes of the slow song Sierra and Beckett had chosen filled the evening air.

Molly turned to look for Noah, since the maid of honor was supposed to dance with the best man. She spotted Poppy standing at the edge of the grass with Jase, waiting for their cue to join the bride and groom.

"Hey," Noah said, coming up beside her to put a hand on her waist and lead her toward the others. "Great day, huh?"

"Amazing." Her eyes stayed on Jase with every step, but he never looked her way.

At their cue, Jase tugged Poppy out onto the dance floor, and Molly followed Noah. She reached up to grasp his offered left hand and settled her other on his shoulder, making small talk and smiling as they danced with the rest of the bridal party and the guests looked on.

Noah responded to everything she said, polite and charming, but she noticed his gaze kept wandering to his girlfriend and that he was gradually maneuvering them toward Jase and Poppy. When they got close enough, he leaned his head to the side and said to the other couple, "You don't mind if we change partners so I can dance with my sunflower, do you?"

Molly stopped dead, her gaze snapping to Jase. He'd gone still too, and when their eyes met her stomach balled up at the resignation she read there. Not only did he not want to be around her, he dreaded it.

His lips quirked in a smile at Noah. "Of course not." He handed Poppy over to him, and Molly swore he squared his shoulders before coming to stand in front of her. They stared at each other for several awkward heartbeats, then he held out his hand, palm up.

Swallowing, she laid hers on top, her throat thickening, and ordered herself not to tear up. All her muscles went taut when he settled his warm palm over the small of her back, as though touched by a live wire. That simple touch was like sensual fire against her skin, the imprint of his palm and each long finger clear and distinct.

Her lower belly flipped and her nipples tightened in a rush as the instant connection between them hit her. She stared at the base of his throat just above the black bow tie he wore, her heart thudding a painful rhythm against her ribs.

She didn't dare speak, afraid she would blurt out

something crazy and stupid. *I want you. Please say you still want me back.*

Instead she focused on his hands, the tempting lure of his body heat as he moved them to the music. A gentle sway, the sure, firm pressure of his hands guiding her.

He'd always been an amazing dancer. She used to love dancing with him whenever they went to a bar or club together with Carter, and even that day in the ER in front of Mrs. Wong. Back when they'd been close and she'd thought nothing could ever change that.

Now it was absolute torture. Being inches from him, breathing in his delicious scent and being achingly aware of every square inch of him. Right in front of her. Touching her. Yet completely out of reach.

She couldn't ignore the effect he had on her, in a totally different way than Carter had back when he'd first captured her attention. Jase was far more subtle, with a simmering undercurrent of sensuality she ached to experience firsthand. She wanted his hands and mouth all over her. Wanted to feel his heat and power as he held her in place and sank into her. Filling her, making her his. Taking away this terrible ache he'd created inside her.

His quiet, solid presence had her wanting to lean into him, to feel his strength and care wrapping around her once more. To know that it wasn't too late. That there might still be a chance for them.

Her throat tightened, the searing lump stuck in it all but choking her.

She couldn't stand that he was seeing someone else. It was killing her. He should be *hers*, dammit.

But when the song ended, Jase briefly paused to look down at her, gave a tight smile and let go. "Thanks for the dance." Before she could summon the words she needed to say, he was striding off toward the crowd gathered at the edge of the dance floor.

Tears stung the backs of her eyes, his name sticking

in her throat. She wasn't going to follow him or call him back and risk making an ass of herself in front of everyone. She'd wait until later when she could get him alone.

An upbeat song started up. The guests all rushed onto the dance floor, couples and groups of friends, all having a great time.

Molly moved out of their way and endured the rest of the reception, breathing a sigh of relief once everything finally wrapped up. When all the guests began to leave, she walked Ella and Tiana up to the lane. As she was saying goodnight, a red car parked across the road. A pretty young woman in a blue dress got out as the driver left, her face lighting up with a smile as she spotted someone in the dispersing crowd.

"You made good time," a familiar masculine voice said.

A sharp pain twisted inside Molly when she saw Jase walking toward the newcomer. They were both smiling, clearly lost in each other.

The woman he was seeing. He'd brought her here as a date.

Which meant things were a hell of a lot more serious between them than Molly had realized.

She whirled around and quickly retreated back to the house, unable to stand there and watch while the remnants of her heart were ground into dust.

It seemed that life had just dealt her yet another crushing blow.

She was too late. Jase had already moved on.

****

The rest of the reception went by way too damn slowly.

Standing at the edge of the lawn, Jase resisted the urge to check his watch for the tenth time as the evening finally came to a close almost an hour later than Beckett had planned.

The groom had just crawled under the skirt of Sierra's dress to retrieve the garter with his teeth and fling it over his shoulder. Noah had caught it and immediately rushed over to slip it on Poppy's wrist while he kissed the breath out of her and everyone cheered.

Jase gave it another month, tops, before the sheriff popped the question.

That thought only made him feel more alone, even though Lauren was meeting him soon. And even still, Jase found himself preoccupied by thoughts about Molly, glancing around for her.

Holding her, even just by the hand and the small of her back had been the most exquisite torture, breathing in her familiar scent while all the feelings he'd been trying to suppress had come roaring painfully back to the surface. She'd left the lawn after their dance and hadn't come back, even though she loved to dance. Now she was over in the far corner, talking with Tiana and Ella.

She laughed at whatever Tiana said, and something twisted deep in his chest. She was so beautiful it made him ache.

The party broke up minutes after Sierra and Beckett left. Molly was nowhere to be seen, and Noah and Poppy were headed for their car with his parents.

Lauren was just crossing the lane when he got to it. He didn't feel like going out now, but he'd promised so he put on a smile. "You made good time."

"I may have paid the driver extra to step on it. And wow, you are gorgeous in that tux."

"Thanks," he said, feeling awkward.

She slipped her hand into the crook of his arm as he led her toward his truck, smiling up at him. Yeah, she definitely wanted to be more than friends and would be expecting him to make a move tonight.

It made him dread the rest of the night, because he had to end things. He couldn't see her anymore, that much was clear.

He wasn't over Molly, and from where he stood, never would be. He'd felt like he was about to come out of his skin for those few minutes during the dance, touching her, his entire body flooded by need and an overwhelming possessiveness.

Spending any more time with Lauren when she clearly wanted more than friendship was wrong. It wasn't fair to her.

Lauren leaned into him slightly, the lush weight of her breasts pressing into his side. "Where should we go with you all dressed up? Maybe out for a drink?"

"Sure." He didn't push her away. He didn't want to hurt her, she was great. Just not the one for him.

He put her in his truck, shutting the door before she could try to kiss him, and immediately drove away. She tried to initiate conversation several times, but he could only summon a half-hearted response, too busy figuring out how he was going to tell her.

She was quiet when he parked in front of her house after taking her for a drink at a bar in an upscale hotel on the water, waiting for him to look at her. Searching his eyes, she smiled tentatively and leaned forward across the cab to kiss him.

He gently caught her chin between his thumb and forefinger, at least having the balls to look her in the eye before he dropped a kiss on her cheek instead and pulled back.

Hurt flashed across her face as his meaning registered. "What's wrong?" she whispered.

Shit, he felt bad about this. "I can't give you what you want," he said, echoing Molly's exact words to him in her note. "I'm sorry."

A heavy beat of silence passed. "Is it Molly?"

Taken aback by her astuteness, he lowered his hand and gave a grudging nod. He owed her the truth at least. "Yeah." It had always been Molly.

"I wondered. You get this…look on your face whenever you talk about her."

He covered a wince. He hadn't realized he'd brought Molly up that often, but if Lauren had picked up on the intense connection between him and Molly, then others would have too. "I'm really sorry." He meant it. Wished with all his heart he could have fallen for her and let go of Molly.

Her smile was sad. "Me too. I hope it works out for you. And I hope she knows how lucky she is."

Jase gave a tiny, stiff smile, not bothering to dissuade her of her assumption that he and Molly would ever get together.

"Well." She gathered her purse, opened the door and paused to look back at him, the dome light shining on her hair and pretty face, and he wondered what the hell was wrong with him. "Thanks for the ride home."

"Of course."

He didn't walk her to her door, but waited until she was safely inside. Letting out a long exhalation, he pulled out his phone to do what needed to be done.

Sever the cord.

He'd saved the most recent text from the guy from the private security company who had been trying to recruit him for contract work, offering Jase an interview whenever he wanted one.

He stared at the message for a moment, though he'd already made up his mind about this two hours ago. Staying here near Molly, watching her raise her baby and move on to some other guy eventually? He'd rather take a hollow point round to the chest and pour acid into the wound. It would hurt less than living here and having a front row seat to watch from while she moved on with her life.

Once Molly was safe from the threat hanging over her, he needed a fresh start, somewhere far away from her. There was no other way.

If the job's still available, I'd like to schedule that interview, he typed back, and hit send.

If the company wanted him immediately, he'd work out Molly's security details with the other guys. Maybe he'd even give Beckett his notice once he and Sierra got back from their honeymoon late next week, depending on how things went.

Having made the decision, his heart was surprisingly heavy on the drive back to Crimson Point. All things considered, he was going to miss this place, and his friends. Most of all Molly, but with any luck that was a wound time and distance would heal eventually.

The moon was up when he pulled into the driveway, and he was surprised to see Beckett's truck parked in front of the house. Why were they here? Weren't they supposed to be at the hotel by now?

He let himself into his suite and pulled off the bow tie before striding to the door that separated his space from the rest of the house. Molly's house, though she hadn't lived here for a couple weeks now.

Just as he reached for the doorknob, a knock sounded from the other side. He pulled it open, expecting Sierra or Beckett.

His heart did a painful, backward somersault when he found Molly standing there instead.

The moonlight filtering through the windows at the front of the house made her lavender dress shimmer with an unearthly light. It caught on her dark curls in brushstrokes of silver and made her gold-and-green irises glow like cat's eyes.

"Hey," he managed once he found his voice. "What are you doing here?"

She didn't answer right away, the expression on her face tugging at something inside him. "I borrowed Beckett's truck in case anyone was watching the house and came to grab a few things. No one followed me. I didn't think you'd be home so soon, so when I saw your truck pull up I…wanted to say hi."

He nodded, feigning nonchalance even though he was all twisted up inside. She shouldn't have come here alone. What was going on? "Wedding was perfect, huh?" For Beckett and Sierra, at least.

"Yes." She kept staring at him. "You're home early."

Was she fishing for information? Why? "Yeah. Been a long day."

She nodded, her gaze shifting behind him into his place. "Am I interrupting?"

He frowned. "No, why?"

"I saw you leave with your date, so I wasn't sure if you brought her back here…"

"I took her home." He would never bring someone back here while Molly lived upstairs anyway.

"Oh." She looked away, a small sigh escaping her. He wanted to believe it was relief, but that was just wishful thinking.

He was wired too tight right now to try and decipher the mixed signals he was picking up from her, and not in the mood for bullshit small talk. "I told her I couldn't see her anymore. And I never even kissed her." He wasn't sure why he felt compelled to add that last bit, but he did.

At that her gaze snapped to his, and he swore he saw a spark of hope there. What the hell?

No.

He shook himself. He was seeing what he wanted to see, not what was really there.

"What do you want, Moll," he finally asked, weary and wanting this night to be over already. He loved roller coasters, but not this kind.

She kept staring at him, those cat's eyes searching his, as though she wanted to say something but was afraid to. He could see the indecision warring in her face.

And something else.

Yearning. A soul-deep yearning that shoved the breath from his lungs and made him go completely still. What the hell? *Am I nuts?*

No. He *knew* her, dammit. Could read her face and expressions better than anyone.

She looked away, losing her nerve. But he knew what he'd seen and now it felt like an invisible vise was squeezing his ribcage.

"Moll," he said, his voice a quiet rasp in the silence, his heart thudding hard against the back of his sternum. Did he dare hope that…? "Look at me."

She hesitated for an endless moment, then raised her eyes to his once more. And the unspoken plea he saw there almost brought him to his knees. "Why are you here?" he repeated, needing her to be honest with him. He refused to get his hopes up anymore. He was sick of having his heart mashed.

Her fingers fidgeted in front of her belly. "I…miss you, and I want…"

His aching heart swelled, pushing back against the pressure of the invisible vise. He'd already put himself out there once and received a sledgehammer blow to the chest in return. He wasn't doing it again. If she wanted him, then she had to tell him. "What do you want?" *Say it. Please, God, say it.*

When she didn't answer, frustration punched through his cautious façade. She was killing him, standing two feet away in the moonlight in that gorgeous dress with her heart in her eyes and leaving him guessing. "*What* do you *want*, Moll?"

A sheen of tears glistened in her eyes. "You," she whispered, so soft he could barely hear her.

Stunned, Jase exhaled in an unsteady rush as that sweet word splintered through him, damn near making his knees buckle. *Thank. Fucking. God.*

Hardly able to believe this was happening, he reached for her, hauling her to him and crushing her in his arms, half-afraid that she might disappear before his eyes.

His throat was so tight he could barely get any words out, his voice a hoarse rasp in the quiet. "Angel, you've always had me."

Chapter Twenty

Molly felt like she'd just jumped off a tall building without a parachute. She was falling, hurtling through the air, and only Jase could stop her from hitting the ground.

Her heart knocked against her ribs, a knot of emotion making it hard to breathe as his heavy arms closed around her, drawing her tight to his body. Sensation burst along all her nerve endings, a soft cry locking in her throat. She was still afraid, afraid this might wind up being a terrible mistake she would pay for later, but she would rather take the risk than lose him.

She'd almost lost him. Had come precariously, terrifyingly close to missing her chance to find out what it would be like to be his.

It was almost like she'd been asleep these past few months, and watching him with his date tonight had shocked her wide-awake. Even though this step could mean the end of their friendship, and that there was a tiny chance he could end up like Carter had.

With pure determination, she pushed the whispers of caution aside. There was no place for that here, with him.

Pulling in a shuddering breath, she hung on tight, her hands curled around the tops of his thick shoulders. Her insides were a quivering mess, her entire body vibrating with suppressed longing.

She pressed closer to his hard frame, digging her fingers deeper into his muscles, conveying her silent desperation because she was afraid to voice it aloud.

He didn't say anything, just held her tight, so tight the mound of her belly pressed into his stomach, his cheek resting against hers.

Finding her courage, she eased her head back until he straightened and met her gaze questioningly. She gave him a smile tinged with nerves. "Will you dance with me?" She wanted a complete dance, not the few stiff minutes they'd shared earlier. Something to ease them into the scorching flames that awaited. After the chilly distance between them these past few weeks, it was more than a welcome change.

A slow, sexy grin spread across his face. "Of course I will." He stepped back a little, putting just enough space between them that he could still curl his hand around to rest on the small of her back and held up the other, waiting.

She slid her hand into his and settled her left one on his shoulder. Just as it had during the reception, that invisible zing of electricity arced between them, curling through her, filling her with heat. She didn't want to think about what would happen tomorrow; she wanted to lose herself in the magic of the moment and see where it led.

In the background a woman was singing an old jazz song she recognized. "Who is this?" she whispered, not wanting to speak too loudly for fear of breaking the spell.

"Billie Holiday."

She recognized the song, the sultry notes and voice adding to the underlying sensuality of the moment. Jase was moving her in a pattern. Slow and steady.

It was effortless to follow him. He guided her with total assurance and ease, and the skill of a man who was completely confident in himself and at home in his body.

She hadn't anticipated how much of a turn on that would be. She'd danced with him before, but never in this intimate context. The way her body moved with his while fully clothed was a revelation.

Molly let herself drift to the music, getting lost in the growing intimacy between them and the lovely, heightening sense of anticipation. So much so that it took her a moment to realize they were no longer moving.

Slowly, she lifted her head. He stared down at her, the unmistakable heat and longing in his eyes undoing her.

"Jase," she whispered unsteadily, unsure how to put her feelings into words. The need and surprise, the lingering worry that something would go wrong. There was no way she could go slow now. Her entire body was keyed up, ready to come apart at the seams with desire.

"Shhh, it's okay," he murmured, kissing her nose, her cheeks. "We're okay. Just follow my lead."

His words took the edge off her building anxiety, but not the wild hunger inside her. Her skin was alive, craving the feel of his hands. She shook her head. "Touch me. Please touch me." It had been so long since she'd been touched the way she needed to be. So many weeks that she'd imagined what Jase's naked body would feel like against hers.

Jase took her face in his hands and lowered his mouth to hers, scattering her thoughts like a flock of startled birds. He took ownership of her, kissing her slow and deep as one hand gripped the back of her head to hold her still, the tender possession making her insides quiver.

His tongue delved into her mouth to stroke hers, caressing, teasing until she couldn't get close enough. Her breasts ached, the nipples hard and throbbing, the rush of heat between her thighs making her wet and needy.

She gasped as he tipped her head to the side and nibbled his way down her jaw to her neck, the glide of his hot tongue making her shiver. Her hands moved restlessly over the powerful width of his shoulders and back, unable to get enough of him, frustrated by the fabric barring her from his bare skin. She reached for the top button of his shirt, fumbled to get it undone.

"Rip it," he commanded, his voice deep and dark against her neck.

Yes. A wave of desire shot through her, pushing her arousal level even higher. Gripping each half of his collar, she yanked. Hard.

Buttons popped, some of them hitting the floor.

Jase growled in approval and scraped the edge of his teeth against a sensitive spot on her neck but she was too busy trying to see what she'd revealed and pulled back a little to stare hungrily at the sight before her. He was stark, masculine beauty standing there in the dimness with his shirt ripped open, that expanse of bare chest and abs on display.

She pressed her lips to the spot just below the notch at the top of his sternum, allowing her tongue to steal out to taste him. His sharp intake of breath sliced through the air, the hand in her hair tightening.

She inhaled his scent, drinking that dark, masculine spice in. He smelled incredible, and having more than six feet of aroused, ripped man in front of her had her head spinning. She started to kiss her way across his chest but he pulled her head up and slanted his mouth across hers in a deep, blistering kiss that made her forget how to breathe.

He kissed her like he was staking a claim. Like she had always been meant to be his.

She was panting, her legs unsteady when he broke the kiss and suddenly grasped her by the shoulders to spin her around, facing away from him. A heartbeat later a solid wall of heat pressed all along the back of her.

His hands went to her hips to steady her for a moment, then coasted slowly up her sides. Molly closed her eyes, absorbing the sensation, the delicious build of anticipation, her breasts tightening in expectation.

He followed every curve of her new shape, the heat of his hands making her throb and ache for the moment when they closed around her breasts. His mouth was at her nape now, nuzzling and nibbling his way across her bare shoulders.

But instead of going for her breasts, he skimmed his fingertips across her collarbones in a teasing caress that left goosebumps in their wake. They brushed over the tops of her shoulders and across the top of her back, coming to rest on the zipper at the top of her spine.

"Your skin's so soft," he whispered, easing the tab downward. Slowly, with excruciating precision.

A cool wash of air brushed over her hot skin as the fabric parted, inch by inch. He drew the zipper down with deliberate slowness, the fingers of his other hand stroking gentle patterns over the flesh he bared.

Without thinking Molly grabbed the front of the bodice to keep it from falling.

Jase shifted behind her, sinking to his knees as he drew the zipper down all the way to the base of her spine. Then his big hands curled around her hips in a firm but gentle grip, and squeezed softly. She shifted restlessly, ready to melt into a puddle at his feet.

Warmth bathed the base of her spine. His mouth. Kissing. Licking. Moving over her bare skin with a slow, torturous lack of haste.

Her head tipped back, her body caught under the spell he wove with each decadent caress of his mouth. His hands held her steady, his tongue gliding over the new erogenous spot she'd never known was there.

The tide of emotions flooding her was almost too

much. She couldn't believe this was really happening, that Jase was here, touching her this way, holding her.

Loving her.

She felt it in the way he held her. In every caress and shift of his strong, skillful hands. In each hungry, passion-laced kiss.

He was Carter's best friend. It should have felt wrong, but it didn't. Instead it felt incredibly, overwhelmingly right.

Yet when he started to pull the fabric of the dress down her body, she held the bodice tighter, suddenly overwhelmed by a wave of self-consciousness. She'd imagined this moment so many times in the past few weeks, but Jase had never seen her naked and now she was so pregnant, her body alien even to her.

"Let go," he said against the base of her spine, steel underlying the soft command.

She swallowed, hesitating.

"Moll. Let go." His voice was low. Quiet. He tugged at the fabric with insistent pressure, his open mouth on her skin, tongue caressing, making her anticipate the moment when he licked other, more sensitive places. She wasn't sure whether she could stand it.

Molly loosened her grip and let the dress fall to the floor, leaving her in just her pushup bra and low-cut panties.

"Turn around."

Just the sound of his voice, all low and seductive, turned her on. Letting out an unsteady breath, she turned, the sight of him kneeling there in front of her now in only his pants making her heart pound.

"Ah, Moll," he breathed, reaching for her hips once more as he leaned forward to nuzzle the mound of her belly.

She swallowed and ran a hand through his thick hair,

desperate for him to take the edge off this need he'd ignited in her. His hands smoothed up her ribs and over her back before coming to rest just beneath the band of her bra. Her whole body was hypersensitive, the slightest brush of his fingers sending ripples of sensation through her.

With a deft, sure movement he undid her bra. She cupped the front of it to her briefly, holding his gaze a moment, then let it fall.

His groan vibrated between them as her breasts spilled free, tight and aching. Heat sizzled across her skin as he cradled them in his palms. Learning their shape, their weight. Then his mouth was on her skin.

She sighed, sinking both hands into his soft hair as he worshipped her breasts, his tongue finally curling around her aching nipple. She pulled him closer, unable to stand the teasing. He obliged her, taking the tight center into his mouth to suck.

Molly whimpered and held him closer, her body craving release from the incessant pressure inside her. "Oh, God, I'm so wet," she whispered. It was almost embarrassing.

His eyes lifted to hers, his mouth tugging on her nipple one last time before his gaze slid down to her panties. "Are you?" he murmured, bending his head to skim his lips down the curve of her belly, pausing just above the edge of her panties to look up at her. A slight smile tugged at the corner of his sinful mouth. "How wet?"

"Find out," she whispered back boldly. She'd never been shy sexually and didn't see any reason to start now. She wanted him. Wanted him to know it, and do something about this terrible need.

His low growl turned into a deep purr as he rubbed his face against the lower swell of her belly, his chin just barely grazing her mound. She gripped his hair, her fingers flexing. She was drenched, her pulse racing, and it was getting hard to breathe.

His lips caressed her belly while his fingers trailed lower, skimming over the delicate lace covering her. "I'm gonna slide my tongue inside you," he murmured. "Taste you. You don't know how long I've wanted to."

She sucked in a breath and tugged on his hair, ready to combust. That was so freaking hot to hear. "Jase…"

A deep, dark chuckle answered, then he was peeling the lace down, over her hips, down her thighs. Before they even hit the floor, he was gripping her hips, his face coming closer and closer to where she needed it.

She pressed her lips together, stemming a shudder when the heat of his breath caressed her. *Oh, please…*

The feel of his hot, intimate kiss loosened her knees.

She gasped and flung a hand out behind her to grip the edge of the table. Oh God, his tongue. His hot, perfect tongue.

"Ohh," she cried, coming up on her toes as he caressed her pulsing clit. Slow. Soft. Watching her reaction.

He made a deep sound that might have been agreement and nuzzled closer, making good on his promise as he licked and stroked her most sensitive place and finally slid his tongue inside her.

She whimpered, her thigh muscles quivering, her fingers locked in his hair.

Jase kept going, seeming to enjoy tormenting her, building her pleasure until she was gasping and trembling, her hand on the table and his grip on her hips the only things keeping her from sliding to the floor.

Then he stopped.

Her eyes flew open, a protest ready to burst from her lips, but he'd been waiting for her to look at him, because he resumed, carefully stroking the side of her clit before easing down and making her watch while he sank his tongue into her.

And suddenly coming wasn't enough. Not nearly

enough. She'd wanted him too long, she needed more. "I want you inside me when I come," she gasped out, trembling.

Even in the dimness she saw the quick flare of heat in his eyes. He withdrew his tongue, paused to gently suck on her throbbing clit.

"Ah," she gasped, shaking.

He stopped, squeezed her hips and stood, turning her to face away from him again. "Lean forward," he muttered at her ear, his naked chest pressed tight to her back. Searing her with his heat.

Molly reached forward and gripped the far side of the narrow table, her entire body trembling. A big hand came forward to capture one of hers, lifting it to his mouth for a tender kiss before guiding it down and back to cover his straining length, still trapped in his tux pants.

He growled at the feel of her fingers curling around him, then undid the fastening with maddening slowness and eased the fabric down until he sprang free into her grip.

She sucked in a breath at the heat of him, the width. Her insides clenched.

"I want to make you open for me," he said against her ear. "I want to make you melt all over me. Want to make you *feel*."

Molly wriggled her hips, impatient. Ohhh, he was going to feel so good inside her—

"Do I need to get a condom?" he murmured.

"No." She was clean, and obviously he was too, or he would have told her by now.

"Then hold on, angel." He pulled her hand from his cock and stretched her arm back across the table.

The marble was icy cold against her palm compared to his heat. His mouth raked along the side of her neck, making her eyes close, a thick, syrupy pleasure mixing with the anticipation.

His hot, hard length branded her bottom. One of his hands curled around her right hip, holding her in place while his free hand played with her nipples for a moment, then eased down between her thighs to slide through the evidence of her arousal.

Pressure and heat lodged against her opening. "You ready for me?" he asked.

She nodded, searched for her voice. "Yes. Yes, I—" Her words cut off on a slow, deep inhale as he began to sink into her from behind.

The position, the angle, made him feel huge. A strangled sound escaped her, her fingers clenching around the edge of the table as pleasure and pressure mingled, melting hotter, softer.

"I've wanted you for so damn long." His voice was rough, unsteady, but his grip never changed and he forced his length into her so damn slowly she thought she might die.

Molly couldn't answer, sensation robbing her of her voice, of thought. He was thick. So thick as he stretched her, hitting nerve endings that were suddenly screaming with sensation, the pleasure rising with every second, aided by the sure glide of his fingers against her swollen clit. She whimpered, tried to rock back into him, but he held her fast.

"No. Feel me, Moll," he rasped out, keeping her in place, forcing her to experience every moment of him claiming her. "Feel me loving you."

She felt it. Had no choice but to feel it. To take it.

She made a soft, choked sound as he finally buried himself inside her and reached back for him, locking her fingers around his nape. Unable to voice her desperation, this clawing need.

"Ah, yeah." He groaned and dragged his tongue up the side of her neck, his hips moving slow and steady, the pleasure amplifying with each slick thrust.

The growing pleasure was almost frightening in its intensity. Molly had no choice but to endure it. The pregnancy had made her more sensitive all over. Her skin tingled with every touch. Each time he stroked across the sweet spot on the upper wall just inside her, the sensations expanded, a slow, melting pleasure that made her gasp and quiver all over.

"Jase," she begged, unsure what she was begging for—mercy, or for him to never stop. "Don't make me wait. I've already waited so long for you."

"Long?" He made a savage sound. "I've wanted to do this to you for fucking *years*, Moll. You can wait a little longer."

"No." She shook her head, her body ready to explode. "Please just..."

He picked up the tempo, and her voice disintegrated. It was even better than she'd imagined. Jase was so unbelievably sensual as he pushed her higher and higher, in complete command of her body, until she could see the shimmering brink of that cliff looming at the edge of her consciousness.

"Oh, *Jase*," she moaned, shaking.

He growled deep in his chest. "Yeah. Melt for me, angel," he murmured against the side of her neck, sliding a hard forearm around the front of her hips, locking it just beneath her belly. "I wanna feel you clench around me when you come." His voice was rough, as desperate as her.

Molly consciously relaxed in his grip and surrendered to him, to the pleasure he gave her. It spread through her in ever-expanding ripples, the pressure rising, rising until at last it snapped free.

She barely heard his rough growl through her desperate, ecstatic cries, then his grip tightened, his big body tensing behind her as he thrust deep, groaning out her name as he came inside her.

Molly struggled to open her eyes. She was still gripping the edge of the table but her fingers were numb. Her legs were so weak she wasn't sure how she was still standing as the orgasm began to fade. She sagged forward to rest her cheek on the cool marble tabletop, Jase still buried deep inside her.

He murmured something in a tender tone and kissed her nape, his big hand smoothing down the length of her spine. Easing out of her body, he immediately scooped her up his arms.

Molly curled into him, sighing in contentment while he carried her to his bed and laid her down. After cleaning her up with some tissues he disappeared into the en suite and came back to slide under the covers beside her.

She rolled into him, savoring the closeness of lying naked in the dark in his arms. "Can I stay the night?" she joked, sleep tugging at her. There was no way she could move. No one had followed her here. She had Jase and the security system to keep her safe if anyone came looking for her.

"You thought I was gonna let you leave my side tonight?" He gave a short laugh and squeezed her tighter, his grip fierce and protective. "Not a chance, angel."

Molly smiled and cuddled closer, savoring every tiny detail about this moment. She didn't want to think about the repercussions of what they'd just done. She didn't want to think about tomorrow or the conversation they had to have.

All she wanted was to bask in the feel of Jase's arms around her and savor the beat of his heart beneath her cheek. The feeling of being cherished and safe.

Loved.

And as much as she was scared to think it, as much as the logical part of her said it was too soon, this sure felt like she was in love with him too.

Chapter Twenty-One

Last night seemed like a dream. So surreal that when Molly opened her eyes in the morning light, it took her a moment to realize she was still in Jase's bed. He'd held her through the night, stroking his hands over her naked skin whenever she'd stirred, then pulling her close as she dropped back to sleep.

She ruthlessly blocked the guilt and anxiety trying to intrude into her happiness. She had absolutely nothing to feel guilty about. Carter was gone. She was a grown woman. This was her life, and Jase was a good man. She deserved to be happy. They both did.

That didn't mean she was looking forward to having a serious discussion about their future, however. She didn't want to force anything or put undue pressure on either of them this early on, she just wanted to take things as they came until they both became comfortable with this major shift in their relationship. She was also still a bit nervous of how everyone else would react when they found out about them, though deep down she knew she shouldn't care.

She could hear Jase moving around out in the suite kitchen. Facing him in the daylight after what they'd shared last night made her stomach buzz with butterflies and nerves.

Though she was tempted to stay snuggled under the covers to see if he came back in, a flash of self-consciousness made her roll out of bed and head into the adjoining bath. She closed the door for privacy and showered, the spicy scent of his soap and shampoo putting a smile on her face as she recalled every detail from last night. Her heart squeezed at the way he'd made love to her.

She found a spare toothbrush in a drawer and tried not to think about why he had them there as she brushed her teeth. She'd never considered herself a jealous person before, but picturing Jase with another woman definitely brought out the green-eyed monster in her.

Since all her remaining clothes were upstairs, she put on Jase's bathrobe instead, finger combed her hair and left it to dry loose around her shoulders. The curls would tighten as they dried, and brushing it was an exercise in futility whether wet or dry.

A hint of nervousness hit her when a tap came at the bathroom door. She took a deep breath and opened it, her heart rolling over at the sight of Jase standing there shirtless, wearing only a pair of jeans.

"Morning," she said, wanting to laugh at herself for feeling shy. It was just strange to face Jase now after what he'd done to her last night.

"Morning." He ran his aqua gaze slowly down the length of her before moving back up to face. "I like seeing you in my clothes."

A stupid smile spread across her face. "I think you like me out of them more."

"Oh, I definitely do." He curled an arm around her waist and drew her to him, making her sigh and melt against his strong frame. There'd been no reason to be nervous. "Sleep okay?"

"Like a rock. You?"

"Best sleep I've had in forever." He ran his nose

along the side of her neck, making her shiver. "You hungry?"

"For breakfast?"

"Hmmm. Why, you hungry for something else?"

The way her body was heating and coming alive, she could easily be persuaded. "Maybe."

His deep chuckle ruffled the hair at her temple. "Later. I made you something and it's not going to waste." Snagging her hand, he led her out to the kitchen with the scent of cinnamon filling the air.

"What did you make?" she asked, smiling as he put her on one of the stools at the island.

"Crepes with cinnamon apples and whipped cream." He crossed to the stove.

She shook her head, admiring the view of his muscular back and the way his jeans hugged his ass. "I'm impressed. I had no idea you could cook something so fancy."

He shot her a heated look over his bare, muscular shoulder. "You have no idea about a lot of things I haven't shown you yet."

The sensual implications had her all but squirming in her seat. "Can I help with anything?"

"Nope. You just sit there and drink your juice."

He'd put a glass of orange juice out for her, and she noted from the carton it was her favorite brand. "I feel so spoiled."

"That's my plan, angel."

Molly couldn't stop marveling at the difference between him and her ex. Carter had had two speeds when it came to sex: playful, usually involving lots of tickling or play fighting—or seek and destroy.

Jase was the opposite, seeming to have figured out that building a woman's anticipation was an important part of foreplay, because he was getting her all hot and bothered without even looking at or touching her.

He came back to the island to slide a plate of crepes topped with the caramelized apples and whipped cream. "This looks and smells amazing," she moaned, leaning over to inhale the fragrant, spicy scent. That worried flutter started up in her belly, the one that refused to let her forget that they had to have a hard, honest talk soon. She pushed it to the back of her mind, refusing to let it spoil this fragile new beginning.

"Hopefully it tastes even better." He took the stool beside her, his body turned toward her as they ate.

Molly hummed in appreciation and closed her eyes as she chewed. The crepes were tender and thin, the apple topping sweet and tasting of autumn. "Yum."

Jase chuckled softly and leaned over to kiss her. A warm, slow melding of lips that made her forget all about breakfast. He pulled back when she reached for him, a sexy grin on his face. "Yeah," he said, licking his lips. "Yum."

Tease. She forked up another bite, set her hand on her growing belly. "Baby likes it too."

His eyes dropped to her hand, his expression curious. "What does it feel like?"

She thought about it a moment. "Tickly little somersaults inside. It's really neat." She watched him. "Do you want to feel it?"

He nodded and reached out, an enthralled look on his face. Molly shifted forward in her chair, her heart thumping when that strong hand splayed gently across her robe-covered belly. The baby kicked. "There, did you feel that?" she asked.

He frowned, staring at his hand. "No."

She shifted his hand and pressed his palm more firmly to the side of her belly, and together they waited. The intimacy of the moment struck her. In some ways it was more intimate than what they'd shared the night before.

They were both silent, Jase watching her belly while she studied his face.

The baby moved again. "There," she said excitedly. "Feel it?"

A look of wonder crossed his face. "Yeah. Wow."

How could a man as tough as him be so gorgeous and adorable at the same time? "Pretty neat, huh?"

He nodded, surprising her by keeping his hand right where it was when she let go. He stroked his warm palm over the mound of her belly, his expression absorbed, and her heart all but exploded with tenderness. Oh, he would be the most incredible father. He—

Don't look too far ahead. You'll just get hurt.

The happy bubble deflated a little.

She was determined not to let it shrivel. They would have a grown-up conversation about everything soon, within the next day or two. "Have you got plans for the rest of the day?"

He looked up at her, and she felt herself falling into that clear, steady gaze. "I do, with you, and my elderly neighbor Mrs. Wong. She got her new bionic hip and I owe her a dance. Better eat up, then go and change into something you can wear to the beach."

****

Fall on the Oregon Coast could be hit or miss as far as the weather went, but today was picture perfect. The sun was out, burning off the light layer of fog and glinting off the waves. Jase laced his fingers with Molly's as they walked down the sandy path through the dunes to the beach.

"I'm keeping that video of you dancing with her in her living room," Molly said of Mrs. Wong. "The woman looked like she'd died and gone to heaven."

"She was high on pain killers. And we were barely

moving."

Moly snorted. "She didn't care, she was thrilled just getting to put her hands on you. I thought I was going to have to pry her off you."

Jase chuckled. "She's got a pretty strong grip for such a frail little thing. Anyway, it made her day and helped her forget the pain for a few minutes, so that's all that matters."

"She's a flirt."

"Oh, big time." His grin said he loved it.

Molly shook her head at him. "You're incredible, you know that?"

He just smiled. Keeping her at the house with him was a selfish risk with people tied to the Russian mob after her money, but he wasn't ready to let her go and the money hadn't been transferred to her account yet, so he'd felt okay with bringing her here for an hour or so. He'd checked the security camera feed for the house while she was asleep and nothing had shown up, so he would take every minute he could get with her before he drove her to Poppy and Noah's tonight.

He wasn't ready to let her go *ever*, and hoped she felt the same way. But he knew Molly, and was smart enough to know he shouldn't demand an answer on that front yet. He needed to prove to her that he wouldn't hurt her. That he would always be there. She'd been through so much, she might not be ready to believe that yet. But she would.

She had to.

Tufts of sea grass waved in the breeze, the salty scent of the ocean filling the air. At the bottom of the hill, miles and miles of sandy beach stretched out before them. People were out walking their dogs, young children darting around gathering shells. Come spring it would be Molly down here with her baby. Jase would give everything to be beside them.

"It's so different than the Outer Banks, isn't it?"

Molly said over the sound of the waves. She'd changed into maternity jeans and one of his button-down flannel shirts that hugged her belly. She was more beautiful now than ever, and he couldn't wait to explore her in the daylight.

"Yeah, way more rugged." Jase let go of her hand to wrap his arm around her shoulders, pressing a kiss to the top of her head. He'd never felt this fulfilled before. He still couldn't believe the sudden turn his life had taken last night. Never in a million years had he expected Molly to show up and basically offer herself to him.

"And wilder somehow." She'd pulled her hair up into a ponytail but little curls had escaped around her face, blowing around with the breeze. "Oh, I needed this," she said with a sigh. "Been too long since I took a walk on the beach."

"I agree." He sipped at his coffee. They'd stopped at Whale's Tale on the way here to grab him an Americano and Molly a spiced chai latte.

They walked another mile or so up the beach while he kept a covert eye out for anyone who might be watching them, then turned around and headed back. Partway there, he led Molly over to a group of huge driftwood logs on the sand where he would still have good sightlines and sat against one, drawing her down between his splayed thighs.

She immediately cuddled close and he wrapped his arms around her, enjoying the peace of being able to hold her out here in the open, her head resting on his chest.

"Thanks for bringing me here," she said over the breeze a minute later, then looked up at him, her gorgeous eyes glowing in the late morning sunlight. "I feel so safe with you beside me."

Her words turned him inside out. She'd been under so much strain lately, and knowing she was relaxed, that she trusted him to watch out for and protect her satisfied him on the deepest level. "I'm glad. And you are safe," he vowed, tucking her tighter into him, his chin on the top of her head. "And I'm sorry for being kinda distant lately. It was too hard for me to pretend we could just go back to the way things were before."

"I understand, but thank you. And you're forgiven—as long as you don't go cold on me again the next time we fight about something. You can't do that to me again."

He winced, knowing she was right. "Fair enough." There were so many other things on his mind. He'd been careful not to push her about the future, but he had to level with her. "There's something else you should know."

"Okay, do I need to brace myself?"

He huffed out a laugh. "No. I'm not trying to pressure you for more than you're ready for, but I've got an interview tomorrow with a security firm back east."

She twisted around to stare at him, worry in her eyes. "You want to do security work?"

"I've been thinking about it."

"And would you have to move?"

"Yes. To Virginia. And I'd be gone a lot."

Her face fell, the worry in her eyes deepening. He had no doubt she was thinking of Carter and how he'd been wounded, the terrible aftermath that had cost them all so much. And that it could be Jase if he went back into harm's way. "Oh."

He stroked his fingers through her curls. "I won't take it if you don't want me to."

A frown tugged at her brow. "Do *you* want to?"

He hesitated. How honest should he be with her? He didn't want to spook her. "You want the truth?"

"I always want the truth."

"Okay, then no, not really. I accepted the offer of the interview last night, when I thought you and I were never going to happen. I thought maybe me moving back east would be for the best for both of us."

She searched his eyes. "And now?"

"Now it depends on what happens with you and I."

"Meaning, if we stay together, then you won't take the job?"

"Right, but I don't want to put pressure on you about that now." His heart rolled over when she wrapped her arms around him and cuddled into his chest.

"I don't want you to go back over there ever again," she said softly. "I don't want to live through that kind of worry anymore."

Jase closed his eyes and hugged her tight. She did love him a little. "We don't have to decide anything yet." The words almost strangled him. He wanted to claim her, lock her down, make her his forever.

"I guess I'm still a little…afraid," she admitted.

It was the first time she'd admitted it. And he wanted to understand. "Of what?"

"Of getting hurt."

Ah, angel… "I wouldn't hurt you, Moll. Not ever."

She was quiet for a second. "I never thought Carter would either. And you served as long as he did. You were exposed to concussive forces a lot too. Part of me worries that you might…" She stopped, as if she was too embarrassed to continue.

"You're worried I might wind up like he did one day."

She ducked her head lower against his chest. "I'm sorry. I know that probably sounds stupid—"

"I get it. But I'm not going to wind up like him." There was no way to prove that to her now, though.

"Are you mad?"

"No. I'm glad you told me."

She let out a small sigh. "I am too, actually. Although now it sounds really dumb to me." Then she took his hands and placed them on the mound of her belly, resting hers on top. A thump hit his palm. "Feel that one?" she asked, tilting her head back to look into his eyes.

"Yeah. It's so amazing." He rubbed her belly, awed and overcome by how protective he felt of her and the baby. He already felt like they were both his.

"Do you miss him?" she asked, taking him by surprise.

He nodded. "It's a little easier now, but…yeah. I miss hearing his voice and his laugh. I miss hanging out with him." He tucked a wayward curl behind her ear. He didn't mind her talking about Carter. He was actually glad she wanted to, because it meant she felt really comfortable with him. "You?"

"Sometimes, when I think about how he used to be. He was fun. Remember how fun he was?"

"Yeah." Carter had been one hell of a good time before being wounded.

"But mostly I miss him now whenever I think of him not knowing about the baby. I wish I could tell him. I still wonder whether he drove over that cliff on purpose. If he did, part of me wonders if he would have made a different choice if he'd known."

Jase was quiet a moment. "Remember when I told you I promised him I'd look after you?"

"Yes."

"He asked me to."

She twisted around to face him more. "He did?"

"The night we deployed for the first time after you guys got married. He pulled me aside just before we left base and made me promise to look after you if something ever happened to him." Back then neither of them had imagined Carter would ever kill himself.

"And you have." She lowered her gaze. "I'm not sure this was exactly what he had in mind, but you know what? I think he would have been okay with it. Knowing we got together after he was gone. He trusted you more than anyone."

Jase nodded. "I know." That's why all the damage between them hurt so damn much. "And as far as him being okay with this?" He eyed her. "Not a fucking chance. He'd have torn my head off and reached down my throat to rip my heart out while it was still beating for ever getting near you like this."

She laughed. "Okay, you're right." He put her hand to her belly. "Oh, God, that feels good to laugh." She sighed, still smiling. "He would have found that description funny as hell."

He loved her. Loved her so much it hurt, and there was nothing he wouldn't do to show her that. "Right?"

"I trust you too, by the way." Her lips curved up in a grin as she stretched up to press her lips to his.

"Thank you." He deepened the kiss, cupping the back of her head to take possession of her mouth. Seducing her with every bit of skill he had.

When he released her a minute later her pupils were dilated and she was breathing faster. "I think you should take me home now. I'm getting hungry again, and it's bad to make an expectant mother go hungry."

Her tone made it clear she didn't mean food, and she didn't have to ask him twice.

Even though he was already thinking about them naked and tangled together in his bed, he still had the wherewithal to watch for anyone following them on the way back to the house. A miracle, considering most of his blood had rushed from his brain to between his legs. The gentle stroke of Molly's fingers over his as he drove was distracting as hell, making him imagine them gliding over more enjoyable places.

By the time he made it home he was aching, desperate for the relief only she could give him. She wrapped her arms around him from behind as he let them into his suite, and his brain almost shorted out when she slid her palms down his chest over his stomach, pausing before she dragged them teasingly over the strangled length of his erection shoved against his fly.

Somehow, he got the security system set to home mode, locked the door then grabbed her around the hips, hoisting her off the floor and carried her to his bed, their mouths fused together, her hands in his hair.

He laid her across the sheets and reached for the buttons on the flannel shirt she wore, but she sat up and impatiently grabbed the hem of his shirt instead, tugging it upward. He helped her, tossing it over his head to land on the floor, his heart trying to hammer its way out of his chest at the look of feminine hunger and approval on her face as she stared at him.

She sat up on her knees, pushing at his shoulders until he rolled and lay down on his back. Immediately she straddled his hips, her center pressed against the strangled ridge of his cock, and began undoing the row of buttons on her flannel shirt.

Jase barely resisted the urge to rip it off her, his gaze riveted to the line of smooth skin she revealed. A tempting glimpse of cleavage. The rounded swell of her belly.

She paused as she started to shrug the shirt off, the tiniest flare of shyness flickered across her face. Jase shook his head, not ever wanting her to hide from him. "Let me see you. I need to see you."

She pulled the shirt open, slowly exposing the lush perfection of her breasts cradled in the deep purple bra, and the swell of her belly. Jase groaned and reached for her, gently cupping the sides of her breasts as he sat up to nuzzle the tops of them. She smelled of his soap and salty sea air.

Molly hummed and reached back to undo the bra, pausing for a heart-stopping moment before pulling it free and leaving her soft flesh to slide into his hands.

God.

It had been too dark to see her clearly last night. Jase

drank in the sight of her now like a man dying of thirst, stroking his thumbs across the creamy brown mounds, her tight nipples making his mouth water.

He teased her with his tongue, tracing it around the rigid peaks, enjoying every gasp and shift of her body until she fisted his hair in her hands and pulled him closer. When he closed his lips around one center, her soft moan sent a shiver ripping up his spine.

"That feels so good," she breathed, arching her back, pushing harder against his tongue. He sucked at her tenderly, rubbing his tongue over first one nipple, then the other.

She made a rough sound and pushed away, leaning down to give him a deep, searing kiss before nipping and licking her way across his chest and down to his abs. His muscles contracted, his breathing turning shallow when her delicate fingers undid his jeans and began to drag them over his hips. He helped her, lifting, biting back a groan when his swollen cock sprang free.

Molly hummed in approval and bent to suck at the skin just below his navel, her soft, cool hands curling around him. He hissed in a breath and gritted his teeth as pleasure surged throughout his body.

His hands went to her hair, tugging the ponytail free so he could slide his fingers into those tight, clinging curls. He stroked them, urging her on, dying for the moment when that sexy mouth he'd been fantasizing about for years finally wrapped around him.

She drew the moment out, making him wait, pausing to look up at him with those gold-green eyes for a heart-stopping moment before her tongue darted out to lap at the flushed tip. Jase fisted his hands in her hair, the breath exploding out of him on a strangled groan.

Her eyes gleamed with a mischievous, playful light, a knowing smile lifting one side of her mouth. She brushed her lips over him, watching his eyes the whole time, then slowly, so slowly it killed him, she parted and closed her mouth around the flared, swollen head.

Jesus.

His eyes slammed shut, ecstasy flooding him at the wet heat surrounding him. She sucked, flicking her tongue over the sensitive underside, her hand stroking the shaft.

He wanted to come down her throat so bad, but he didn't want to waste this chance—he wanted to watch her face as she slid down on him, watch her eyes go hazy as she took every inch of him inside her.

He wanted to claim her. Imprint the feel of him into her mind and make her crave the pleasure he could give her.

Sucking in a deep breath, he pulled her head up. He was panting, his hands a little clumsy as he reached for the waistband of her stretchy jeans. She shifted aside to shimmy out of them and the purple boy shorts she wore, and his gaze shot straight to the strip of dark hair between her thighs.

"Come here," he ground out, his voice harsh and guttural, his control almost gone.

He grasped her hips and hauled her up his body, positioning her thighs on either side of his shoulders. She moved willingly, and he loved that she wasn't shy with him now, or about communicating what felt good for her.

Stroking his hands over her sleek curves, he lifted his head and pressed fervent kisses across the firm mound of her belly, the top and inside of her thigh. The scent of her arousal made him insane, the sight of her glistening folds and seeing the evidence of her wanting him almost too much.

With a soft groan he grasped her hips and tugged her upward until he could kiss the tender flesh between her thighs.

Molly's gasp immediately turned into a broken moan, one hand sliding into his hair while she reached for the top of the headboard with the other.

"I love that sound," he whispered against her. "Do it again."

Jase tongued her gently, licking and caressing, using her movements and noises to guide him, drawing that same, perfect sound from her. Her thighs trembled slightly, her eyes closed as she arched, reaching back to grasp his length in her fist. His whole body contracted as he thrust up into her grip, pushing his tongue into her at the same time.

"Oh, Jase," she moaned, her voice unsteady.

"Sink down on me," he commanded. "Take all of me inside you." He helped her shift down his body, mesmerized by the sight of her, her breasts swaying with her movements.

Straddling his hips, she raised him up in her hand, looked directly into his eyes and began to sink down on him.

Jase gripped her hips, fighting the urge to take over and thrust upward as she surrounded him, inch by torturous inch. Her lips parted, her eyelids fluttering closed.

Tight, wet heat engulfed him. A low groan tore from his chest as pleasure swelled.

"You're so thick," she whispered, her words dissolving into a plaintive moan that made him shudder.

She was so fucking gorgeous.

Pushing back the need to come, he reached up to squeeze and roll her sensitive nipples, the feel of being buried inside her so much better than he'd ever imagined. Molly eased all the way down then lifted slowly, rocking her hips. He guided her with one hand on her hip, the other delving between her flushed folds to gently rub at the swollen bud of her clit.

"Ohhh, that's... Mmhmm." She bit her lip and flexed around him, her muscles clenching his cock as she splayed her thighs wider apart. Seeking just the right spot and angle.

God. She was so beautiful, so sensual as she sought her pleasure. "Moll. Ride me," he rasped out.

She grabbed his hand, pressed it more firmly between her legs, rubbing against his fingers as she rode him. He watched her climb to the peak, watched her face contort in ecstasy and felt her thighs tremble as he pushed her over the edge, her cries of release ringing through the room.

Jase sat up and rolled them, still joined, coming up on his knees and taking care not to put pressure on her belly. Molly melted back into the sheets with a sigh and wrapped her arms around his shoulders, a sated, dreamy look in her eyes.

"Moll," he said in a ragged whisper.

She smiled up at him. A secret, intimate smile that twisted him up inside as she wound her legs around his hips and sank her hand into his hair, drawing him down into her hold.

Jase clenched his hand in her curls and covered her smiling mouth with his, moving slow and deep, each slick, sweet glide magnifying the building sensation. He groaned into her mouth, their tongues twining as he pumped in and out, savoring the feel of her slick walls hugging him.

He teetered on the edge of release for an endless moment, not wanting it to end. Molly's hands caressed him, her tongue teasing his, sucking at him. He drove deep, his guttural shout of ecstasy lost in her mouth as he started coming. Every muscle in his body locked tight, pleasure punching through him in endless pulses.

Struggling to catch his breath, he was finally able to force his eyes open. Molly gave him a soft, tender smile, curling her arms around his neck with a satisfied murmur as she lifted her head to kiss him again.

Groaning, Jase rolled them onto their sides and

tucked her into his body, dreading the moment when he had to pull out of her.

I love you.

Utterly and completely. There would never be anyone for him but her. He wanted everything with her. A future, a home, a family.

Wrapping his arms around her, he held her tight and closed his eyes, trying to stay in the moment and not leap ahead. It was damn near impossible to hold back the words crowding his throat but he had to be patient a little while longer and wait for her to catch up to him.

Chapter Twenty-Two

Her first shift back at the hospital the following evening was not for the faint of heart.

Noah had dropped her off more than an hour early so she could get settled and organized. The ER was uncharacteristically busy for a Monday night, with two fractures, a serious stroke and a heart attack patient all arriving within an hour of each other.

"Ms. Boyd?"

Molly looked up from her paperwork at a young nurse approaching the counter of the nurse's station. "Hey. What's up?"

"Mr. Brown is up."

She groaned. "Again? I just settled him twenty minutes ago." She'd been sure that dosage would have knocked him out for at least a couple of hours.

"Yep, again. We're trying to get him back into bed but it's so busy and he seems to respond better to you—"

"I'll handle it."

The nurse gave her a grateful look. "Thank you."

Molly chuckled. "Don't mention it." She set aside her charts and exited the nurse's station. Partway to the patient area, she spotted Mr. Brown, a dark-skinned man in his late seventies, standing there in his hospital gown, looking around in consternation. He also showed signs of dementia.

"Mr. Brown," she said as she approached. "What are you doing out of bed?"

His dark eyes focused on her, clouded with cataracts and confusion. "What?"

"I just put you in bed for the third time a little while ago. Why are you up?"

A frown wrinkled his forehead as he glanced back at the bed he'd climbed out of. "This isn't my bed." He lifted his left forearm and reached for the IV as if he was going to tear it out. Again.

"No." She rushed over to grab hold of his wrist. "That line is there to give you medicine."

He tried to snatch his arm back. "I'm not sick."

"Mr. Brown, you've just had a major heart attack."

His fuzzy gray eyebrows shot upward. "I had a heart attack?"

"Yes, and that's why we need you to lie back down and rest."

He stood there gaping at her in astonishment. "*I* had a heart attack," he repeated.

"Yes. Now let's get you back into bed."

The news seemed to mollify him a little because he lost his belligerent edge and followed her over to his bed, docile as a lamb. "There you go," she said, helping him lie down and tucking him in for what she hoped would be the last time. "We're having a busy night here, Mr. Brown, so we would appreciate it if you would stay put until the doctor says otherwise. Your son is on his way right now to see you."

His brow wrinkled. "My son?"

"Robert."

His eyes flooded with tears and a tremulous smile quivered on his lips. "Robbie. I haven't seen him in so long."

"No?" she said, tucking the sheets around him and adjusting the flow of meds in his line. With any luck the dosage they were giving him would sedate him enough to keep him in bed this time.

"We had a fight a few years back. Stupid." He shook his head, wiped at his tears and nodded his thanks at Molly when she passed him a tissue. His bleary eyes settled on hers. "You make sure you don't have to live with regrets," he warned her. "It's worse than anything, including losing your marbles." He tapped his skull with a gnarled finger.

Molly wasn't sure whether the story was true or not, but his words were heartfelt and they resonated with her. She'd taken a huge leap of faith with Jase this weekend, but she could admit that she was still holding part of her back. She didn't want to regret that later.

She smiled and put a comforting hand on the old man's shoulder. "You know, you're right. I have something I need to take care of, to make sure that doesn't happen."

Mr. Brown mopped at his eyes and wiped his nose, then handed the soggy tissue back to her. Molly hid a rueful smile and put it in the trash. Her job was so glamorous. "Is it a fella?"

He still had plenty of marbles left upstairs if he could figure that out. "It is a fella, as a matter of fact. And he means the world to me. I need to tell him that." She needed to give Jase the words, and ask that he be patient with her a little longer.

He'd had the interview today. It had gone well, and they'd made him an offer. With his service record, resume and personality, of course the company wanted him. It terrified her to think of him doing contract work. He'd asked for a couple of weeks to think about their offer.

Molly was working hard to overcome her secret fears about falling in love with him, but the truth was, she might already be there. Knowing he was considering contract work alarmed her, but she trusted him to honor his promise and not to take the job if they stayed together. More than that, she wasn't going to jeopardize what they had by holding onto the miniscule chance that he would wind up like Carter.

Mr. Brown shook his finger at her. "You fix it."

"I will. Now, you promise to be good and stay here while you wait for Robbie to get here?"

He gave her a gap-toothed grin. "Yes, ma'am."

"Perfect. Try to sleep for a bit. If you need anything, just ring this call button." She showed him where it was and closed the curtains around him for privacy before heading back to the nurse's station.

The next few hours passed in a flurry of activity, but by the time her break rolled around, all she could think about was calling Jase. She hadn't seen him since yesterday afternoon when he'd dropped her off at Noah and Poppy's with Walter, but it felt like an eternity.

She texted him as she headed to the staff room to grab her late night meal. *You still up?*

It surprised her when her phone rang a few seconds later. "Hey," she answered with a grin. "I guess this means you're still up?"

"Better than that. I'm about a minute from the hospital."

"What? Why?" she said, stepping out into the hallway, heading for the exit.

"Haven't seen you in way too long, so I thought I'd bring something to eat together."

She couldn't help smiling as she pressed the release bar on the exit door. The air was cool and slightly damp, carrying the crisp scent of evergreen and turning leaves. "What is it?"

"Fattening."

"Ooh, my favorite kind of food. I'm heading out

back to the sitting area to meet Trisha." It was around the far side of the building, and other nurses on break always hung out there when the weather permitted.

"What are you wearing?"

She chuckled and kept walking, the brisk air chasing away the fatigue she'd been feeling. "A really sexy pair of violet scrubs."

"Hmmm, and what about underneath?"

"You'll have to find that out later."

"You mean in a couple minutes."

Don't take the job. Call them back and tell them no. "Well that depends on whether—" She gasped and jerked to a halt when a shadow suddenly detached from the side of the building and lunged at her.

A man. And he wore a chilling expression on his face.

Rafe Baxter.

Molly whipped around to run, but the exit door was shut now. To get back in she had to enter a code into the keypad and Rafe was too close, she'd never—

"Put the phone down." His voice was ice cold.

Skin crawling, she spun back around to face him. "What are you doing here?" she demanded, the tremor in her voice betraying her fear. They were alone back here and it was dark, the closest light over by the eating area.

"Moll?" Jase's sharp voice came from her phone, now at waist-level in her frozen hand.

Rafe paused a few feet in front of her and pulled something from his pocket. "Drop it," he ordered. "I'm not gonna tell you again."

Molly dropped the phone and her food. They clattered to the pavement. Jase's muffled shout cut through the air a split second before Rafe lifted his foot and slammed his boot down on the phone, once, twice. Smashing it to pieces.

Molly started to turn but he was already advancing

on her. She stumbled back two steps until her shoulders hit the brick wall behind her, her heart lodged in her throat.

Rafe lunged for her, wrapped his hands around her throat. She grabbed them. Couldn't make him let go. "I tried to be nice," he snarled. "I don't want to hurt you. But this is your last chance to make a deal with me."

She gripped his wrists, struggled to pull them off her, her pulse pounding in her ears. He was too close for her to knee him in the balls and her belly was in the way. "Get your hands *off* me," she ground out, adrenaline exploding through her. There were security cameras but she wasn't sure if anyone could see her and what was happening.

He increased the pressure around her throat, until she couldn't swallow and began to fear he would cut off her airway. A new wave of fear rose inside her.

The baby. She had to protect her baby, would do whatever it took. She stilled, stopped struggling.

"You got the insurance settlement," he said, his face inches away, his eyes boring into hers. "I need it."

He switched his hands around, using one to grip the front of her throat. A soft snick sounded, and her eyes widened in terror when he raised his arm and the faint light caught on the switchblade in his hand.

Her entire body went taut, freezing in place, her lungs seizing as he lowered that evil blade toward her belly.

No!

She cried out and grabbed at his wrist, digging her nails in deep, trying to twist away, but couldn't budge his arm. The tip of the blade pricked the side of her belly.

"You've got more than yourself to think about in this situation," he murmured, his eyes glinting like the blade, "and a lot more to lose. So, you're going to transfer that money to my account while I watch, or you'll regret it."

Had the payment gone through? She hadn't even

known it had hit her bank account yet.

"*Answer* me, bitch."

She opened her mouth to tell him yes, she'd do whatever he wanted, but he whipped his head to the side as the screech of tires came from the parking lot.

A white pickup was barreling toward the hospital.

Molly choked back a sob. *Jase.*

Rafe swore and swung his head back around to meet her eyes, his expression full of cold fury. "This isn't over, bitch." He shoved her sideways, sending her hurtling to the ground.

Molly swallowed a cry and twisted to land on her side instead of her belly. Rafe's running footsteps pounded away in the distance to her left as she rolled onto her hip and slowly got to her feet, shaking all over.

"Molly!"

She looked to the right. Jase was running flat out toward her, but she wasn't in danger anymore.

She held up a hand, shook her head. "No, I'm okay," she gasped out. Oh God, oh God, he'd been about to plunge that knife into her belly. Kill her baby.

Jase kept running toward her. He skidded to a stop in front of her and grasped her shoulders. "*Moll.*" He cupped her face in his hands, ran them over her anxiously. "Are you—"

She pushed at his chest. "I'm okay, but he's getting away," she blurted.

He stopped, cast an uncertain glance in Rafe's direction. "Get inside and call Noah. Tell him I'm going after Rafe."

She grabbed for his shoulders. "No, don't—"

"Get inside and stay there. I love you." He planted a hard kiss on her mouth, broke free of her grip then turned and raced back to his truck.

Molly wobbled toward the door as fast as her jellied knees would carry her to punch the code into the pad with shaking fingers.

It was only after she'd called Noah that she realized Jase had told her he loved her…

And that she hadn't said it back.

Chapter Twenty-Three

Fuck. Fuck, nothing was going according to plan. Rafe raced down the pathway, jumped over the wooden barrier lining it, and veered across the strip of grass, heading for the road where the car was waiting. He risked a glance over his shoulder, relieved that guy was no longer chasing him, but the white pickup's tires screeched as it reversed in the lot, the engine roaring as the driver raced away.

Coming after him. Rafe had no doubt Jase Weaver was coming after him. He and Carter Boyd had served together. On a fucking SF A-Team.

There were only two exits to that parking lot, and one of them led directly onto the road where Rafe's driver was waiting. He raced toward the Lexus, the driver already leaning over to throw the passenger door open for him.

"What the hell happened?" Travis demanded.

Rafe jumped in the idling car and yelled, "Go, go!" even as he yanked the door shut.

Travis peeled away from the curb, cutting across a lane of traffic as he gained speed. "What the hell's going on?"

"Just drive." Rafe twisted around to look behind them. The white pickup burst out of the lot onto the street, its back end fishtailing, but Weaver controlled it expertly and sped after them.

Jesus Christ, talk about a nightmare. He had *one day* left to pay back the money he owed.

First, Molly had arrived early for her shift—escorted by the fucking town sheriff of all people—when Rafe had been planning to grab her on her way in. There was no way to get her quietly on the inside, so he'd had to wait and hope that she went outside on her break as she usually did when the weather was nice.

All he'd needed was another three minutes with her, tops, and he would have been able to get the money transferred. She'd been terrified. Would have done whatever he told her to.

Instead, he now had a former Special Forces soldier on his ass, and the cops would be on the way too.

"Where we going?" Travis asked, still trying to lose Weaver.

"Just lose this guy and get us to one of our warehouses." He needed to regroup, come up with another plan. The deadline was tomorrow. He was almost out of time.

Travis swore as he veered around another corner and the pickup followed. "Who's this asshole?"

"Former SF."

"You shitting me?"

"Nope." He pulled his Glock from the glove compartment and shoved a full mag into the base. "If you can't lose him, I'll take him out." Molly Boyd wasn't a typical mark, at all, and she was even friends with the local sheriff. Taking out Weaver would put even more heat on them, but if there was no other option, Rafe would take it.

He would do anything it took to buy more time. Because if he didn't get Molly Boyd's money by midnight tomorrow, he was a dead man walking.

****

Fury pumped through Jase's veins as he raced after the speeding Lexus. "How far away are you?" he demanded of Noah through the phone.

The sheriff's voice came through the truck's speakers. "Ten. I've got Mac with me. I'm off duty and we were out together, but my deputies are a few minutes behind me."

"Tell Mac to track my phone." The company paid for their cell phones, and everyone in management had the custom tracking app activated. Mac could track his movements without Jase having to constantly update them verbally, allowing him to better focus on the task at hand:

Running these bastards down.

"You're sure Molly's okay?" Noah asked.

She wouldn't have been if he'd arrived even a minute later. "I got there just in time." Rage detonated inside him as he remembered the sight of that asshole holding a knife to her.

He flexed his jaw. "I'm not letting this son of a bitch get away."

"Don't do anything stupid, man."

"I won't." Not stupid. But he'd do whatever it took to take these guys off the road and bring them in, and stop any other threats coming at her from the organization.

He whipped around a slower-moving vehicle and sped through a stale yellow light. Two more intersections and they'd hit the two-lane coastal highway. It was pitch dark out, and with no streetlights on the route, he had to be right on the other car's ass because if the Lexus turned its lights out, he could lose sight of it. "You tracking me yet?" he demanded.

"Yeah, Mac's got you."

"Good. Gotta go." He hit the button to end the call and gripped the wheel tighter, wishing he had Mac or

Beckett with him now. That would have evened the odds nicely once Jase caught up to Rafe and whoever else was in the car.

Up ahead in the next intersection the light was red. The Lexus swerved to miss a car as it barreled through the light.

Jase set his jaw and kept his foot on the accelerator as he approached the intersection. An SUV started to turn left ahead of him. Jase yanked the wheel, narrowly avoiding T-boning the other vehicle and ignored the angry blast of the horn as he sped away.

The Lexus was pulling away from him with every passing mile. When they cleared the final intersection and finally reached the highway, Jase drove as fast as he dared given the curves in the road and the darkness.

He glanced at his cell when it rang again, the number unfamiliar.

Molly?

Jase nearly answered, then thought better of it. He couldn't afford to be distracted right now. He had to stop these assholes and hold them until Noah and the deputies arrived to arrest them. It was the only way he could stop this. The only way he could protect Molly from the ongoing threat.

He wouldn't stop. Because he wanted this over with *tonight*.

They played a dangerous, high-speed game of leapfrog as they darted in and out around slower traffic. The Lexus had lost some of its lead now, allowing Jase a chance to get closer.

He took it, keeping his foot hard on the accelerator as he flew after his target. He stayed right with the car until they hit some traffic as they neared the next town.

Jase pulled out over the double solid line to pass the car in front of him, swore when an oncoming truck was too close to give him the chance. He whipped back into his own lane, frustration pounding through him as he watched the Lexus pull away from him.

The moment he had room, he passed the slower vehicle in front and poured on the speed. Up ahead in the distance the Lexus suddenly veered right at a turn off the highway.

"Where the hell are you going," he muttered, pulling onto the narrow shoulder and racing past the line of traffic keeping him from the Lexus, narrowly avoiding taking off the side mirror on the rocky cliff beside the shoulder. Was the driver merely trying to get away? Or was this some kind of ambush setup?

Jase had to play this carefully, but he couldn't let them go. When he reached the turn he skidded around it, straightened out and hit the gas, speeding after the taillights in the distance.

This road was deserted, a side route that connected the outlying area of the small town to the highway. It was even darker here with no traffic. And it got darker still when the Lexus's taillights suddenly went out ahead of him.

Muttering a curse under his breath, Jase put on his high beams and chased after it, determined to keep up. Crazy motherfucker was gonna get someone killed.

He barely caught sight of the Lexus as it took a sharp right ahead. He slowed as he reached the turn, took the corner as fast as he could without rolling his truck, his high beams cutting through the darkness. The road turned to gravel here, crunching under his tires. Forest surrounded him on either side for as far as he could see.

But the gravel gave him an advantage. The Lexus had rear wheel drive, making its back tires slip on the uneven surface. Jase switched on his four-wheel drive, triumph streaking through him when his truck began to gain on the car.

Sixty yards and closing. Fifty. Forty.

Thirty.

His high beams barely caught the flash of the deer as it leaped out of the trees ahead of the Lexus. The car slammed on its brakes and skidded in a wild fishtail, spraying up gravel.

Seizing his chance, Jase drove right at it.

He jerked forward against the seatbelt as he rammed the back right end, pushing it into a hard spin. His truck swerved and skidded. He took his foot off the gas and turned the wheel to counteract it, wrestling with the big vehicle.

It wasn't enough. The front left bumper bounced off a tree with a loud crunch. He battled to keep the truck on the road, finally skidding to a stop on the shoulder, the left side wheels in the forest.

Throwing it in park, he cut the engine and glanced out the back window. He could barely make out the Lexus maybe twenty-five yards behind him, its front end crumpled against a tree trunk.

He undid his seatbelt and lunged across the cab to grab his pistol from the glove compartment. He shoved in a full mag and loaded a round in the chamber before turning off his dome light and opening the driver's door, using it for cover as he stepped out into the darkness.

His eyes adjusted in time for him to catch movement in the front of the Lexus.

A door squealed open in the quiet, then the crack of gunshots ripped through the air.

Bullets punched into his tailgate even as Jase ducked. Swearing, he scrambled back to crouch behind the hood. He could hear those assholes moving around back there, trying to come at him from either side.

He waited there, poised, his ears attuned to every tiny sound, all his training kicking in. He was an expert at hunting the enemy. Even in the dark.

The person on the right was coming closer. Jase

darted around the side of the truck and fired twice in quick succession.

A pain-filled cry filled the air as he ducked back behind cover. "You're gonna die for that, asshole!" whoever it was yelled at him.

"Sheriff and his deputies are on the way. Drop your weapons *now*," Jase shouted back.

"Fuck you," the guy snarled. "You're a dead man."

"Shut up," Rafe snapped back. Jase couldn't get a bead on him. To the left?

"I'm fucking bleeding, man," the other guy ground out. He was no longer advancing.

"Shut up and help me take him out so we can get outta here."

Definitely the left. And neither of these assholes had any intention of surrendering or being arrested tonight.

Jase swiveled on the balls of his feet and crept to the left, keeping the engine block between him and the shooters. Three shots cracked through the air, one round pinging off the front quarter panel.

Jase raised his weapon and returned fire, then ducked back behind the front bumper. There was no painful cry this time. And he wasn't even sure where the shooters were now.

He waited there, poised in the darkness. *Come on, Noah. Where the hell are you?*

Movement to the left again. He started to turn, then heard the telltale sound of someone trying to creep up at him from the right.

He spun around and raised his weapon, tried to pinpoint the shooter's location before darting out to fire.

Hot, burning agony speared through him a split second after he pulled the trigger. He grunted and stumbled back, slapping a hand to his front where the bullet had torn through, high up on the right under his ribs. Blood poured from the wound, hot and sticky against his skin.

Through the haze of pain and shock he could hear the shooter moving back toward the driver's side. Jase clenched his jaw and gripped the pistol with both hands, ready to make his final stand. It was either kill or be killed. And he wasn't going down easy.

He was bleeding bad. Already growing lightheaded.

Molly. Have to end this for Molly.

It was the only way to protect her and ensure she would be safe.

Gritting his teeth against the pain, he sucked in a ragged breath and struggled to his feet, standing behind the open door for a moment before he stepped out into the open. He saw the muzzle flash in the darkness as one of them fired on him.

It was all he needed.

Adjusting his aim, Jase stepped out from behind cover and squeezed the trigger twice.

As if in slow motion he watched the man's silhouette fall to the ground in the distance. The victim thrashed around weakly but didn't get up, didn't raise his arm to return fire.

Jase struggled to stay on his feet. Silence reverberated around him, pulsing against his eardrums. Both shooters were now down, but maybe not out.

He waited, the white-hot fire in his belly intensifying with every passing second. Blood continued to pour down his ribs and side, soaking his shirt and jeans.

A wave of dizziness slammed into him. He sagged, grabbed for the top of the truck's doorframe to steady himself. But he was too weak to hold on.

His legs gave out. His knees hit the ground with a bone-jarring thud that sent another shockwave of pain through his belly.

He bit back a scream, thought for a moment he hadn't been able to hold it back, then slowly realized it was the eerie, high-pitched wail of a siren echoing in the distance.

Noah. Finally.

Jase's right arm trembled as he kept the pistol aimed at the downed men in front of him. And as the pain and dizziness continued to assault him, a wave of fear began to build deep inside.

He knew enough about combat medicine, had seen enough men get gut shot to know he was in deep shit. His strength was already fading, his heart beating out of control no matter how he fought to slow it.

He couldn't catch his breath, the rasping sound of his shallow gasps grating on his nerves. Worse, he could feel the weakness spreading through him like a poison.

No. Have to hold on.

He fought it off, knowing if he succumbed to it, it would mean the end.

Closing his eyes, he bit down hard on his back teeth and struggled to stay upright.

Molly.

He had to hold on for Molly.

Chapter Twenty-Four

"Shite," Aidan breathed as they rounded the bend and saw the carnage ahead.

A dead deer lay in the middle of the deserted back road. Jase's pickup was swerved off to the side of it, the Lexus maybe thirty meters behind it, its front end crumpled into a tree.

He sucked in a breath when the cruiser's headlamps revealed the rest of the scene.

"Jase is down," he bit out, then spotted the other two men lying on the ground between the Lexus and the truck. "They're all down."

Noah swore and got on the radio to his deputies, who were still several minutes behind them. "I need two ambulances, stat. We'll transport all three patients to the main highway and rendezvous with the crews there."

Aidan was already drawing his weapon as Noah sped up and skidded to a stop near Jase's pickup, the cruiser's high beams illuminating the scene. He jumped out and immediately took aim at the two men lying on the ground as he hurried toward Jase.

"Weaver, it's Mac. You with me, wee man?"

"I'm...hit," he said, and Aidan wasn't sure what worried him more, the weakness in Jase's voice or the lack of a comeback. Jase was still holding his weapon, his hand in his lap, his head bowed. The back of his shirt was soaked through with blood. A small pool of it gleamed in the light.

"Where?" Aidan said, dividing his attention between the two downed men, ready to fire if one of them so much as made a move for their fallen weapons. One of them was on his back, groaning and moving around slightly. The other was crumpled on his side facing away from them, unmoving.

"Gut."

The answer chilled Aidan's blood. "Any other shooters?" he asked Jase, scanning for more threats.

"No." His voice was too damn weak.

"I've got Jase. Both shooters down," Aidan called to Noah over his shoulder, then holstered his weapon and rushed up to kneel beside his friend, setting a hand on his back. "Let me see what we're dealing with."

The cruiser's lights immediately showed the extent of the damage but he ripped Jase's button-down shirt apart to get a better look at the wound. A bullet had pierced him just below the base of his right ribcage and exited a few inches down on his side.

Shite. "I'm gonna lie you down now, mate," Aidan told him, taking Jase's weapon from him before grasping his shoulders to lower him backward. Jase grimaced and allowed Aidan to help him back, the pressure on the exit wound hopefully slowing the bleeding in his side.

"They dead?" Jase croaked out.

"One's not. Not sure about the other." He didn't care about them, he only cared about Jase.

Noah came running up, dropped a med kit next to them and paused to set a hand on Jase's shoulder. "You hanging in there, man?"

"Yeah."

"Good. Help's on the way and I'll be right back."

Noah raced off to check on the other men, pistol in hand.

Aidan unzipped the med kit. The contents were sadly basic: some bandages and pressure dressings, gloves, scissors. No IV needles, no blood volume expander that might help stabilize Jase until they could get him to the nearest hospital. He needed surgery immediately.

"Molly," Jase groaned.

"What about her?" He pulled out the bandages, not bothering to waste time putting on gloves and applied them to the entry and exit wounds. The shot was bad, the amount of bleeding telling Aidan there was significant internal damage.

"She'll be…safe now."

"Aye."

He could hear Noah talking on the radio. One shooter was unconscious but alive, and the other was wounded but in serious condition.

Jase was bleeding bad, and there wasn't much Aidan could do to help him. Finally, he picked up the sound of approaching sirens. Lights appeared in the distance a moment later. Three police cruisers speeding toward them.

"Here's the cavalry. We'll get you loaded up and take you to the hospital," he said, pressing down hard on the bandages to slow the bleeding. "Noah's got ambulances dispatched already."

Jase didn't answer. He closed his eyes, his face eerily pale in the beam of the headlamps.

The deputies arrived within a minute. Noah appeared next to him. "He unconscious?"

"No, but he will be soon. He's losing a lot of blood."

"Let's get him to the cruiser. Ambulance is six miles south of us."

Aidan took Jase under the shoulders while Noah took his legs and together they hustled him to the back of the cruiser. Jase groaned and twisted, his whole face tight with pain.

"I know it sucks, brother," Noah told him as they laid him down across the backseat. "It'll be better when we get you to the ambulance."

Aidan let Jase go and was easing out of the door when a bloody hand shot out and grabbed his forearm. He looked down into Jase's pinched face, his friend's eyes haunted. "Tell Molly…"

Oh, no. Screw that shite line of thought. "You tell her yourself."

Jase shook his head and dug his fingers into Aidan's arm, his lips pressed tight together. "Tell… Tell her…I love her."

Aidan's stomach dropped. Jase didn't think he would make it. And if they didn't get him to that ambulance in the next few minutes and start transfusing him, he wouldn't.

Aidan couldn't risk letting Jase die without honoring this request. "All right, wee man," he agreed. "I'll tell her."

Chapter Twenty-Five

Molly looked up when another nurse poked her head into the staff room. She'd been in here ever since calling 911 and reporting the incident. She'd been on edge the entire time, waiting for word from Jase or Noah about what was going on. But still nothing.

"We've got multiple gunshot victims inbound, coming in two ambulances. Two critical, one serious. We need all hands on deck," the nurse said, and ducked back out.

Molly jumped up and hurried after her into the hallway, a sense of foreboding forming in her gut. They rarely got gunshot victims here. The last time she'd treated one was a few weeks ago when a local hunter had accidentally shot himself in the leg while cleaning his rifle.

And it was way too much of a coincidence that the patients were coming in soon after Jase had chased after Rafe.

It can't be Jase.

Pushing that disturbing possibility from her mind, she focused on her job, getting everything prepped and set up in anticipation of the ambulances' arrival. She informed the senior surgical resident and called in the on-call surgeon, then helped get both operating rooms ready.

Back down in the ER, her heart rate kicked up when she heard the distant, eerie echo of the sirens approaching.

It's not Jase. It's not Jase. Someone would have called to tell her if it was.

The paramedics opened the back of the first ambulance and began unloading both gurneys. Their faces were covered with oxygen masks. "Two adult males, approximately early thirties, GSWs to the upper torsos, and one to the abdomen."

Molly directed her team, organizing everyone and putting them into action. One team rushed the critical patient into the trauma room, while the other took the seriously wounded man into another treatment room. She turned around and hurried for the automatic doors just as the third victim came in.

Her heart seized, the blood draining from her face when her eyes landed on the third gurney, Noah rushing alongside it.

Jase.

"Adult male, gunshot wound to the right upper torso," the paramedic said. "Entry wound below ribcage, and exit wound a few inches lower on his back."

A strangled cry locked in her throat. She ran toward Jase, scanning his bloody chest and abdomen, trying to assess the severity of the damage but there were too many bandages in the way. His eyes were closed, his face way too pale beneath the oxygen mask.

She grabbed his bloodstained hand, scared by how cold it was. "Jase. Jase, can you hear me?" She couldn't keep the tremor out of her voice.

"He lost consciousness about a minute ago," Noah told her, keeping pressure applied to the bandages on Jase's belly.

Oh God... From the placement of the bandages the bullet could have hit his liver, gallbladder or even his small intestine.

"BPs ninety over sixty, pulse one-twenty," the paramedic told her. Molly snapped back into work mode. She took in the information, grabbed the IV bag from him and began issuing orders to her staff.

She called out to the remaining group of nurses, ordering them to start a transfusion, and helped rush him into the third room standing ready. They hooked him up to various machines to monitor his vitals. His blood pressure was dropping fast. Too fast.

"Jase," she said more sharply as she leaned over him, fighting tears. There was no time for CT scans or x-rays. They had to get the internal bleeding under control and transfuse him immediately or they would lose him.

His eyelids fluttered. They opened slowly, his bleary gaze focusing on hers. "Moll," he croaked.

Thank God. "Yes, I'm here." She squeezed his hand while another nurse started the transfusion, and fought to keep her voice and expression calm when she was anything but inside. "You're in the hospital now. You're going to be okay, but we need to get this bleeding stopped. The surgeon is scrubbing in right now and the team's standing by in the operating room. You have to hold on for me."

He nodded weakly. "Told you…"

She leaned closer, pulled the oxygen mask away from his mouth slightly to hear him better. "What did you tell me?"

"Only way…you lose me is if…you walk away."

Molly bit the inside of her cheek and forced a smile. "That's right, you did. And I'm never walking away from you again, so that means you have to keep your promise." She stroked his hair back, wishing she could take away his pain and heal him right now.

He returned the pressure of her grip, but it was weak. Too weak. "Not going anywhere…now that you're mine."

"I know you won't," she told him. "And we're going to take good care of you." Fear flooded her but she mentally shoved it back and focused on what needed to be done to help stabilize him.

Someone brought another gurney in and she got the rest of the group ready to transfer him. "On three. One, two, three," she directed, lifting him with the others and placing him on the new gurney. "OR team ready?"

"Surgeon's just scrubbing in now."

"Well tell him to get his ass in gear." She glanced over at the BP monitor. "Let's go."

She and another nurse rushed Jase into the OR where the surgical team was standing at the ready. As quickly as possible she brought them up to speed on his injuries and vitals while the anesthetist got ready to put Jase under.

Molly stood in his line of vision, holding his hand. Looking down into his face, she forced back the sadness and fear. She wanted him to feel as calm as possible as he went under. "They're ready to get started now, sweetheart." She leaned down to kiss his forehead and straightened to give him a reassuring smile. "I love you. See you when you wake up."

His beautiful aqua eyes focused on her for a second, but he was already fading and she wasn't even sure if he'd heard her declaration or not. His eyes closed and his hand went lax in hers.

The surgeon took over, directing his team. "Friend of yours?" he asked, stepping up beside her, his voice and demeanor calm.

She nodded and backed away from Jase, staring at his face as a sense of helplessness took hold. She didn't want to leave, but he was in the best hands possible at the moment. She couldn't do anything more to help him. "Take good care of him."

"We will."

It took an act of will to make herself turn around and

leave the OR, but protocol dictated that she couldn't stay.

The double doors shut behind her.

Alone in the hallway, the iron hold she'd had over her emotions ripped apart. Tears flooded her eyes, spilling down her cheeks as she slid down the wall to sit on the cold linoleum floor. Sobs shook her, painful and raw.

Why Jase? Why, after everything they'd gone through? When she'd finally made up her mind to give herself to him completely?

She didn't know how long she sat there before the tears stopped. She wiped her face with the sleeve of her scrubs and stripped off her bloodstained gloves. Jase might own her heart and be her priority, but there were two more patients downstairs and she was the shift supervisor.

Numb inside, she took the stairs back down to the ER. Rafe was in surgery. The other man had been stabilized and was on his way up to the surgical floor where the police would question him.

She stopped in surprise when Noah appeared in front of her. "How is he?" he asked, his expression full of concern. The front of his tan uniform was spattered with blood.

"He'll be in surgery for a while yet. Are you heading up to question the other suspect?"

Noah nodded. "In a bit." His eyes were worried. "Are Jase's chances good?"

"Depends on how much internal damage was done. What the hell happened, anyway?"

Noah cursed under his breath and took her by the arm to lead her into an adjoining hallway where it was quieter. "He chased them twenty miles east and rammed the back end of their car to force them off the road. Both drivers lost control and crashed into the trees."

It made her cold all over just to imagine it. "They got out and started shooting at him?"

"Yeah, two against one. He used the driver's side door for cover. Without his training, he'd have died out there. But he managed to hit them both center mass, even with a bullet in his belly. When I got there, he was on his knees on the road, still holding his pistol. I was a minute too late."

Her throat closed up as though an invisible fist was choking her. Jase had gone after Rafe to protect her. Had willingly gone into harm's way to end the threat and ensure she was safe.

Why the hell had she been too afraid to give him all of her? She loved him, and what was left of her heart would die with him if he didn't make it. "I can't lose him," she choked out. "I can't, Noah."

Noah eased her into a comforting hug. "You won't lose him. He won't leave you after everything you guys have been through."

Molly pushed out a shaky inhalation and returned the embrace, sending out a prayer for Jase. All she cared was that he pulled through the surgery.

Please let him come through this. I love him and I need him to hear me tell him so.

****

Jase slowly became aware of a blazing pain below his ribs as he came to. *Oh, shit, that hurts.*

He tensed, his brow puckering into a tight frown, his mind fighting to stay below the surface where the pain didn't exist.

"Hey, you're awake."

He knew that voice. That sweet, slightly husky voice edged with the hint of a North Carolina drawl.

He turned his head toward it, forcing his heavy eyelids open. The sight of her leaning over him instantly made him relax, and the sharpest bite of the pain faded as he focused on her face, her pretty hazel eyes. "Moll," he whispered, his throat sore and dry.

"Hi, sweetheart." She bent closer to slide a hand beneath his nape, cradling it while she kissed him and pressed her cheek to his. Her sigh of relief gusted against his ear. "How do you feel?"

"Sore." Weak. Tired. Glad to be alive.

"Yeah." She straightened, smoothed his hair back from his forehead. "We've got meds in your line but I can't up the dosage just yet."

"'S okay." He could handle the pain. Maybe. Hopefully.

"You thirsty?"

"Yes."

"Here, I got you some ice chips. No water yet for a while." She lifted a spoon to his mouth. The ice was cold and sweet on his tongue. It dissolved fast and didn't do much to quench his thirst, but it was better than nothing.

She gave him three more then lowered the cup and spoon. "That's it for now, sorry."

He slid a hand down his chest to the edge of his ribcage, gingerly laid it on the bandages he could feel beneath the front of his hospital gown. "What's the verdict?"

"Good news is, they stopped all the internal bleeding and got everything patched up."

That was good news. "And the bad?"

"They had to remove a piece of your liver and a section of your small intestine, and your right kidney's badly bruised and swollen from the shockwave of the bullet impact."

"Oh. No wonder it hurts," he said with a crooked smile.

She shook her head at him, her eyes sparkling. "No wonder. But the liver can regenerate, and you should be able to make a full recovery *if* you take it easy." She gave him a stern look, raised one dark eyebrow.

"What about Rafe and the other shooter?"

Her expression sobered. "Rafe died on the table."

Good. He hoped the bastard was frying in hell right now. "He fired first."

"I know. Noah questioned the other guy. He tried to pin it all on Rafe, tried to make it seem like he was a helpless lackey, just along for the ride."

Jase made a growling sound, then grimaced and covered his incision.

Molly gently captured his hand in hers. Her fingers were warm and soft. "You're in the clear, legally speaking. All you have to do now is heal up."

He searched her eyes. "Are you okay?"

"Now that you're awake and talking to me, I'm fine." She leaned down to kiss him again, but this time she didn't stop at just one on his mouth. Her lips traveled across his face, trailing kisses over every inch. "I was so scared when I saw you come in on that gurney," she whispered against his cheek. "If you'd died, my heart would have died with you."

He made a low, negative sound and opened his mouth to reassure her but she captured his face in her hands and the tear-bright intensity of her gaze made him silent.

She searched his eyes, a tremulous smile on her lips. "I don't want you to take that job offer and move away. I love you, Jase. Love you so much I can't handle the thought of you not being in my life."

His heart swelled and rolled over in his chest. He gripped her wrist and squeezed, her admission meaning everything to him. "I'm not taking the job. I've loved you forever. It's always been you, Moll."

A watery laugh escaped her, then she kissed him on the lips. "You can't make me cry again, dammit. I'm all cried out," she said, but there was a catch in her voice.

"This baby has already had way too many floods of cortisol in its system."

Jase couldn't stop, though. From the moment the bullet had hit him, he'd thought about her. What she meant to him, that she was his reason for living. He'd held onto that, even when he'd faded into unconsciousness. "I want to marry you and be this baby's father," he told her, reaching out his hand to place it on her swollen belly.

"Jase," she whispered, her voice unsteady.

"I know it's fast, but I don't care." He'd almost died. To hell with waiting and being patient. "I want everything with you."

Molly leaned in and gently rested her forehead on his. "Yes, I'll marry you, Jase. But only if you swear never to try to be a hero for me again."

The stern edge to her voice made him smile. She'd said yes. She was going to be his forever. That made all the pain in the world worth it. "No promises, angel. I'd do it all over again in a heartbeat."

Chapter Twenty-Six

Jase woke up in an empty bed to find a note sitting on Molly's pillow.

Up and at 'em, birthday boy. Get showered and dressed and meet me downstairs at ten.

A slow grin spread across his face. He sat up gingerly, placing a protective hand over the right side of his belly. He'd been home recuperating for almost two weeks now and was finally on the mend. The incisions had healed and the staples were long gone, but the surgeon had warned him that given the damage to his liver and bowel, he was facing a long recovery.

The house was so quiet. Had Molly left? It had rained nonstop for the past week but now bright fall sunshine flooded through the large windows overlooking the backyard, spilling over Molly's king-sized bed. Their bed. Since coming home from the hospital she'd settled him upstairs with her for good.

Knowing she was truly safe now had made his recovery a lot easier. With all the media attention on Rafe and his cohort after the night Jase was shot, there was no way the Russian mafia would touch her now—a pregnant widow who'd had nothing to do with her late ex-husband's debt.

Rafe had been the one desperate to get the money from Molly anyway, to cover his own ass, and now he was dead. His boss, Mick, had his hands full with the federal investigation the FBI had launched. He wasn't coming after Molly either. No one was.

Which meant he and Molly could get on with their life together.

He swung his legs over the side of the bed and took his time getting to his feet. His insides still hurt, but as long as he moved slowly and was careful, it wasn't too bad.

In the master bathroom he found a towel and facecloth already laid out for him on the quartz vanity, along with fresh clothes: jeans and a light cream sweater. What did Molly have up her sleeve? As soon as he could drag his ass around town by himself, he was going ring shopping. He planned to formally propose on Christmas Eve.

He brushed his teeth, pausing to look at himself in the mirror. Thirty-four years old. He almost hadn't made it. Wouldn't have made it if not for the quick, decisive action of Noah, Mac, Molly and the surgeon who saved his life.

The incisions slashed across his middle like an angry, lopsided purple cross. He'd lost enough weight so far during his recovery that all his clothes were loose, but he was getting stronger every day. Molly made sure he was eating three times a day, plus Poppy was always either coming by with treats from Whale's Tale or sending them home with Molly.

It was nine-thirty, giving him plenty of time for a long, hot shower. Standing up straight was a luxury he now appreciated more than he used to, and made the most of it now while the water pounded down over his head and shoulders.

Drying off and getting dressed wasn't quite so fun. Or easy. But he managed. Yay, him.

A sharp, familiar whistle from downstairs cut through the quiet.

Beck? "What the hell are you doing in my house?" Jase called through the master bedroom door.

"Molly asked me over, to make sure your crippled ass doesn't fall down the stairs or something," Beckett called back.

Jase huffed out a laugh and made his way out to the landing. Beckett stood at the base of the stairs. He held out his arms to Jase, grinning like an asshole. "Come on, Sergeant, you can do it," he coaxed as though Jase was a toddler afraid of navigating the stairs.

"Shut up," he muttered, and gingerly made his way down, tread by tread. By the time he reached the bottom, he was sweating.

"Good job. Proud of you."

Jase didn't have the breath to tell him to go screw himself.

A car honked outside in the driveway. Jase looked at Beckett. A sly grin lifted one side of his friend's mouth. "She's here."

Molly?

Beckett grabbed Jase's bomber jacket and thrust it at him. "Put this on. And this," he added, shoving his grandpa's newsboy flat cap at him.

"What's she done?" Jase asked, obligingly putting on both treasured items.

"You'll see."

Jase shot him an amused look on the way to the front door. Beckett had his phone out and raised it to start filming. "Here's the broken birthday boy on his big day. He's got no idea what's going on," he narrated.

Jase grinned and opened the front door, wondering what they were up to.

Shock blasted through him when Beckett swung open the door and he saw what awaited him outside.

Molly was standing in front of a gorgeous, cobalt blue 1932 Ford, dressed in a blue polkadot 40s-style dress and red high heels. Her hair was pulled up at the front and sides, little spirals curling around her temples, and her lipstick was a bright, glossy red.

"Surprise," she said with a huge smile. "Happy birthday."

Jase couldn't stop gawking at her. She was the sexiest pinup model he'd ever seen. "Oh my God, where did you find it?" he asked, shaking his head in wonder at her and the car.

"Found my outfit at a retro shop, and rented this baby from a man in Portland at a car show." She patted the glossy, deep blue hood. "Don't get too excited, I have to return it in the morning." She cocked a hip and raised an eyebrow. "It's a gorgeous day for a drive down the coast. Think you can handle a short cruise?"

"Hell yeah," he said, starting down the front steps, unable to wipe the grin off his face. Molly was an awesome nurse, but the recovery had still sucked. On top of being in constant pain and unable to sleep well, being cooped up in the house this entire time had made him nuts. "I thought maybe you were gonna take me swing dancing." He'd promised to teach her when he was better.

"Yeah, no. Swing dancing is gonna have to wait another few months at least." Molly opened the passenger door for him and stood there with a sexy smile. "I'm driving, by the way."

"I can live with that." Jase slid his arms around her waist, his heart thumping at the way she looped hers around his neck and lifted up on tiptoe to kiss him. They hadn't had sex since the day before he'd been shot. He hated that part of the recovery most, and couldn't wait until he was up for it again, hopefully any day now if Molly would allow it.

"You're so gorgeous," he whispered against her

mouth. "This is the best present ever, thank you."

"You're welcome. And you deserve it. It's been a tough few weeks, so I figured getting you out for a while was the best medicine."

Jase couldn't wipe the smile off his face as he eased onto the leather passenger seat. Molly shut the door for him and hurried around the hood, giving him an additional present of being able to watch her breasts bounce in her cute dress, the front of it stretched over her prominent baby bump. Sexy and adorable and all his.

He was the luckiest guy on the planet.

She slid behind the wheel and reached for the ignition, pausing to shoot him an excited grin. "Ready?"

"Yeah. Turn her over."

She turned the key and the engine came to life with a satisfying growl.

"Is it the original engine?" Sounded like it.

"I knew you'd ask that, so I checked, and pretty much. The owner said the only thing not period specific is the paint color. Otherwise, he's maintained it with mostly original parts he's bought over the years."

"It's amazing."

She looked pleased with herself. "Knew you'd like it." She laughed as she put it in drive and looked through the windshield. "My God, this thing is like a tank. Beckett drove it back from Portland last night, I was too scared to drive it in the dark. And I didn't realize there weren't any seatbelts in it until I picked it up. I made Beckett take all the back roads instead of the freeway, because I felt like we were already risking our lives."

Jase chuckled. "She's a beauty." The car eased forward, the tires crunching over the pea gravel driveway.

"I feel like we've just gone back in time," she said, still smiling as they passed the trees still ablaze with the colors of fall, even the tall cedars filled with the rusty-orange parts on their branches. "Which reminds me, grab my phone and turn on the playlist I've got there."

Jase fished her phone out, seeing that she'd made up a playlist of 40s tunes. He laughed. "You're awesome."

She grinned. "I wanted you to get the full effect."

He hit play, and the resonant tones of Bing Crosby filled the interior. Instantly he was transported back to his grandparents' farmhouse in Nebraska.

Feeling more alive than he had in weeks, he reached across for Molly's hand, wound their fingers together and squeezed. "This is my best birthday ever," he told her. Being with her like this was more than he'd ever imagined.

"Glad to hear it. Ready to cruise the strip? Got one more surprise for you before we head down the coast."

"Sounds good."

She took the long way into town and finally turned onto Front Street where the speed limit was only twenty miles per hour. People walking along the sidewalks in front of the shops and restaurants all stopped to stare at them as they drove past, and a few drivers honked in approval. Jase loved every second.

"Let's see if I can park this old lady," Molly said under her breath as she steered into a spot in front of Whale's Tale.

"This is gonna sound weird, but it is so insanely hot to watch you drive this thing." It would be even hotter to bend her over the hood, pull up her dress and slide into her from behind. Not that it was gonna happen, but it was fun to fantasize about.

She laughed and put it in park. "Glad you think so. Weirdo."

He opened the door before she could come around to do it for him and slowly got out.

"Doing okay?" she asked, scanning his face with a nurse's critical eye.

"Doing fantastic," he murmured, tugging her close for a slow, thorough kiss. Yeah, he was in pain. He wasn't letting it ruin this.

She smiled against his mouth and grasped his hand. "Come on, everyone's waiting."

He followed her into Whale's Tale, a startled laugh coming from him when he saw his friends all standing there in period clothing. Poppy and Sierra both wore 40s dresses, Noah and Mac both wore zoot suits with fedoras, and Beckett had somehow arrived ahead of them, dressed in WWII Army summer khakis complete with a tie and cap.

"Happy birthday," they all chorused at once.

Jase's cheeks were starting to ache from smiling. "You guys look awesome," he said with a laugh.

Beckett came up to slap him on the shoulder and shake his hand. "Happy birthday, Sergeant."

The formal, respectful address made Jase's throat tighten. "Thanks, Cap." It had been a while since they'd served together in uniform, but the memories and the bond would always be there.

"Glad to see you up and about," Noah said, shaking his hand next.

"Glad to be up and about."

Mac grinned and held out his hand. "Happy birthday, wee man. Nice car."

"Isn't it?"

"Aye. A lot bonnier than the '32 Ford in your garage."

"Because I like you, I'm gonna pretend you didn't say that. Nice hat, by the way."

Mac doffed it. "Aye."

Poppy and Sierra both hugged him gently, and Poppy thrust a plate containing a cupcake with a candle burning in the center. "For you."

"Thanks." He stood there holding it, waiting while they sang happy birthday to him.

"Make a wish," Molly said, taking pictures of him on

her phone.

Jase met her gaze. *She* was his wish, and she'd already come true. But he pretended to think one up and blew out the candle anyway.

They stayed to visit for a while, then Molly called a halt to the celebration, announcing he'd had enough excitement for one day, and they got back in the car. Their friends stood on the sidewalk, waving at them as they drove away.

Jase couldn't remember ever being so happy as Molly drove them to the 101 and they started south along the coast while the autumn sunshine lit everything with a warm glow and the rolling waves crashed into the rocks below with an explosion of white foam.

He glanced over at Molly, reminded again of how lucky he was, then took her hand and raised it to his lips for a kiss. She'd gone to a hell of a lot of work to pull off this surprise and he appreciated all of it. "I love you."

Her mouth curved up. "I know. Love you too."

Jase leaned back to enjoy the ride. Everything was finally right in his world. He had his girl, a child on the way, and the rest of their lives together to look forward to.

Without a doubt he would do it all over again, endure every moment that had brought them here. Even the taking a bullet part.

Epilogue

"Just one more push, Molly," the doctor said.

"No." This *sucked*.

She'd changed her mind. She didn't want to have the baby anymore. She hadn't wanted to have the baby for the past twelve hours, not that anyone seemed to care. In hindsight, she should have taken Zoe the author up on her offer and called, because no one had warned her it would be *this* bad.

"The baby's head is right there."

Yes, she was fucking well aware of where it was, because it felt like her entire vulva had been submerged in sulfuric acid for the past fifty-plus minutes. She growled and squeezed her eyes shut even tighter, trying to escape the pain.

"You're so close, angel," Jase said, his low voice breaking through the haze of pain and fear. It was like being caught on an out of control roller coaster from hell, and there was no way to get off until it rolled back into the station. "Just one more. You can do this."

Molly shook her head, gritting her teeth against the urge to shout at him to go fuck himself. "Can't," she gasped out. This was way worse than she'd ever imagined it would be, even though things were going "perfectly" according to everyone in the room. Screw them all. She was a freaking ER nurse and she couldn't believe this was what it was like to give birth.

Jase set her leg down and leaned over her to cup her face in his hands, getting her full attention. He wiped away the sweat and tears from her cheeks, his gaze solemn and steady on hers. "It's almost over, sweetheart. I know it hurts—"

Oh, *hell* no. "You don't have any clue what this feels like," she snapped, realizing even as she said it that he'd been shot in the abdomen not too long ago. Maybe he did kind of know. "You—" She broke off, a strained groan pulling from her as another contraction squeezed and twisted, lighting her entire lower body up in pain.

Jase straightened and grabbed her leg again, pushing her thigh up and out while the hideous burning sensation intensified. Folding her into the equivalent of a human pretzel while she was enduring hideous amounts of pain. She wanted to kick him.

"There," the doctor encouraged. "Slow, now. Nice and slow."

Molly didn't have a choice. Her body was forcing this on her, and she screamed as the baby's head popped through the awful pressure.

"You're doing fantastic, Molly," Dr. Smithers said.

She used to be Molly's favorite doc, but not anymore. The woman was a heartless sadist, refusing to give Molly an epidural or even knock her out with a rubber mallet because it was too late. "One more gentle push."

Molly opened her eyes to stare up at Jase, her body caught in a vise. "So close, Moll," he told her, his expression intent but excited. "I'm right here, angel, and I'm so proud of you."

Well, he should be proud. She was being ripped in half, trying to shove what felt like a concrete bowling ball out of her hooha.

"One more," he encouraged.

Okay. Okay, only one more. I can do one more.

She closed her eyes and summoned her strength, bracing for the agony she knew was coming. This was gonna hurt like a bitch no matter which way she sliced it, so might as well just get it over with.

Crushing Jase's hand in her own, she locked her molars together and pushed with all her might, holding it, an animal sound of pain and exertion coming from her throat.

Another pop, a gush, and the baby slipped from her body.

Instantly the hideous burning stopped. Molly's eyes snapped open and she scrambled up on her elbows to see. "What is it?"

A tiny wail rang through the room, making Molly's racing heart squeeze.

Holding the baby, Dr. Smithers smiled at Jase, who answered for her. "It's a girl," he said, his voice rough.

A girl.

"Ohh, is she… Is she okay?" She tried to sit up, but she was too weak, and held out her limp arms instead. Jase was there in an instant, sliding a powerful arm behind her to help raise her up as Dr. Smithers placed their daughter on Molly's chest.

Nurses wiped the baby gently with soft towels while Molly cradled her newborn to her. She had a cap of thick black hair, and her skin was a shade or two lighter than Molly's.

"Oh my God, she's beautiful," she choked out, tears flooding her eyes. They came out of nowhere, the release of pent-up emotion hitting her like the mallet she'd wished for moments ago.

"She's perfect," Jase said in awe, reaching out to stroke the baby's hair with a gentle finger.

"What's her name going to be?" the doctor asked.

"Savannah Carter Weaver," Molly answered. Today

was February eleventh. That was her daughter's birthday, just a week after Carter's. Incredible.

The tears came faster and she gave up trying to stop them, pulling her hospital gown aside to put the baby against her bare skin. Carter had never even known he was going to be a father.

He should have been here. Not in Jase's place beside her, but at least out in the hall with the others, waiting for word. Though he would never know his daughter, a part of him would live on through her forever.

"Would you like to cut the cord?" Dr. Smithers asked Jase, who took the surgical scissors from her and did the honors.

Molly reluctantly allowed the nurse to take the baby to weigh her and check all her vitals. Molly tore her gaze from that tiny form to look up at Jase. "Oh my God, I did it."

"You sure as hell did," he told her, wrapping both arms around her and pushing his face into her sweat-soaked, matted curls. "You deserve a medal."

"I totally do." She stared across the room at her daughter on the scale while Dr. Smithers gave Molly a shot of oxytocin in the thigh that burned like a wasp sting.

Delivering the placenta thankfully didn't hurt at all, and they mercifully froze her before putting in the stitches. Through it all, she was distracted by what was going on with the baby.

Finally, the nurse turned to Jase, holding out Savannah, who was now swaddled in a receiving blanket. "You want to hold her?"

"Yes." Jase stood and wiped his hands on his jeans, looking adorably nervous as he reached for their daughter. The way he carefully tucked her into the crook of his arm, the sight of her tiny body cradled so protectively against that broad chest, made Molly's heart turn inside out.

But the look on his face. The absolute awe and pride

and joy there brought on another wave of tears as the nurse stood by taking picture after picture on Jase's phone.

He'd been her rock through this entire ordeal. Through every hellish step of her marriage's painful decline with Carter, through his death and beyond and through the ordeal of childbirth. He'd been at her side. She loved him more for that than anything else.

He was all choked up, his voice rough and raw as he stared down at their daughter. "You're mine in every way that counts, and I'm gonna be here for you forever." His gorgeous aqua eyes shimmered with tears when he looked over at Molly, but he was smiling. "I love her so much already," he said with a rough laugh.

If the man hadn't already owned her heart and soul, those words would have done it.

Molly smiled back and reached out a hand for him. "Me too."

He came and sat beside her, carefully transferred Savannah to Molly's hold. The nurse had put a little knit cap on her perfect head to keep her warm.

Molly cuddled her close, pain forgotten, cataloguing every little thing about her face. Savannah had Carter's cleft in her chin. Her eyes were a deep, slate gray right now. Would they be dark, like his had been? Or hazel-green, like hers?

She looked up at Jase. "Do you think he knows?" she whispered, meaning Carter.

He understood exactly what she meant. "Yeah, he knows. And he's damn proud of you both."

She smiled, believing it was true.

Molly sighed in relief as soon as everything was done and the staff filed out, leaving them alone. "That's better," she whispered, bending her head to kiss the center of her daughter's forehead.

"Much," Jase agreed, and stood.

She was so preoccupied by the baby that she didn't notice what he was doing until he sat a hip on the edge of her bed next to her thigh and held up one hand. The gray morning light coming through the window caught on her gold wedding band as he took her left hand and slid it onto her finger. He'd proposed on Christmas Eve and they'd eloped the first week of January with just Sierra, Beckett, Poppy, Noah and Aidan there.

"I'm putting this back where it belongs now," he murmured, leaning down to kiss her softly. He cradled her cheek in his palm, his gaze so tender and fierce all at once that her heart skipped. "I love you so damn much, Moll, and I'm in awe of how incredibly strong you are."

She was only strong because she'd had him beside her through everything. "I love you too, sweetheart."

He glanced toward the door. "Guess I should tell the cheering section out in the hall. Your mom and grandma are probably ready to claw the door down."

"Not yet," she begged, wanting to hold onto this moment forever. She loved that her mom and grandmother had made the trip out for the birth, but she wasn't ready to give up this solitude yet. "I want a few more minutes with just us."

He kissed the top of her head. "Me too."

Together they gazed down at their newborn daughter, a forever family.

No matter what else life threw at them, Molly would always have Jase at her side. And not a single day would pass when their daughter didn't know how much she was loved.

—The End—

Dear reader,

Thank you for reading **_Shattered Vows_**. I hope you enjoyed it. If you'd like to stay in touch with me and be the first to learn about new releases you can:

Join my newsletter at:
http://kayleacross.com/v2/newsletter/

Find me on Facebook: https://www.facebook.com/KayleaCrossAuthor/

Follow me on Twitter: https://twitter.com/kayleacross

Follow me on Instagram: https://www.instagram.com/kaylea_cross_author/

Also, please consider leaving a review at your favorite online book retailer. It helps other readers discover new books.

Happy reading,
Kaylea

**Excerpt from *Rocky Ground*
Crimson Point Series**

By Kaylea Cross
Copyright © 2019 Kaylea Cross

Chapter One

A womanizing deadbeat, a not-so-high-functioning alcoholic, and a pedophile.

The sad truths of her three longest-lasting relationships. Not exactly a track record to be proud of, or a recommendation for mother of the year.

Tiana Fitzgerald pulled the hood of her coat up as she got out of her car and dashed through the rain from to the Crimson Point police station to face more fallout from her most recent disaster of a romantic relationship. Her week had already gone from bad to shit on Monday after receiving another blow, this one by mail.

One crisis at a time.

Sheriff Noah Buchanan rose from the chair behind his desk with a broad smile on his handsome face when she knocked on his open door. He'd been so good to her and her daughter through everything that had happened. Over the past year he and his girlfriend Poppy had become her friends. "You look half-drowned," he said with a chuckle. "Come on in."

"It's monsooning out there." April showers brought May flowers and all that, except here on the Oregon Coast when it rained nonstop for weeks on end and saturated everything.

"Is Ella at afterschool care?"

"No, I dropped her off at Beckett and Sierra's before coming here." She took off her soaked jacket and draped it over the back of the chair in front of his desk before sitting and folding her hands in her lap, maintaining at least the outward appearance of calm and collected. "So, you said you had an update for me about Brian."

She still hated saying his name. Hated even more than she'd fallen for his fake charm in the first place and not seen the monster underneath. It disgusted her to think that she'd slept with him. Filled her with rage that, unbeknownst to her, he'd exposed himself to her then eight-year-old daughter, and would have molested her or worse if Ella hadn't told someone.

Ella hadn't told her. No, she'd told their neighbors, Beckett and Sierra. Noah's best friend and sister.

It broke Tiana's heart that her daughter hadn't trusted her, but once Ella's reasoning had become clear, she understood her decision better. Ella had been trying to protect her.

"I do." Noah reached one muscular arm back into a file cabinet and took out a folder that he placed on his desk. "The latest report came back from the computer forensics people."

Her insides curdled. They'd seized Brian's electronics after he'd been arrested last spring, but they'd found a personal laptop of his a month ago. She hadn't been shown any of the information about the ongoing investigation until now. "Let me guess—they found all kinds of child porn and a whole bunch of other disgusting stuff on his hard drive."

Noah confirmed her suspicions with a nod. "Right."

Gross. "And I'm also betting Ella's not the first girl he's done this to."

"Right again. We identified three other possible victims. All girls, aged eleven and under, and there may be others we don't know about yet. His pattern seems to be targeting single moms with young daughters."

The news sickened her. It was horrifying to think that predators like him were walking around in plain sight but undetected, and that she'd fallen for his act. His clean cut good looks and impressive professional image as a successful and highly sought after investment banker working for a large firm based in Portland. "Well that's…disturbing."

Noah's deep blue gaze was steady. "Yes it is." The night of the confrontation with Brian, Noah had been especially wonderful. Beckett too, whom she'd never be able to thank enough for intervening on Ella's behalf.

Tiana had arrived home that evening, clueless as to what had been going on, and walked into a chaotic scene straight out of her nightmares. Brian in cuffs in the back of Noah's cruiser, his nose and mouth bleeding from Beckett's powerful fist. When she'd found out what Brian had done, she'd wanted to rip him apart. "I can't say any of this surprises me, though. Not now."

"I showed you this because I wanted you to know you're not the only one. You're not the only person he's fooled. He's done this before and gotten away with it, at least three more times that we know of. But because Ella spoke up and he's been charged, two of the other girls are willing to testify as well."

"A tiny bit of a silver lining in this whole mess."

"Yes." He opened up the file, leafed through some papers and began to read. "The forensic psychologist's report says the usual things common to most child predators. He was likely sexually abused himself as a child himself and blames external factors to explain and justify his actions in an attempt to diminish his guilt. He'll also go to great lengths to hide his behavior."

"Boy, did he ever," she said bitterly. She'd been completely oblivious to what was happening behind her back.

Noah closed the file. "They're experts at it. That's why it's so hard to catch them. And they control their victims, making it hard for them to speak out. But not Ella."

He sat back in his chair, a slight smile lifting one side of his mouth. "You've got a brave little girl there."

"I know it." She pulled in a breath and shook her head. "How do you do this job, Noah? Seeing this kind of thing day after day?"

"Thankfully around here that kind of thing is rare, but yeah, I've seen my fair share of shit. It's always harder when kids are involved. And I do it because I can make a difference and protect kids like Ella by taking the monsters off the street and putting them away for as long as possible."

If it were up to Tiana, Brian and all the other child predators in the world would rot in prison for the rest of their lives and never see the light of day again.

Noah's parting words resonated with her as she drove home to her rental house on the other side of town. If Brian refused the plea bargain that was about to be offered him—and it was sickening enough that he was being offered any kind of a deal at all—then Ella would have to take the witness stand and testify in court in front of him.

The only reason Tiana had agreed to the terms of the plea bargain was to spare her daughter that additional trauma. Ella had been through more than enough, and Tiana was determined to protect her daughter from any more harm.

That plan included steering clear of any more romantic relationships, and men in general until Ella was all grown up. Maybe longer.

Maybe forever.

Her cell rang as she drove down Front Street along the water, past all the charming wood-framed shops and businesses and the wide expanse of sandy beach and rolling ocean beyond it. Aunt Lizzie, her mother's younger sister. The closest thing Tiana had ever had to a real mother, and the only family she had any contact with. "I'm just on my way home, so perfect timing," she told her aunt.

"It's a gift," Lizzie replied. "So, how did it go at the sheriff's office?"

"Depressing as hell, as expected." She relayed everything Noah had told her.

"When will you hear about the plea bargain?"

"Not sure. Last I heard the State Attorney's office was still finalizing it."

Lizzie grunted. "I hope the pedo takes it. It's more than he deserves, especially if he's molested other girls, but I'd hate for Ella to have to go through the stress of a trial to put him away."

"Me too."

"And what else? I can tell there's something else. Spill."

Aunt Lizzie knew her too well. "It's Evan."

A shocked pause followed her announcement. "As in, Ella's deadbeat sperm donor who ditched you both before her first birthday and disappeared to chase women and his dream of being a famous musician?"

A perfect summation. "That's the one."

"What did he do now?"

"Our mediation is over. If I don't grant him visitation—they call it parenting time here—then the court will enforce it."

"*What?*"

Tiana winced and turned the volume down on the car's Bluetooth system. "Yep. Got the letter couriered to my office Monday morning."

"That's insane. He didn't want anything to do with Ella for her entire life up to now, hasn't paid you a dime in support, left you both to fend for yourselves, and now he suddenly wants access to her?"

The weight that had been sitting on Tiana's chest for the past several months as the start of the trial loomed suddenly grew heavier. "Yes, and since he's agreed to pay the child support he owes, the court will side with him if I keep fighting it." She hadn't gone after him for child support when he'd left because she'd just wanted him out of their lives permanently and had been willing to go without the money to get that.

"What are you going to do? Does Ella know?"

"The initial visit would be here with a court liaison to supervise. It's better for everyone if Evan and I can work out something amicably between us in terms of a visitation schedule, but since he's in California it's even harder. As for Ella, I've brought up the subject to see how she reacted."

"And?"

"She actually seemed excited about meeting him." It had surprised Tiana. "According to my lawyer, I can't fight this unless I can prove he's a criminal or poses a threat to her. Which, given my track record with men, he probably is, and I won't be able to prove anything until it's too late."

"Then you're not going to fight it?"

Part of her desperately wanted to. She wanted to keep Evan as far out of their life as possible, because as far as she was concerned, he'd forfeited any rights to Ella the day he walked out on them. "I can try, but it won't look good in front of the court and it'll burn through money I'd rather put into a mortgage and a college fund for Ella."

"God, I hate that man. Why the hell does he want to see her now?"

"I don't know, but I don't trust his motives even with the money he's willing to pay to see her." He'd abandoned her and Ella when they'd needed him most. There was no reason to let him back into their lives now. Raising Ella alone had been the hardest thing Tiana had ever done, but she'd never once regretted her decision. "I may have to come to terms with him having supervised visits. But if he tries to file for any sort of custody, I'll fight him for as long as it takes."

"Good girl."

"My lawyer's looking into what can be done about that, but right now it's all up in the air."

"Honey, the universe owes you a big break."

"God, don't I know it. Now let's change the subject before the last of my determination to stay positive disappears and I'm forced to eat both quarts of ice cream currently sitting in my freezer when I get home."

"Is one of them mint chocolate chip?"

She smiled at her aunt's hopeful tone. "You're coming to visit this weekend, so of course."

"You always were my favorite niece."

Tiana laughed under her breath. "By process of elimination, that's not saying much, is it?" She was Lizzie's only niece.

"You'd still be my favorite even if I had twenty nieces. Which, considering the crazypants, whackadoodle family we both come from, I'm thankful I do *not*."

She grinned at the apt description. "Imagine how boring we'd have been without their influence, though."

"True. I'm still determined to write my memoir one day and sell a million copies, wind up on Oprah and all that. I'll save a few chapters for you to put in your story."

"You're too kind." She sighed. "I miss you so much."

"Hang in there, sweetie. I'll see you in a few days."

"You can't get here soon enough."

"Love you, Tia-bear."

A lump formed in her throat. Lizzie had been there for her when no one else was. She had taken Tiana in when she had nowhere to go, and given her the only unconditional love she'd known through her life. "Love you too."

She ended the call, but even the prospect of Lizzie's impending visit couldn't ease the awful pressure in her chest. Ever since that night last summer when she'd learned the truth about Brian it felt like her world was caving in.

Now she was flat out scared. The thought of Evan trying to take Ella away even part time was enough to put her into a panic.

Rain continued to splatter across her windshield as she drove beyond the town and finally turned onto Salt Spray Lane. Tall cedars and Douglas Firs bordered either side of it, and at the top of the rise her first destination came into view. Beckett and Sierra's gorgeous heritage Victorian stood proud in the center of its ocean view lot. Warm light spilled from its windows into the gloom.

Knowing her daughter was safe and warm and cared for there put a smile on Tiana's face. The first she'd had all day.

But as she pulled into the driveway, she spotted Ella sitting on the side porch not with Beckett, but with that man who worked for him—Aidan MacIntyre.

Her jaw tensed and her spine went rigid.

Hell no.

She'd taken all she could take today, and he was the last damn straw.

End Excerpt

About the Author

NY Times and USA Today Bestselling author Kaylea Cross writes edge-of-your-seat military romantic suspense. Her work has won many awards, including the Daphne du Maurier Award of Excellence, and has been nominated multiple times for the National Readers' Choice Awards. A Registered Massage Therapist by trade, Kaylea is also an avid gardener, artist, Civil War buff, Special Ops aficionado, belly dance enthusiast and former nationally-carded softball pitcher. She lives in Vancouver, BC with her husband and family.

You can visit Kaylea at www.kayleacross.com. If you would like to be notified of future releases, please join her newsletter: http://kayleacross.com/v2/newsletter/

Complete Booklist

ROMANTIC SUSPENSE

Crimson Point Series
Fractured Honor
Buried Lies
Shattered Vows

DEA FAST Series
Falling Fast
Fast Kill
Stand Fast
Strike Fast
Fast Fury
Fast Justice
Fast Vengeance

Colebrook Siblings Trilogy
Brody's Vow
Wyatt's Stand
Easton's Claim

Hostage Rescue Team Series
Marked
Targeted
Hunted
Disavowed
Avenged
Exposed
Seized
Wanted
Betrayed
Reclaimed
Shattered
Guarded

Titanium Security Series
Ignited
Singed
Burned
Extinguished
Rekindled
Blindsided: A Titanium Christmas novella

Bagram Special Ops Series
Deadly Descent
Tactical Strike
Lethal Pursuit
Danger Close
Collateral Damage
Never Surrender (a MacKenzie Family novella)

Suspense Series
Out of Her League
Cover of Darkness
No Turning Back
Relentless
Absolution

PARANORMAL ROMANCE
Empowered Series
Darkest Caress

HISTORICAL ROMANCE
The Vacant Chair

EROTIC ROMANCE (writing as *Callie Croix*)
Deacon's Touch

Dillon's Claim
No Holds Barred
Touch Me
Let Me In
Covert Seduction

Printed in Great Britain
by Amazon